# A.N.G.E.L.S.
## INC

Robert W. Bliss

*Val*

*Thank you for all you do to make life smooth for me at Saddleback. Hope you enjoy Angels —*
*Bob Bliss*

The McGraw-Hill Companies, Inc.
Primis Custom Publsihing

*New York St. Louis San Francisco Auckland Bogotá
Caracas Lisbon London Madrid Mexico Milan Montreal
New Delhi Paris San Juan Singapore Sydney Tokyo Toronto*

**McGraw·Hill**

A Division of The **McGraw·Hill** Companies

A.N.G.E.L.S. INC
Copyright © 1998 by The McGraw-Hill Companies, Inc. All rights reserved. Printed in the United States of America. Except as permitted under the United States Copyright Act of 1976, no part of this publication may be reproduced or distributed in any form or by any means, or stored in a data base retrieval system, without prior written permission of the publisher.

McGraw-Hill's Primis Custom Publishing consists of products that are produced from camera-ready copy. Peer review, class testing, and accuracy are primarily the responsibility of the author(s).

1 2 3 4 5 6 7 8 9 0   BKM BKM   9 0 9 8

ISBN 0-07-229823-5

*Editor: Lorna Adams*
*Cover Design: Rob Winter*
*Printer/Binder: Book-Mart Press, Inc*

# ACKNOWLEDGMENTS

I wish to thank the two ladies who have made the publishing of this novel a reality: Julie Jahn, of McGraw-Hill, and Lorna Adams, of PRIMIS Custom Publishing, a McGraw-Hill Company. Lorna's expertise in the areas of book design and production were especially invaluable.

I wish to thank the members of the Saddleback Valley Writers Guild, who have helped me through two years of rewrites, one chapter each week: Jacqueline Hanson, Bob Anton, Mel Packard, Janice Carbone, Ben Leviton, Judy Jacovitz, Jerry Gould, Mel Zimmerman, and Mary Machtig. Their constructive criticism and wonderful encouragement have made the difference. I must especially thank "Jackie" Hanson, who edited the entire manuscript. As a Stanford graduate in nursing, her suggestions adding to the medical credibility of various incidents described in the story were invaluable.

I wish to thank three others who read the manuscript and provided excellent suggestions for improvement: Kathleen Leighton, an ABC-TV newsanchor in Buffalo, whose encouragement and friendship mean so much; my tennis buddy, Bill Christie, a retired teacher, who spotted several errors and "graded my paper" appropriately; and my brother-in-law, Don Roberts, an engineer whose technical knowledge I greatly admire, who wrote a thorough critique of an early draft of the book.

I also wish to thank my colleagues at Saddleback College and my family, for their patience and forbearance, in the years that this project has been so all-consuming in my mind. My daughter, Pam, and my step-daughters Lori, Kathy, and Jeni, will, I think, be especially grateful to hear me speak of something else in the future.

Finally, and most importantly, I would like to thank the woman who has endured many years of my sitting at the computer until 2:00am: my wife, Dee, who gives me honest criticism when needed, encouragement always, and faith that "it's going to happen." Darlin', if I can borrow a line from the song, "You are the wind beneath my wings."

# AUTHOR'S NOTE

This is a novel, originally written as science fiction; but with the announcement of the successful cloning of Dolly the sheep in March, 1997, it has become, perhaps, more mainstream.

Some elements of the book are, however, still science fiction. Although we *are* presently inserting human genes in cows, to make their milk more suitable for children, the transgenic manipulation of genes from other species, to accelerate growth in the human clones of this story, is certainly far from today's reality.

The cloning of humans is, of course, highly controversial. In his 1998 State of the Union address, President Clinton asked Congress to pass legislation banning it. While I do not advocate cloning humans (certainly, the old-fashioned way of reproduction is a good deal more fun), I think it foolish to assume that it will never be done. Indeed, many scientists believe such efforts may be secretly underway, today.

This novel is intended as an entertainment for people who enjoy imagining what the future might hold. Although all of the characters are fictitious, references to genetic scientists James D. Watson and Leonard Hayflick are factual, as are references to various heavyweight boxing champions. My father saw Gene Tunney take the title from Jack Dempsey in 1926 (a fight mentioned in the book), and the program from that event is one of my treasured mementos. References to Joe Louis' terrific beating of Max Schmeling in 1938, are also factual.

Mention of "The Eudaemonic Pie", a book which details the attempt by a group of Santa Cruz physicists and computer scientists to use computers and radios in their shoes to beat roulette wheels, is also true. The book was authored by Thomas A. Bass, and published in 1985 by Houghton Mifflin.

# CHAPTER 1

Finally, the big day arrived. Capodilupo knocked on the door of their suite at the Parthenon. Jack checked the view through the peephole, recognized the security director, and swung the door open. "Right on time, Cappie."

The former LAPD cop allowed a half-smile. "We don't wanna be late for this one, Coach. How's Joey doin'?"

Joey strode briskly into the sitting room. "I'm ready, Cappie."

Capodilupo searched the fighter's face with a professional eye. He could see the tension in his face. As Joey stood for a moment beside his brother, Cappie marveled, as always, at their resemblance. Almost twins, but with his trained eye, the ex-cop could spot the differences. Joey appeared younger, and a little bigger.

Harry strode into the room, as he fussed with his small canvas bag of ringside gear, and threw Cappie a nervous glance.

"Hi, Doc," Cappie offered.

"Hi, Cappie," Harry replied, not looking up from his work.

Cappie half-smiled again, this time at the contrast between Harry and the rest of them in the room. Harry weighed 150 pounds, wore glasses, and looked every bit the stereotypical scientist that he was. The ex-cop, and the fighter, and his brother were all well over 200 pounds.

"OK," Joey said to Cappie. "Let's do it."

Cappie turned and opened the door. Four of his best men stood waiting. They all walked quickly to the elevator. Cappie inserted his master key in the security lock to prevent the elevator from stopping at any floor except the one he selected, and they dropped to the employees parking garage. A large unmarked van stood waiting outside the elevator door and the eight men quickly climbed aboard. A few minutes later, they slipped through a delivery entrance at the rear of Caesar's Palace. Caesar's security men escorted them through a maze of "employees only" corridors to Joey's dressing room.

Cappie and his guards stood outside the door, stoically protecting Joey. Benito swept into the room and stared at Joey for a long moment, searching his face. He saw the cold hardness in Joey's eyes, and the former Mafioso's face relaxed into a smile. "You're a winner, Kid." Nodding to Jack and Harry, he left without another word.

Jack and Harry taped Joey's hands and laced his gloves with care. Joey pounded each fist into the other's palm, several times. His eyes grew even colder, and Jack knew he was running through one of his scripts. As Jack studied his brother's face, he realized he had seen that look once before. "Oh, Jesus," he said quietly.

"What is it?" Harry asked, looking up. Following Jack's gaze, he caught the look in Joey's eyes. " 'Oh Jesus' is right," he said grimly.

None of them spoke again. One of Cappie's guards knocked on the door and announced, "They're ready, gentlemen."

Joey slid off the table and strode toward the door. Jack and Harry had to move fast to stay with him. As they stepped through the door, a cordon of security guards and Las Vegas policemen surrounded them. They moved quickly down a concrete corridor. As they approached the arena, the crowd noise grew louder.

When Joey stepped through the door and came into view, the boisterous audience roared. His loyal fans started chanting "Bam! Bam! Bam!" as he strode down to the ring. Jack could feel the crowd's anticipation. The air seemed charged with electricity. Radio and television announcers yelled into their microphones, while pressing their earphones against their ears, straining to hear themselves in the bedlam. Television cameras swung to follow every move Joey made as he trotted up the stairs and ducked between the ropes. Joey's fans roared their approval as the challenger stepped into the ring.

Joey paced nervously and pounded his fists alternately into his palms. Jack and Harry fussed in his corner, checking his towels, sponges, water bottles, spit-bucket, hydrogen peroxide, and swabs. The champion kept them waiting for five full minutes. Part of his strategy, Jack supposed.

When he stepped through the door, another roar went up. A popular champion, he waved and smiled all the way to the ring.

Finally, the tuxedo-clad announcer strode into the center of the ring. He yelled into the microphone, "Ladies, and gentlemen. Caesar's Palace takes great pride in presenting the feature bout of the evening . . ." The screaming fans prevented him from being heard for ten seconds.

"Fifteen rounds of boxing for the heavyweight championship of the world . . ." Again the crowd noise forced him to pause.

Then pointing to Joey, "In this corner — wearing black trunks, with white stripes — weighing 240 pounds — with a record of 30 wins — all by knockouts — and no losses — from Irvine, California — the challenger — Joey — 'Bam-Bam' — *Hanley!*"

The crowd went crazy. They yelled for 30 seconds. Joey's fans started their chant again, "Bam! Bam! Bam!" It was infectious. "Bam! Bam! Bam!" The room rang with the sound. Jack looked at the champion. He smiled calmly and seemed amused.

Finally, the announcer yelled into his microphone, "In this corner — wearing white trunks with red and blue stripes — weighing 235 pounds — with a record of 44 wins — 35 by knockouts — and no losses — from Trenton, New Jersey — the Heavyweight Champion of the World — Willy — *Kramer!*"

Kramer leaped into the center of the ring and jumped up and down with both arms raised high above his head. The place went crazy for him, too. The referee allowed the champion a full minute before he called the fighters into the center of the ring.

While the referee gave them their instructions, both fighters stared coldly at each other. Jack recognized Kramer's attempt to "psych" Joey out, and he also knew that the champion wasted his time. Joey's mind focused on another place and another time. In his mind, Joey stood in Yankee Stadium — in June, 1938. He faced Schmeling, the hated Nazi, and he wanted revenge.

They touched gloves, turned, and went to their corners. Harry took Joey's robe, and ducked between the ropes. Jack looked at his brother and yelled, "Go get him, Joe!" Not Joey — Joe.

The bell rang and Joey sprang like an uncaged lion into the center of the ring. He attacked with a fury that surprised everyone in the arena except Jack and Harry. He threw a series of vicious punches that would have devastated any of his previous opponents; but Kramer, a superb boxer, reacted instinctively and blocked all but one. Joey's last punch in the flurry landed solidly in Kramer's midsection.

The champion took the punch, stepped inside quickly, and landed a right cross to Joey's head that staggered him. Sensing his advantage, Kramer bored into Joey with a fury of his own. He landed two solid body blows, and another right cross to the head, which knocked Joey down. The place suddenly became a madhouse. Experienced fans expected the fight would start slowly, with the men cautiously feeling each other out during the first few rounds. The fight had begun as a slug-fest, and the crowd loved it.

Joey climbed slowly to his feet and took the mandatory eight count. When the referee let him loose, Joey seemed to hesitate before he moved back toward the center of the ring. Kramer, sensing Joey's vulnerability, moved in quickly for the kill. The champion launched another right cross. It never landed. Joey had sucked him in. He bobbed under the cross, wove to his left to avoid the next punch, and he came out of the weave with the left hook.

The champion saw it coming and tried to bob under it. It caught him solidly enough to knock him down, but not enough to end the fight. Kramer got up quickly, took the eight-count, and moved briskly back into the battle. The bell rang to end the first round, and the crowd roared its approval.

Joey sat down angrily on his stool and spat out his mouth-piece, "Jesus Christ! This son-of-a-bitch can fight!"

"He sure as hell can, Joey," Jack said grimly. "He can box. He can slug. And he can see your punches coming better than anyone you've ever faced before. That's why he's the champion. And he's a great one. But he can't go at your pace for fifteen rounds. Be patient. Wear him down."

Joey nodded his understanding. The horn blew, and Jack put Joey's mouth-piece in. He jumped off the stool and the bell rang. In Round Two, Joey moved around the champion like a well-oiled machine. He fired three sharp jabs and moved quickly away, circling to his left. He sprang back in, landed two more jabs, then stepped smartly back, out of range again. The crowd did not like it. They wanted more of the slug-fest they had been given in Round One, but when the bell rang, Jack knew that Round Two belonged to Joey.

"You're right, brother," Joey said hoarsely as Jack took his mouthpiece. "His legs aren't as good as mine." He took a mouthful of water and spat it into the bucket. "That's how I'm gonna to beat him."

Round Three seemed a repeat of Round Two, with one minor variation. The champion's corner-men had coached him to cope with Joey's new strategy by taking the fight to him. Kramer tried hard to catch Joey and make him slug it out. But Joey stayed tantalizingly just out of his reach. Joey landed jabs, almost at will, then moved away from anything Kramer threw.

In Round Four, Kramer began to show his frustration. He took more chances, lunging at Joey, trying to land a solid punch. Near the end of the round, as Kramer lunged too far to recover quickly, Joey hammered him with a right cross that knocked him down. Kramer got up quickly, and the bell rang before the mandatory eight count.

When Joey sat down, Harry yelled, "Kramer felt that one! They had to help him find his stool!"

"Don't believe it," Jack cautioned. "He's smart enough to play possum too. Stay on your bicycle, Joey.

You're ahead. The last three rounds were yours, and Round One was even. Make him chase you. Wear him down. He hasn't got your stamina. Be patient."

When the bell rang for Round Five, it quickly became clear that Kramer had not been badly hurt. He seemed renewed, and he attacked with even more energy. He tried desperately to catch Joey, but he fanned a lot of air.

The next few rounds were more of the same. By the end of Round Nine, Kramer was visibly tiring. When Joey came back to his corner, Jack said, "I'll bet he's gonna go for the knockout this round. He hasn't got much left. Be careful." Joey nodded, then jumped up for Round 10.

Kramer attacked Joey with a vengeance, going for the knockout. He took the risk, and caught Joey with a flurry of hard punches. One of them landed below the belt. The referee cautioned Kramer. Jack caught Joey's look of pure rage. When the referee finished his warning and allowed the fight to resume, Joey lunged at Kramer with a fury that surpassed anything they had seen before.

Kramer finally got his toe-to-toe slug-fest, and he gamely threw everything he had, while Joey's attack pummeled his body and his head. The screaming crowd almost drowned out the bell at the end of the round. Blood from a cut over Kramer's left eye ran down his face, and he had to be guided to his stool. His cornermen worked feverishly on the cut.

Joey still seethed with anger. When the bell rang he leaped at Kramer, and immediately landed a body blow that knocked the champion backward. Joey bored in and threw a series of six more body blows. Most of them landed, and Kramer's legs wobbled. Joey raised his sights to Kramer's head. Two hard jabs, and a cross. Kramer staggered. The crowd chanted: "Bam! Bam! Bam! Bam!"

Joey backed Kramer up with the unrelenting fury of his attack. He fired punch after punch, landing them all. Heavy body blows and solid punches to the head drove Kramer into the ropes. The crowd screamed, "Bam! Bam! Bam!" begging for the left hook they knew would end the battle. But Kramer somehow stayed on his feet, absorbing punch after punch.

Then Joey gave them what they wanted. The hook lifted Kramer off the floor. He slammed to the canvas and lay motionless on his side. Joey immediately went to a neutral corner, and he clung to the ropes on either side, as if to restrain the uncaged animal within himself. His face still showed his rage.

Bedlam ruled. The instant the referee yelled "Ten!", the doctor and Kramer's handlers rushed to his side. The referee grabbed Joey's hand and held it up. Jack could not begin to hear what he said. But he knew at that moment, his brother had become the Heavyweight Boxing Champion of the World.

# CHAPTER 2

Radio and TV announcers rushed into the ring. They surrounded Joey, stuck microphones in front of his face and yelled questions at him. Although he had just fought ten rounds with the toughest opponent he had ever faced, Joey grinned and did his best to field their questions.

Noticing Joey's heavy breathing, one reporter shouted, "Never seen you out of breath after a fight before. Was this one that much tougher?"

Joey grabbed a towel from Harry and wiped the sweat pouring down his face. "Yeah. I went anaerobic — the last two rounds."

"Anaerobic?"

"Opposite of aerobic."

Jack jumped in, to give Joey a chance to recover his breath. "In aerobic exercise, such as in distance running, the idea is to work just below the point at which you get out of breath. So you can run for two hours or more without stopping."

"So you don't usually go anaerobic?"

"Well," Joey grinned, "most of my fights — have only gone a few rounds."

"Was there any time in *this* fight when you thought you would lose?"

"No. I try to focus — on the positive. You know, the self-fulfilling prophecy — kind of stuff."

"You were that confident? Even when Kramer knocked you down?"

"Willie Kramer — was a great champion. A truly great one. I knew he had the power — to knock me out. I knew I had to stay away from him — until he tired."

"How about a re-match?"

"It's in the contract."

"When?"

"As soon as he wants it."

"Any prediction?"

"Like I said, Willie Kramer is a great fighter. I won tonight — but that doesn't mean our next fight's gonna be any picnic. I'm sure he'll study the films of this fight — and work hard to prepare. And if I'm not at *my* best — it could be a totally different story."

Jack stepped between Joey and the reporters. "C'mon fellas. He's just boxed ten rounds. How 'bout lettin' him catch his breath an' grab a shower?" Jack nodded to Cappie.

The security director and his crew, backed up by even more Las Vegas policemen, formed a wedge around the new champion and helped him make his way out of the ring. Jack and Harry followed Joey up the aisle and through the screaming crowd. Exuberant fans tried to reach through the wall of security guards and policemen to touch the new champion. Cappie had trained his crew well. Being careful not to use any more force than necessary, they deflected the outstretched hands and protected their charge. Joey smiled graciously and waved to his adoring fans.

When they finally reached Joey's dressing room, Cappie unlocked the door and they dashed inside. Their women waited for them. Sheila rushed to Joey and threw herself into his arms.

"God," he breathed, holding her tight. "I've missed you, Babe."

"Me *too*, Honey," she said with an urgency that made him grin. Then playfully tugging the belt of his robe, she whispered, "Want some company in the shower?"

Jack overheard her whisper. "Oh, it's a *shower* you want? We got a shower. Right here!" And he poured champagne on their heads. Joey grabbed the bottle, clamped his thumb over the opening, shook it, then sprayed a stream at Jack. Squealing with delight, Stephanie and Maria grabbed bottles of their own. All six of them laughed like children, and squirted each other with the bubbly wine.

Cappie opened the door to let Sollie Benito into the room. Sollie froze in the doorway. "Jesus! Hold your fire, will ya? I got an expensive suit on here!"

They all stood dripping champagne, looking sheepishly at the boss for a moment. Then Stephanie broke the tension, "OK, Mr. Benito. It's safe to come in. We won't waste any more of this good stuff." She giggled and took a sip out of her bottle.

Benito strode into the room. "Congratulations, Champ! I tol' you, you was a winner. Didn't I?"

Carter followed Benito into the room, with Mae and Gwen in tow. He grabbed an open bottle and poured glasses of champagne for Benito, himself, and their women. "Here's to the new Heavyweight Champion of the World!" he toasted Joey effusively. Jack, Harry, and their wives solemnly raised the bottles they each held, and joined in the salute to the new champion.

They continued to celebrate for another fifteen minutes. Then Benito said, "I got to get over to the Parthenon. We got a huge party. Should be gettin' started. You guys come as soon as you can. OK?" He gave Joey a final pat on the back and swept out of the room with Mae clinging to his arm.

Carter said to Jack, "The revenue from tonight's fight is going to make you all millionaires." Gwen, noticing Carter engrossed in his favorite topic, moved toward Joey. She stared at the bulging muscles of his extraordinary physique, glistening from the champagne that still trickled down his arms and chest.

Wearing a low-cut, red satin blouse, she inhaled deeply and smiled at Joey. "Well, Mister Champion, you're sittin' on top of the world now." She spoke with a slight lisp, affecting the image of a helpless little girl, as she stared up at the fighter. "I guess everybody's so proud of you," she dropped her voice to a suggestive purr, "you could have just about anything you want."

Looking over Carter's shoulder, Jack noticed that Stephanie and Maria jerked to attention. "Red alert," Maria said out of the corner of her mouth.

Sheila had already moved. She stepped quickly between Gwen and Joey and gave Gwen a big hug. With a smile frozen on her face, Sheila spoke quietly but firmly. "Stay away from my man, Cookie, or your next date will be with a paramedic."

As a former mannequin, Gwen knew that dancers were exceptional athletes. She looked into Sheila's eyes for a moment, and saw her strength and determination. Gwen dropped her eyes, turned on her heel, and walked back to the attorney's side.

Jack heard Stephanie say to Maria, "Secure from battle stations."

Then Sheila threw her arms around Joey's neck, licked a drop of champagne from his cheek, and breathed, "OK, Champ. How about that shower?"

Joey lifted her into his arms, and carried her into the shower room. Grinning at Harry, Jack yelled, "OK, kids. Let's give 'em some privacy."

\* \* \* \* \* \*

The party Sollie Benito threw that night would become a legend in Las Vegas. The guests included politicians, entertainers, sports-writers and sports-broadcasters. Sollie beamed as he ushered Joey from table to table where he proudly introduced the new champion to several Nevada state legislators and one of the state's national congressmen. A famous actor, who had played a boxer in one of his films, clowned around with Joey in a mock fight while delighted photographers shot pictures.

Later, after Sollie finished introducing the champion to his guests, Joey took Sheila in his arms and they danced while the orchestra played soft, romantic music. After several songs, Stephanie studied her brother's face from a distance, then turned to Jack. "This looks very serious, Honey."

Jack looked up from his lobster. "Huh? What is it?" Following his wife's eyes, he saw that Joey and Sheila had stopped dancing in the middle of the floor. Suddenly, Sheila kissed Joey. As she clung to him, he lifted her completely off the floor. Several couples nearby watched and smiled.

"Ah, yes." Jack did his W. C. Fields impression. "It's the famous Joey-Sheila clinch, my dear."

Finishing their kiss, they walked hand-in-hand back toward the table where Jack, Stephanie, Harry, and Maria sat. "He asked her to marry him," Stephanie said.

Maria nodded. "And she said 'Yes.'"

"Could you Wonder-Women hear them — that far away?" Jack asked.

"Didn't need to," Maria replied. "Look at their faces."

Jack looked at them closely as they approached the table. Joey wore a huge grin, and Sheila glowed with happiness.

"Sheila and I are gettin' married," Joey blurted as he reached for Jack's hand. Stephanie and Maria rushed to Sheila. As the three women hugged and laughed together, Sollie strolled over to the table.

"What's all the excitement?"

"The Champ's takin' a wife," Jack grinned.

As Sollie shook Joey's hand, he said earnestly, "Joey and Sheila, I would be very honored if you would let me give you this wedding, at the Parthenon."

Joey looked at Sheila and raised his eyebrows.

Without hesitation, she nodded emphatically.

Turning back to Benito, Joey said, "Thank you very much, Sollie. We accept."

Sheila added quickly, "And, Mr. Benito, since my father has passed away, I would be honored if you would walk me down the aisle."

Sollie's face took on a warmth that Jack had not seen before. He took Sheila's hands, kissed her on each cheek and said, "Thank you, Sheila. If I'm gonna walk you down the aisle, then I think you should start callin' me Sollie."

# CHAPTER 3

That night, Jack Hanley had trouble sleeping. The excitement of the championship fight, his brother winning the title, and the celebration afterward, including the announcement of Joey and Sheila's wedding, had him "pumped up". As he lay sleepless, he began to reflect on how it all began. His mind drifted back to that hot Saturday afternoon in July, several years before . . .

Jack had driven the 405 Freeway, muttering to himself. "This isn't the kind of day to leave Newport Beach and drive inland to Irvine. Unless you've got a damn good reason." Jack had a good reason. His best friend, Harry, had invited him over. He wanted to introduce Jack to his girl-friend's sister.

"Absolutely gorgeous!" Harry had raved exuberantly. "She's a blonde. Life guard. Just flew in from Hawaii. You'll go *nuts* when you see her!"

Jack had the top down on his red sports car as he cruised the freeway, ten miles-per-hour over the speed limit. A carload of female teenagers drew alongside. Jack glanced over, and saw the girls staring at him. Hanley, at 35, kept himself in good shape. He pumped iron three days each week, and ran eight miles on three alternate days. Not really a religious man, he joked, "On the Sabbath, I *resteth*." An All-State tail-back in college, he still ran at six minutes-per-mile. He held his old "playing weight" at 220, and at six-feet, two, he made an impressive figure. As he drove, he rested his arm on the car door and lightly drummed his fingers to the beat of new-age music flowing from his radio. Well-defined biceps bulged under the sleeve of his red polo shirt. Dark brown, collar-length hair whipped in the wind. Staring openly at Jack's tanned, rugged, good looks, one of the girls rolled her window down. Hard-rock blared from their radio, and she yelled, "Where ya goin', dude?"

Jack gave her a brief smile. *All under eighteen*, he thought. *No thank you, Lolita!* Spotting his exit coming up, he cut across two lanes of traffic and downshifted as the sports car entered the off-ramp.

Harry lived in Irvine, in a housing development called "The Ranch," just a few miles from UCI where he taught Computer Science. He owned a two-story, four-bedroom house with a pool. At the end of a cul-de-sac, a row of tall eucalyptus trees stood in a parkway against one side of his property. Jack always liked that about Harry's place. It made it more secluded.

Jack pulled into the driveway, hopped out of the car, and strode briskly up to the double-width entrance. The door swung open almost the second he punched the doorbell. Jack almost gasped out loud at the vision that stood before him. At first, he thought of Helen Lockhart. He knew, of course, it could not be, but Harry had not exaggerated. Absolutely stunning, with long blonde hair and eyes so blue he stared straight into them for several seconds and could not speak. *My God*, he thought, *she must know the effect those incredible eyes have on a man.*

"I'll bet you're Jack." She gave him a warm smile and held out a graceful hand. "I'm Stephanie."

Jack took her hand and found her skin soft, but her grip firm. She continued to gaze straight into eyes. Finally he found his voice. "Ahhh — yes. I'm Jack. Jack Hanley. I'm glad to meet you, Stephanie." He felt like a teenager as he stood for several more seconds holding her hand.

Jack gazed at her lightly-tanned complexion, smooth and unblemished. Her taut cheek muscles seemed to confirm an athletic life-style, yet he found the expression around her eyes to be soft, and sweetly feminine. She looked as though she'd be equally at home on a surfboard or baking cookies. He guessed her age at about 28. She wore a modest, yellow sundress that revealed a stunning figure.

Still holding his hand, she said, "Come on in. Harry and Maria are getting dressed. They just got out of the pool."

Reluctantly, he released her hand and followed her into the house. She led him to the kitchen. "Can I fix you a drink?"

"Yes, please. Scotch, if you've got it, with soda."

She poured two generous shots of Cutty Sark into a glass with ice, added some soda, and handed it to him with a smile that made him lose his train of thought again.

"Harry and Maria have told me so many nice things about you, Jack. I'm so glad to finally meet you."

"Yes, I pay them well." He smiled at her.

She laughed as she poured herself a glass of Chardonnay, then asked brightly, "Shall we go sit by the pool?"

He followed her out onto the pool deck. She moved with an easy grace and the slightest, feminine sway of her hips. A set of patio chairs surrounded a glass-topped table. An umbrella "grew" up through the center of the table, and they sat in its welcome shade.

"Tell me about yourself, Jack?" She looked at him as though she really wanted to know him.

"Sure. Where should I start?"

"Well, I know you and Harry go back to your college days. Why don't you start there?"

"OK. I've known Harry since we were freshmen at Saddleback College back in '88. I guess you couldn't find two guys with less in common. I played football. Not much of a student. Harry was five-ten, weighed 150 and wore thick glasses. A brilliant computer science student. He sat down front in my English class.

"The whole class knew he was a brain. He always had the right answers. And everybody knew the only thing I studied in that class was Sherrie Tyler, the head cheerleader. I had a good season at Saddleback, and Sherrie and I had gone together since she saw me score my first touchdown." With a sheepish expression, he added, "And I saw her jump up and down, cheering."

Stephanie laughed easily, and nodded.

"Anyway, Harry earned extra money as a tutor. He helped me write a term paper that saved my butt in English. And from then on, we've been good buddies."

"And after Saddleback?" She sipped her wine and looked at him over the rim of her glass.

He stared into her lovely blue eyes for a long moment. Butterflies danced in his stomach. He wondered whether the Scotch or her extraordinary beauty affected him so strongly.

She raised her eyebrows and tipped her head slightly to one side, encouraging him to continue. He looked down, away from her devastating eyes, trying to gather his thoughts. To his dismay, he found himself looking through the glass table-top at one of her shapely, tanned legs swinging gracefully while she waited for his answer.

Finally, he tore his eyes away from her altogether, and gazed over her head at the eucalyptus trees. He cleared his throat. "Saddleback was only a two-year college," he said at last. Then, daring to look at her again, he continued, "After we graduated, I transferred to USC, and got a full-ride, football scholarship. I never made first-string, but I managed to play in a few games including one Rose Bowl. I knew I'd never be drafted by the pros, so I decided to hit the books. I made decent grades, and earned my Bachelor's in Marketing."

"How about Sherrie?"

"Who?"

"The cheerleader."

"Oh," he laughed, "Sherrie posed for 'Playboy' and was Playmate of the Year. Then she married a famous tennis pro."

"No foolin'?"

"Yeah. Saddleback's President, a woman, was furious. Sherrie had worn her Saddleback sweater — partly, in some of the pictures."

"She must have been something."

"Well, she had a great figure. But to be honest, Stephanie, you're more beautiful. In fact, you're the most stunning woman I've ever seen."

Her face lit up. "I'm glad you like me, Jack." With a radiant smile, she added, "I think you're kind of OK, too."

A warm feeling crept over him when she said that. "Tell me about yourself, Stephanie?"

"Well . . ."

At that moment Harry and Maria came out of the house. Harry yelled, "Hey, Jack. How're you doin', Buddy? Steph taking good care of you?"

"Just great, pal. She makes a mean highball."

"Good," Harry beamed, pumping his friend's hand.

Maria hugged Jack and kissed his cheek. "Well, how do you like my kid sister, Jack?"

"I thought she was a movie star when I first saw her."

"Really?" Maria arched her eyebrows. "Which one?"

"Helen Lockhart."

Jack noticed that Harry, Maria, and Stephanie exchanged glances, but did not say anything. He wondered if he had missed something.

After a moment, Maria said brightly, "Oh, Jack, you're such a romantic. The first time you saw me, you said I reminded you of Denise Moran."

"I still think so. And like I told Harry, if he doesn't treat you right, someone'll take you off to Newport Beach in a minute."

They all laughed. Maria moved against Harry and put her arm around him. "Well, that's a nice compliment, Jack. But so far, he's treatin' me pretty good."

"OK," Jack said, "but how come you've been keepin' your sister such a big secret? I've never even seen a picture of her."

"Oh . . . " Maria hesitated for a moment. Then she quickly said, "I've never been much for family pictures."

Harry reached for Jack's hand again and turned it over, studying the cuts on his knuckles. Looking Jack in the eyes, he said, "That was *you* last night. At Charlie's Wharf. Wasn't it?"

"What are you talking about, Honey?" Maria raised her eyebrows.

"It made today's paper. Some anonymous white knight kicked the you-know-what out of two scum-bags who were tryin' to rape a woman in the parking lot at Charlie's Wharf. That's your favorite hangout. Isn't it, Jack?"

Everyone looked at Jack.

He didn't answer, but finally nodded his head.

Harry exploded into laughter. "I *knew* it was you! You put 'em both in the hospital. Did you know that?"

"Yeah. Well, they deserved it."

"What happened?" Stephanie asked Jack.

"I was gettin' into my car, and I heard some noise in a parked van. I went over to check it out, and a woman inside yelled for help. The van was locked, so I broke a window. One of the creeps came at me with a hammer, so we went two fast rounds in the parking lot.

"Then this other guy tried to drive off in the van, so I banged his head a couple of times on the window frame, until he stopped. That's about it." Jack shrugged. "No big deal."

"No big deal?" Harry laughed. "According to the paper, Pal, one of 'em got four broken teeth, and a broken nose. And the other one has a broken cheek bone, two cracked ribs, and a severe concussion."

"My God!" said Stephanie. "Are you a boxer, too?"

"No, not really," Jack replied. "But I pump iron a little. And when I played football, there was a certain amount of hand-to-hand combat in the game." He chuckled.

"Well, it sounds like you could have been a Golden Gloves boxer." Stephanie stared appreciatively at Jack.

Maria asked, "What made you think Jack was involved, Honey?"

"Remember I told you how he rescued me from that mugger, years ago? Put that guy in the hospital, too. The story in today's paper sounded like the same 'white knight' to me."

"What happened that time?" Stephanie asked.

"Jack spotted this thug pounding on me in a campus parking lot, and he ran over to break it up. The other guy took off, but Jack caught him. Then the guy tried to kick him. That was Mistake Number Two."

"What do you mean?" Stephanie asked.

"Well, Mistake Number One was trying to outrun an All-State tail-back. And Mistake Number Two was getting him mad. Jack was still hitting the dirt-bag when the campus police pulled him off."

Jack said quickly, "It turned out the guy had a record for mugging people. And he really liked to hurt them."

"Jack broke the guy's jaw, his nose and two of his ribs," Harry said emphatically. "Anyway, I got my money back, and I healed up OK. I was so grateful I helped Jack write a term paper, and we've been good buddies ever since."

"I thought you were a paid tutor," Stephanie pointed out.

"Well, I was. But I sure wouldn't charge Jack anything. Not after what he did for me." Harry patted his friend's shoulder.

Jack looked at Stephanie. "I hope you don't think I'm the kind of guy who goes around lookin' for fights all the time."

"What I'm thinking, Mr. Hanley," Stephanie looked him straight in the eyes, "is that you are a man who doesn't like to see people victimized. By robbers or rapists. And you're a man," she ran her eyes appreciatively over the well-defined muscles of his arms and shoulders, "who is pretty darn good with his dukes." She smiled, then turned to Harry, "What did you call him? A white knight? . . . Yes." She nodded, then turned back to Jack. "I like that. I like that *very* much." She smiled at him, and her incredible blue eyes held him for a long moment.

# CHAPTER 4

Harry asked, "Well, is everybody hungry after hearing the tales of Sir Hanley?"

Trying to keep a straight face, Jack declared, "Why, yes, my Lord. I am most eager to partake of your gracious hospitality."

Maria and Stephanie laughed and nodded their agreement.

"Excellent. You take care of the damsels, Sir Hanley," Harry called over his shoulder as he headed back toward the house, "whilst I shall fetch the beef."

"How's work, Jack?" asked Maria.

"Good. Busy. Sales up fifteen percent this quarter. Makes my boss happy."

"What do you actually do?" asked Stephanie.

"I'm Marketing VP for a vitamin manufacturer."

"Oh, which one?"

"Well, you might not have heard of it. Global Nutrition."

"I sure have. You're one of the biggest in the country."

Harry came out of the house with the steaks on a large platter. As he walked past Maria, he asked, "Honey, please fix me a drink?" Then turning to Jack and Stephanie, he called out, "How're you guys doin'? Ready for a re-load?"

Glancing at their nearly empty glasses, Stephanie and Jack followed Maria into the house. As they walked, their hands bumped. She casually took his hand in hers, looked up at him, and smiled. He got that nice, warm feeling again. Maria fixed Harry a Jack Daniels and water, and poured a glass of Chardonnay for herself. Stephanie made another Cutty Sark for Jack and re-filled her own glass.

"So how did you get from USC to VP of Marketing?" she asked, as they walked back out to the pool deck.

"I spent a few years in advertising. Worked for a small agency in L.A. as an Account Exec. Good experience. I learned sales and advertising at the same time."

"Then what?" Stephanie encouraged him to continue as they reached the patio and sat in their chairs. Maria gave them some space by walking over to Harry at the barbecue. She put her arm around him, and leaned her head on his shoulder.

"Lucky guy," Jack said quietly.

"No one special in your life right now, Jack?"

"No." He remained silent for several seconds.

"Same here," said Stephanie, and she slid her chair around the table to be a little closer to him. "So after the ad agency?"

"Oh," he said. "Sorry. I lost my train of thought. After the ad agency, I interviewed for a job in sales at Global. The owner took me under his wing. I guess he saw some potential I didn't know I had. He brought me along, and in a few years he made me Sales Manager, and eventually his Marketing VP."

"He must be a very smart man." She leaned toward him. She smelled sweet and clean. Not an overpowering scent. Jack did not want to move too fast and scare her off, but it seemed obvious that she found him attractive. He leaned a little closer toward her.

Just then, Harry yelled, "Steaks are ready!"

That broke the mood and they both pulled back. She laughed and blew a little kiss at him.

Harry and Maria arrived at the table with the food. Maria poured a nice Beringer Cabernet, and they eagerly cut into their steaks. During dinner, Jack asked Stephanie, "I've told you a little about myself. How about you do the same?"

"Well," she responded thoughtfully, "I'm a graduate student at the University of Hawaii, Psychology major. I also got my Bachelor's in Psych there, and was on the swim team for four years. I love the ocean, and surfing, and I've been a lifeguard in the summer for the past few years." She looked down at her plate. "I also like Cabernet Sauvignon with a good steak." Then looking directly at Jack, she said, "and slow dancing."

The early-evening dusk still gave enough light for him to see the incredible blue of her eyes as she gazed at him. He felt as though he could have studied those eyes for a very long time.

"How about ice cream?" asked Harry.

"I like that too." Stephanie continued to hold Jack with her eyes.

Harry and Maria picked up the dishes and headed for the house.

Stephanie smiled, "Just before the steaks were done, you were about to say?"

He slid his chair closer to hers. She leaned toward him again. As he leaned toward her, her lips parted and she closed her eyes. He kissed her, and she responded with a tenderness that moved him.

Afterwards, she caressed his cheek with her hand. "Very sweet, Jack."

"Yes," he nodded, trying to control his emotions. He wondered why this incredibly beautiful woman would kiss him so soon. They had just met. *She must have had men falling at her feet since junior high,* he thought. Finally, he decided to just accept it. *Maybe,* he thought, *it's just that old adage: "being in the right place at the right time."*

He wanted to learn more about her. "What are your plans after you get your Master's?"

"Well, maybe family counseling. But it's hard to set up a practice without a doctorate. You have to intern forever at starvation wages. I might teach. I'm a Grad Assistant now, and the Prof I work for lets me take her class about half the time. I really enjoy teaching."

"What class is it?"

"It's a Senior-level course in personality disorders."

"Uh, oh," he said. "I'm not schizophrenic . . ." then lowering his voice he added, "and neither am I."

She tossed her head and laughed, "You're about the most normal man I've met in a long time, Jack. Your only problem is," she tipped her head slightly, "you're not kissing me enough."

He bent forward and kissed her again. After a few seconds, Harry set the ice cream down on the table with a bang. Stephanie jumped, and Jack looked up sheepishly at his friend.

Harry grinned at them. "So sorry to see that you guys aren't hitting it off better."

After dessert, they had coffee and Kaluha, and talked for about two more hours. Finally, Harry stood up, "Well, gang, I'm ready to hit the hay. Jack, please stay later if you like." Harry shook Jack's hand, and Maria kissed his cheek as he thanked them for the dinner. Then Harry and Maria took the last of the dishes and disappeared into the house.

"I've never seen my sister so happy," Stephanie smiled.

"Yes," Jack said, "Harry's a good man. He was badly hurt in a lousy marriage a few years ago. I'm glad that he's found Maria."

"What happened, I mean, in Harry's marriage?"

"He caught her cheating on him. More than once. It tore him apart. He finally divorced her. But for a long time, I was afraid he'd take her back if she tried hard enough."

"Looks like that's not a problem now," she smiled, as the light flicked off in one of the upstairs windows.

"Yes, I'm really happy for him. He deserves the best."

"How about you, Jack?"

"Huh? Oh, I hope I deserve the best too," he laughed.

"I mean," she asked with a stern half-smile, "have you ever been married?"

"Yes. After USC. Another Sherrie."

"What? Another centerfold?"

"Well, not quite. But she was a model, and had hopes of making it big in show business. It's very hard for anyone committed to a career in that business to be married. If they get a chance, say, to be in a movie, and it means they've got to spend six weeks in Africa while they're shooting, the marriage gets put on the back-burner."

"Where is she now?"

"New York, last I heard. I've seen her in a few television commercials. And she's had some small parts in movies. But hasn't really hit it big yet."

"Any children?"

"Oh God, no! That was the last thing she wanted."

"How about you?"

"Kids? I guess so. But to be honest, I haven't given it a lot of thought. If I got married again, and my wife didn't have a career, that would be the next logical step, I guess."

Stephanie looked closely at him for a moment, and appeared to be about to say something, but then she looked down and remained quiet.

Jack wondered if he had said something wrong. Finally, he broke the silence, "How about a swim tomorrow?"

She looked up quickly and smiled. "At the beach? I'd love it. But we don't have to wait 'till tomorrow. There's a pool right here. Wanna?"

Jack found her enthusiasm infectious. "It sounds great, Steph, but, I don't have a suit with me."

"Borrow one of Harry's," she urged.

"I don't think so." He smiled, shaking his head. "I weigh 220, and Harry's only 150."

"Well . . ." she said, with a mischievous twinkle in her eye. She glanced toward the pool.

Jack's heart leapt as he thought she might suggest they skinny-dip.

Then she turned quickly back to him and said, "OK, Sir Hanley, I'll wait — for a day at the beach, tomorrow."

She took his hand and led him back through the darkened house to the front door. She gave him one more very sweet and tender kiss and softly said, "Goodnight, Jack."

Jack drove home more slowly than usual, his thoughts filled with the extraordinary woman he had just met.

# CHAPTER 5

The next day Jack arrived at Harry's house at 1:00PM. Stephanie opened the front door before he reached it. "Hi, Jack," she said brightly. "You're right on time."

He thought, *she must have been watching for me.* He smiled with pleasure.

She returned his smile, took two quick steps toward him, and kissed him. That pleased him even more. Her manner said, *I really like you. I'm glad you're here.*

She wore white shorts and a blue, sleeveless blouse that brought out the incredible blue of her eyes. She had tied the shirttails in a knot around her slim, tanned waist. "C'mon in while I get my stuff." She turned and reentered the house. He could not keep from staring. She had just about the most beautiful pair of legs he had ever seen.

"Harry and Maria went out to brunch," she said over her shoulder. She caught him staring at her legs, but she just smiled. Her large, straw beach bag lay just inside the door. A blue beach towel overflowed the top, and the bag bore large letters: *Here today, gone to Maui*.

"Uh, oh," he said. "I hope you won't be gone — to Maui."

"No, I've got all summer." She smiled again. "I've fixed us some lunch. Would you grab the cooler?"

\* \* \* \* \* \*

A few minutes later, Jack pulled his car onto the freeway and headed for Newport Beach. On the way, they talked about music. She asked, "What's your favorite song?"

"The Power of Love. By Celine Dion."

"That is a great one," she said, "but my all-time favorites are 'When I Fall in Love' and 'The Wind Beneath My Wings'."

"Any particular singers? I mean, renditions of those songs?"

She appeared a little embarrassed, "Well, one of them is a real oldie. I've always loved the way Doris Day sang 'When I Fall in Love'. She must have done that in a 1950's movie. She cried while she sang it, and so did I — when I saw the movie, I mean. 'The Wind Beneath my Wings', that was Bette Midler. The theme from 'Beaches'. Another tear-jerker." Then laughing nervously, she added, "About now you're probably wondering if I only like movies I can cry to."

"What I'm thinking, Steph, is that you're a very sensitive lady. And I like that, very much."

"Good." She nodded and smiled at him.

They drove the rest of the way to Newport, talking about movies, books and the theater. They had both seen "Cats", "Les Miserables" and "The Phantom of the Opera." He confessed that he had cried two or three times during "Les Mis."

Stephanie said, "I know."

"You knew? How?"

"You saw it with Harry and Maria. She told me."

"I didn't know she saw me," he said, embarrassed.

"Jack, when Maria told me how deeply you had been moved by 'Les Miserables' — that's when I decided I wanted to meet you." She reached across the seats and squeezed his hand. "That, and the picture she showed me."

"What picture?"

"The one where Saddleback had just won the National Championship, and somebody poured a big tub of water over you."

"Oh, no!" he groaned. "Harry took that one in the locker room. I only had my shorts on!"

"Like I said," she grinned, "that and 'Les Mis' are why I'm here."

They arrived at his tiny, one-bedroom cottage on the Lido peninsula. He parked in front of the house. The owner had converted the garage to an apartment even smaller than Jack's, which he rented to a couple of students.

Jack opened the door and led her into the tiny living room.

"Oh, I *love* it, Jack!" Stephanie exclaimed. "It's a *terrific* beach house!" She stepped into the even tinier kitchen. "Pretty neat and clean for a bachelor. I'm very impressed."

"Thank you," he said, with a slight bow. "Do you need to change?"

"Nope. Got my suit on under this."

"OK, make yourself comfortable. I'll just be a second." He went into the bedroom and pulled on his bathing suit.

When he came back, she stood looking at the pictures on his wall. He joined her and pointed out his mother and father, who lived in Florida, his sister, Joanne, her husband, and their two children. They also lived in Florida, which provided the reason his parents had moved there after his father retired. "My Mom and Dad couldn't stand to be 3,000 miles away from their grand-kids," Jack chuckled.

Stephanie suddenly looked away, and he wondered if he said something wrong. After a moment she turned to the pictures of Jack in his football uniforms, high school, Saddleback, and USC, which covered the rest of the wall. Clearing her throat, she asked brightly, "No pictures of the cheerleader, or the model?"

"Nope. Ancient history. No artifacts on file."

"Good," she nodded. Then, waving her camera, she added, "We'll start a new file."

They walked the two short blocks to the wide, clean beach on the ocean side of the peninsula. "Newport's a zoo on summer week-ends," Jack said.

"But because parking is so tough, it holds down the number of people who actually get onto the beach. Most of the kids just want to cruise around and look at each other."

They found a spot close to the water. Steph noticed the yellow flag on the nearest lifeguard tower. "Does yellow mean rip-tides?"

"Yeah. You have them in Hawaii?"

"Sure do." She untied her blouse, undid the buttons, and slipped it off her tanned shoulders. She wore a blue bikini. He tried not to stare, but her brief top revealed a more voluptuous figure than he had noticed the previous night. Then she slid her shorts off her hips. He could not tear his gaze away from the daring French-cut style of her bikini bottom. When she turned toward the ocean, her body sideways to him, she appeared to be almost naked.

Tipping her head toward him, she smiled, "Well, am I OK?"

"Steph, Sherrie what's-her-name just lost in all remaining categories."

"Good. Wanna get wet?" She ran for the water.

He dropped his towel and the cooler, and took off after her. He took great pride in his excellent physical condition, but she raced like a gazelle over the hot sand and easily beat him to the surfline. When she hit the water, she swam like a porpoise. He couldn't touch her.

She swam effortlessly, so much in her element that he smiled with pleasure as he watched her. Finally, she came to him, cutting the water with clean, easy strokes. She stood in waist-deep water, leaned her head back, and wiped her hands over the top of her hair. She gave him a radiant smile and laughed with such delight that it filled him with happiness just to be with her.

In her natural, matter-of-fact way, she wrapped her arms around his neck, and kissed him. He tasted the salt water on her lips, and felt her body against his. Then, just as quickly, she sped off again. He swam after her as hard as he could and touched one of her feet. She instantly went into high gear and pulled away from him effortlessly.

She played in the water for a long time, diving, and swimming circles around Jack. Then they body-surfed. She caught the waves like an expert, Jack noted. She glided across the sloping faces, head up, guiding herself with one arm stretched ahead of her.

After thirty minutes of non-stop surfing, Jack's chest heaved from the exertion. "Hey, Lady," he yelled. "How about a break?"

"OK," she grinned. "The next one's a 'shore-boat'." But after riding that wave in, she laughed, and asked "One more?"

Before he could answer, she swam out to catch another wave. After six more, they finally ran up to the beach and threw themselves down on their warm towels. Jack lay on his stomach, trying to catch his breath. He turned toward her. She smiled as she watched him. Jack thought her breathing appeared completely normal.

"My God! You aren't even out of breath. You must be in *fantastic* condition."

She just shrugged, then asked brightly, "Hungry?"

"Sure. I can always eat." Then he added, "Especially after I've been trying to keep up with a mermaid for an hour."

She laughed and handed him a sandwich.

He bit into it and groaned with pleasure as he tasted the charcoal-broiled flavor of the meat.

She smiled, pleased at his reaction. "That's some left-over steak from last night. Maria told me it's one of your favorites."

"Ah, yes, my dear," he said, imitating W. C. Fields, "an excellent repast, indeed. Most deserving of a reward."

"OK," she said, laughing. "Let me take your picture." She snapped several shots of Jack, as he mugged for her.

"OK," he said. "Now I want some of you."

She handed him the camera, and as he looked through the viewfinder, she turned sideways to the camera, cocked her head to one side, and smiled.

"Wow!" he exclaimed, after he squeezed off several shots. "Are you sure you're not a model?"

"Nope." She laughed, as she pirouetted on the sand. Then she planted her feet, legs spread slightly apart, with her hands on her hips, and a pouty half-smile on her lips. "Just an ordinary college girl on vacation," she said breezily.

Jack quickly took several pictures of her in the new pose. Then he said, "Steph, if you're just an ordinary girl, I've been dating aliens from another planet."

He thought he saw the smile fade from her face for an instant, and wondered again if he had somehow offended her.

She quickly recovered her composure and took still another professional-looking pose. She raised one leg, bent at the knee, like a majorette. Then she made her hand into the shape of a gun, her index finger pointed at him, and her thumb up. "Phasers to stun," she said, giggling. The she flexed her thumb, and said, "Zap! Now you're helpless, Captain Hanley. You're my prisoner."

*Oh, yes I am. I am indeed*, he thought, as he quickly took several more shots of her.

A man's voice asked, "Would you like me to take some pictures of the two of you, together?"

Jack looked up from the viewfinder and saw a couple about 60 standing nearby. "Thank you very much." He handed Steph's camera to the man. Then Jack put his arm around Stephanie's slim waist. She leaned toward him, and he could feel the warmth of her sun-drenched skin against his side.

After the man had taken two pictures of them, he handed the camera back to Jack, and said, "That is one lovely young lady."

"Yes, she sure is," Jack agreed. "Thanks for taking our picture." After the older couple had left, Jack guided Stephanie back to their towels. As they lay beside each other, he stared at her lips again, and said, "Now, the pictures will be very nice, but the reward I really had in mind, for that excellent lunch . . . "

Before he could finish, she kissed him, more sensuously than before, he thought. Suddenly, she broke the kiss, raised herself up on one elbow and looked toward the water in alarm.

"What's the matter, Steph?"

"There's a bad rip setting up, and about six kids are caught in it."

"How could you tell that?"

She shrugged. "I've got pretty good peripheral vision." She looked toward the lifeguard tower, "He's gonna need some help."

Jack looked at the tower, and saw the guard yank the phone off the hook. He grabbed his "torpedo" buoy, jumped off the platform, and hit the ground running. Jack turned back and started to say, "You were right about that . . . " But she had already sprinted half-way to the water.

He ran down to the water's edge, but really did not think he belonged out there. The guard and Steph were both in the rip, stroking at high speed toward the young swimmers. The powerful current had pulled the children 100 yards from the beach, and, with unyielding force, dragged them further out every second.

A siren wailed, and a jeep with two more lifeguards pulled up near Jack. The guards sat in the jeep and watched. The older man barked into a microphone, "This is Horne. We're at Tower Eight. We've got six kids in a rip. Gimme the boat."

The radio squawked, "Roger, that." A moment later the radio blared again, "Headquarters to Horne. The boat is rolling."

Horne turned to his driver. "Who's the girl?"

The younger man replied, "No idea, but she sure can swim."

"She's my date," Jack offered. "She's a lifeguard from Hawaii."

"She's pulling away from Scott," the driver said, his voice edged with surprise.

The older guard watched the scene through his binoculars. "She's not breathing."

"What do you mean?"

"Look for yourself." He handed the binoculars to the younger man.

The driver looked for about 30 seconds, and exclaimed, "Jesus, you're right! I haven't seen her breathe yet."

As Jack watched Stephanie, and listened to the conversation in the jeep, he could not tell whether she breathed or not, but she swam relentlessly. Her arms flashed in the sun like high-speed paddlewheels as she pulled further ahead of the guard.

The senior man got out of the jeep, and walked over to Jack. "What's her name?"

"Stephanie . . . " he paused, as it dawned on him he had never asked her last name. Then, realizing it must be the same as Maria's, since neither of them had been married, he added, "Winthrop."

"Stephanie Winthrop," the guard repeated thoughtfully. "Is she an Olympic swimmer or somethin'?"

"I don't think so. She said she swam in competition, but I thought that was just in college."

"Well, the guy she's swimmin' the pants off out there is Scott Klein. He's the Cal State U. Champ in the 1650. If she ain't an Olympic Swimmer, she oughta be."

A crowd had gathered around the jeep, including the children's families. Several of them appeared badly frightened, and two of the women wept. In the distance, the lifeguard boat roared toward the swimmers, but remained at least a half-mile away.

# A.N.G.E.L.S., Inc.

At that moment, Stephanie reached the youngsters. She grasped two of them by their arms and held them up as she treaded water.

"Looks like she's got the ones who were in the most trouble," commented Horne as he watched the scene through his binoculars.

In a few more moments, Scott Klein reached them. Two of the children grabbed his torpedo, and he held the last two. But the rip kept them all in its powerful grip, pulling them further and further out to sea.

Finally the boat arrived. The pilot expertly veered out to sea, cut the engines, shifted into reverse, then backed slowly toward the swimmers. One of the guards on the boat dove in to help. In a few moments, all six children, Stephanie, and the guards had clambered through the open doorway in the stern. When all were safely aboard, the parents near the jeep breathed a collective sigh of relief.

The pilot then steered out of the rip-current, and carefully backed the boat as close as possible to the beach. Stephanie and two lifeguards swam with the six youngsters in to shore. The children, rested by now, came in on their own power to the waiting arms of their relieved parents.

Jack ran to Stephanie. "You OK, Steph?"

"Just a little tired, but I'm OK."

"That was very impressive. You sure had the guys in the jeep talking. You pulled away from that guard like you had fins on, and he's a distance swimming champion."

The older lifeguard walked over, "Hi, Stephanie," he said, sticking out his hand. "I'm Dick Horne,

Captain of the Marine Safety Department. Good job. Thanks for the help. You guard in Hawaii?"

"Yes. The last few summers. Honolulu City-County."

"Well, I'd sure like to send my guys to train with you. Geez, you're a fish. You swam in college?"

"Thanks. Yes, I swam for the University of Hawaii. Four years."

"Stephanie, can I ask you somethin'?"

"Sure."

"How long did you hyperventilate before you went in? I never saw you breathe."

"I breathed. Every three strokes. Alternate sides."

"I watched you through my binoculars. I never saw it. Not once."

"Well," she laughed, inhaling deeply, swelling her impressive chest, "I do breathe, honest."

"Yes, I can see that," he smiled, and then looked at Jack. "Well, you have a good day. And thanks again, Stephanie." He walked back to the jeep.

"I think I may have overdone it, Jack," Stephanie said with a sigh. "Do you mind if we go back to your place?"

"Not at all. I've had all the beach I need for today."

When they reached his cottage, he asked, "Would you like to take a shower and change into some dry clothes?"

"I'd love it. Thanks." With a heavy sigh, she went into the bedroom, and he heard the shower come on. A few minutes later she emerged, dressed in her blouse and shorts, with a towel wrapped around her hair.

He looked closely at her. The corners of her mouth turned down with fatigue, and her eyes had lost their sparkle. "You look really tired."

"I am. Do you mind if I lie down for awhile? I think a nap will revive me."

"Go right ahead, Steph. Can I get you anything? Hot coffee? Tea?"

"No, thanks. I'll just crash for awhile." She returned to the bedroom and closed the door.

# CHAPTER 6

Still in his damp bathing suit, Jack wrapped a beach towel around himself and sat on the couch. He picked up the remote control, turned on the TV, and "surfed" until he found a football game.

About an hour later, Stephanie walked slowly out of the bedroom. He again looked closely at her face. Her eyes had circles under them, and her skin had lost its healthy glow, replaced by a ghostly pallor. "Are you OK, Steph?" he asked, his voice edged with concern.

"I'm sorry to be such a pill, Jack. But I guess you'd better take me back to Harry's."

"Can't I get you something? Coffee? Soft drink? Water?"

"No, thanks." She managed a little smile. "I probably just need a good night's sleep."

She clung to his arm as they walked to the car, and she napped while he drove to Irvine. When they arrived at Harry's, Jack found her sound asleep. He tried to rouse her, but she could not keep her eyes open. He ran to the door and punched the bell. Harry opened the door, and Jack yelled, "Something's wrong with Steph!" As they ran to the car, Jack continued, "She helped a lifeguard save some kids. She's been out of it ever since."

Harry looked closely at her. "How you doin', Steph?"

She replied so faintly that Harry had to crouch beside her, his ear close to her mouth. Jack thought he heard her say, "Overdid it — oxygen debt too great — glycogen way down."

Harry seemed to understand. "Carry her into the house, Jack."

"Jesus, Harry! Shouldn't we take her to emergency? Or call the paramedics?"

"Jack, believe me, she'll be OK. I know exactly what I'm doing." Harry seemed so sure of himself, Jack picked Stephanie up and carried her into the house. He took her upstairs, and laid her gently on the bed in the guest room. Maria hurried in with a worried expression on her face.

"Maria will take it from here," Harry guided Jack out of the room. Then he turned back to Maria, and said quietly, "Oxygen. D5 in saline."

Harry led Jack into the kitchen. "Want a drink, Jack?"

"What I want, Harry, is some answers. Is Stephanie a diabetic?"

"No."

"Does she have some other kind of disease?"

# A.N.G.E.L.S., Inc.

"No."

"Well, what the *hell's* goin' on, Harry?"

"I understand your concern, Jack. Let's have a drink."

"Jesus! Am I going to need one?"

Maria walked into the kitchen, "She'll be fine after a few hours, Jack."

"Is she sick? What?"

"Jack," Harry said, "let's sit down." Turning to Maria, he asked, "Honey, would you please fix us a couple of drinks?" He led Jack to the couches in the family room, and they sat.

Jack tapped his fingers impatiently on the table, as he waited for his friend to gather his thoughts. Maria brought their drinks, sat on the couch beside Harry, and draped one of her arms over his shoulders. "Think it's time to tell Jack about me and my sis, Honey."

Jack took a gulp of a strong Scotch. "OK. What? Please."

Harry asked, "Jack, have you heard of genetic engineering?"

"Yeah. Clones, gene-splicing. So?" Suddenly, things started fitting together in Jack's mind. Stephanie had outswum a male champion. Two lifeguards had said she didn't breathe, and they had watched her through binoculars.

Jack's jaw dropped open, and he stared at Harry in disbelief, "Jesus! Are you telling me — that Stephanie is some kind of . . . " his voice trailed off. "What? Artificial woman? Like a robot or something?"

Maria cleared her throat, "Jack, Stephanie and I are not mechanical machines, robots. Our bodies are made of biological cells, just like other living creatures. But we were not *born* in the usual sense, and did not *grow* from birth to adulthood. We were created and incubated in a laboratory."

Jack jumped to his feet, spilling his drink. "What the *hell* are you talking about?! *Incubated*? What's *that* supposed to mean? Grown in *pods* like — 'The Invasion of the Bodysnatchers'? For Christ's sake!"

"Jack," Harry said quietly, "please sit down, and try to be calm. I created Maria with the help of a Molecular Biologist, and a bunch of graduate students who worked on small parts of the problem without knowing the true nature of the project.

"It took several years, and Maria is actually the result of a kind of evolution. My early attempts actually *were* robots. They had elegant Artificial Intelligence programs, and could carry on sophisticated conversations. They were beautiful to look at. Their skin was a plastic developed by DuPont for prostheses. Amazingly life-like and warm to the touch. And like the robots in the movies 'West World' and 'Cherry 2000', they were also capable of having romantic relationships with humans. But, in the final analysis, they were machines. Clever imitations. But not living creatures."

Harry paused and took a long pull of his Jack Daniels. "Then I met Jim Feingold, a biologist working on the Human Genome Project. That's a Government funded project to map all of the genetic information encoded in the DNA of a human being. Jim knew it would take 50 years for the best mainframe computer to handle all of the computations.

"So he came to me, to see if I could help him. He knew that I specialized in Artificial Intelligence, and hoped I might have some technique that could help him solve the Genome problem — in his lifetime. I did. It's called Massively Parallel Processing. I connected 256 microcomputers together. One master computer, and 255 workers. The master divided the Genome problem into many segments, and assigned specific segments to each worker.

"It worked. We had the Genome in two years. Jim was so grateful he then put all of his effort, and the considerable resources he had available, into helping me. Using the Genome information, we were able to create a being of living cells. Not a robot. A living human being." He turned to Maria with great pride in his eyes, and she casually caressed his shoulder.

"Unfortunately, Jim died suddenly of a heart attack. But Maria studied everything available in the field, and, using Jim's notes, she helped me create Stephanie."

Jack sat dumbstruck for several moments. Harry and Maria waited patiently for him to recover from the shock.

Finally, he asked, "And Stephanie looks like a movie star, because you *made* her that way?"

"That's right, Jack," Harry smiled. "And by the way, you were also correct last night."

"What?"

"The sources of Stephanie's genes were two female students. One was an Olympic class swimmer, the other a dead ringer for Helen Lockhart."

Looking at Maria, Jack asked, "And was I right about you?"

Maria nodded. "Yes, Jack. I'm a clone of a young lady who won a Denise Moran look-alike contest."

"Why did you pick her, Harry?"

"I had the world's worst crush on Denise Moran, ever since I saw her cry in 'Phantom'," Harry said quietly.

"Why did you pick Helen Lockhart for Stephanie?"

"*You* picked her."

"*I* did! What do you mean?"

"I knew that you thought she's one of the most beautiful women in Hollywood."

"But — why . . . ?"

"I made her for you, Jack."

"You made her for *me*?!"

"You're my best friend, Jack. When I saw how happy Maria made me, I wanted you to have the same kind of happiness."

"Well, thank you very much, Harry, but I think I prefer *real* women." He looked quickly at Maria. "Sorry, Maria. This is all a shock to me. One hell of a shock. I'm completely off balance. I don't know what to say. I'm not even sure of my own feelings. I'm very confused . . ."

"Of course you are," Harry nodded. "And I have to apologize for this. I should have told you the truth about Maria a long time ago. And I should have gotten your approval before introducing you to Stephanie. All I can say is — because you've always had beautiful women in your life — I wanted to see if you'd notice anything different about her. And if you'd be attracted to her."

"Well the answer is, yes. I was very attracted to her. I've spent — what? Four hours with her last night, and another four today. Eight hours doesn't make a mad love affair. But I was interested in her, very interested. OK?"

"You *were* interested?" Maria raised her eyebrows. "Not now?"

"Yeah. Like I said, I really don't know what the hell to think right now. I'm going to need some time to sort this out."

"I understand, Jack," Harry said. "Again, I apologize for handling it the way I did. I should have been straight with you."

"OK. Let me ask you a couple of straight questions."

"Shoot."

"What's the matter with Stephanie right now?"

"She completely exhausted herself. Depleted the glycogen in her muscles."

"What the hell is glycogen?"

"It's the principal carbohydrate stored in the body. It's converted to glucose, sugar, when needed for energy."

"OK. Another question. Two lifeguards watched her swim. Through binoculars. They said she didn't breathe."

"She breathes, usually. But many competition swimmers don't breathe during short races. They can go faster. Stephanie was so concerned for those kids, she overdid it. She built up a tremendous oxygen debt. That also exhausted her."

"What are you doing for her?"

"We're giving her oxygen, and five-percent dextrose in saline, intravenously."

"Oxygen? Saline? What've you got here? A hospital?"

"Well, in some ways, yes. Genetic engineering is a very sophisticated technology. We set up a pretty decent lab here when we created Stephanie. Some of the equipment is hospital-class stuff."

"Is she going to be OK?"

"She's sleeping now. In a few hours, she'll be good as new."

"Anything else I should know about her?"

Harry hesitated. Maria said quietly, "Neither Stephanie nor I will be able to have children."

"Can . . . " he glanced at Maria, then looked away, embarrassed, "can Stephanie make love?"

Harry replied quickly, "Yes. If your relationship had developed the way mine and Maria's has, she would have made you the happiest man in Newport Beach."

Jack looked down at his drink. "This is a little embarrassing . . . "

Maria looked directly at Jack, and continued to caress Harry's shoulder. "The most important thing in my life is this man."

"It sounds like you're in love, Maria."

"Of *course* I am. Totally and completely."

Jack stared at her, then Harry, for several seconds. "And I have to admit that I've never seen you happier, Harry."

"Are you kidding? Jack, for Chrissakes. I've been, all my life, the stereotypical Nerd. While handsome football heroes like you were nailing all the Sherrie Tylers of the world, I was lucky to get a date. When I finally found a girl who'd marry me, she turned out to be a slut. She broke my heart. I damn near cracked up, and nearly committed suicide.

"After two years of hell, I finally hit on the idea of using my own expertise in Artificial Intelligence, and later, adding the Genome information, to create a woman. A companion who would really care about me." He hesitated for a moment, then smiled at Maria and went on, "A lover who would never cheat on me. Someone I could trust — absolutely — with my heart."

"And do you? I mean, do you love Maria just as much as you would if she were . . ."

"A *born* human being? Yes. I love her. I love her *very* much. She makes me completely happy."

Jack sat for several moments looking first at Maria, then Harry. They remained silent, letting him sort through his thoughts. Finally, Jack looked hard at Harry. "You said Maria would never cheat on you. Does that mean she doesn't have free will? You haven't *programmed* her, somehow — have you?"

Harry smiled at Jack, then turned to Maria. "Maybe you'd like to answer that, Honey."

Maria turned to Jack and did not smile. "I certainly have free will. I am *not* one of those mindless bimboes in the 'Stepford Wives'. Cheat on Harry?

Yes, I could, if I wanted to. Every time I go to the store, men hit on me. Half of 'em want my autograph, thinking I really am Denise Moran, and the other half want to jump on my bones. And some of 'em aren't bad lookin'." She began to smile, and changing her tone to a throaty imitation of the actress she resembled so strongly, she said seductively, "Like the dude who keeps promisin' to drag me off to Newport."

Jack shifted uncomfortably on the couch, and took a large swallow of Scotch.

"But," Maria continued, using her normal voice, "I would *not* cheat on my man, no matter how strong the temptation."

"Why not?" Jack asked.

"Lots of reasons."

"Such as?"

"Well, there's the obvious ones, AIDS, syphilis, gonorrhea, et cetera. More importantly, I know how *I'd* feel if I found out Harry was screwing another woman."

"How would you feel?" Jack interjected.

"Devastated! Hurt beyond belief." Turning to Harry, she continued, "I'd be so pissed at you . . . "

"Not to worry, Sugar," he said, patting her hand. "That's never going to happen."

"I know, Babe."

Jack looked at them for a long moment. "Well," he said, standing up, "I've got a lot to think about. I'm going to head home."

"Harry stood up quickly. "Jack. I hope you'll accept my apology. I made a bad mistake, and I really am sorry."

Jack shook his friend's hand, "You're forgiven, Harry. I know your heart was in the right place."

Maria asked, "When Stephanie wakes up, what shall I tell her?"

"Tell her the truth. Tell her that I was very attracted to her, but I was shocked to learn — the facts about her. Tell her that I need some time to think about all this. I'll call you when I've decided if I can handle — this situation."

"Jack," Maria looked at him, "while you're thinking about it, please keep this in mind. Stephanie knows you far better than you know her. After last night, she pumped Harry and me for every detail of your life."

"And?"

"And she already has strong feelings for you. Very strong feelings."

"I understand. I'll call you later." He didn't kiss Maria good-bye. He just looked at both of them, shrugged his shoulders, and hurried out the door.

# CHAPTER 7

When Jack got back to Newport, he parked in front of his house, but did not go in. He walked slowly to the ocean side of the peninsula and sat on the beach to think. The sun sank into the ocean with a blaze of color. Jack watched it disappear, and then savored the beautiful after-sunset glow on the wet sand at the water's edge. Sand pipers scampered busily after each receding wave, digging for sand crabs. The last few families on the beach packed up their gear, and trudged toward the parking lot. A child laughed as she discovered some unknown treasure. Surfers sat astride their boards, waiting patiently for the last waves before dark. Jack's favorite time of the day. "Worry time", a lifeguard friend of his had jokingly called it.

"What on Earth do you worry about, at a time and place like this?" Jack had asked.

"Nothin'. Absolutely nothin', Jack. That's the beauty of it. Just another perfect day in paradise."

Jack did have something to worry about. He attacked the problem as an experienced business executive, and began by making a mental list of the facts.

First, Stephanie's extraordinary beauty rushed to his mind. "Probably the most gorgeous woman I've ever met," he said aloud. Second, she seemed extremely intelligent. According to Harry, Maria had absorbed all of the knowledge of a Ph.D. in Molecular Biology. He supposed that Stephanie could do the same. Third, she had a playful, affectionate personality.

Fourth, she apparently had strong moral character. He certainly did not get any hint of promiscuity, although she did not seem to be a prude, either. And she had risked her life to help save some kids. "Kids," he said aloud, again. "She can't have any. Is that important to me?" He didn't know. Would it be important later in his life? Same answer.

Next, Harry had said that Maria made him completely happy. Gave him the love he had yearned for, all his life. And Stephanie would be the same.

Finally, she hadn't been born, but had been *incubated*. What the hell did that mean? Did Harry and Maria *grow her*, like a plant in a test-tube, or a greenhouse?

He wondered about Stephanie's age, and if she really studied at the University of Hawaii. Or could that just be a cover story to explain her sudden appearance? Had she really life-guarded? Probably not. Certainly not for four years. Harry and Maria had only been together for two years.

"Damn," he muttered. "I need more information." He walked back to his house and dialed Harry's number. Maria answered.

"Oh, Jack, I'm glad you called." Relief sounded in her voice. "Do you want to speak to Steph? She's fine now."

"No, not yet anyway. I need to talk to Harry."

"Oh — OK, Jack." Her voice reflected her disappointment. "I'll get him."

Harry came on. "Hello, Jack," he said in a guarded tone.

"Couple of questions, Harry."

"Go ahead."

"Is Stephanie really a student at the University of Hawaii?"

"No."

"Never life-guarded?"

"No."

"Some kind of cover story?"

"Yes."

"How old is she?"

"Six months."

"Only *six months*? Jesus! How can she function so fully? How can she know so much about music and the theater? How would she ever know what to do — if our relationship had gotten to the point — that I wanted to make love to her?"

"Jack, Stephanie has, in that beautiful little head of hers, what we computer scientists call 64 giga-bytes of information. That's the equivalent of about 20,000 books of 1,000 pages each. She can access and use that information in a fraction of a second."

"How did she read 20,000 books in six months?"

"They were read to her, by a computer, equipped with a speech synthesizer, during her incubation."

"That's another thing. What the hell is this *incubation* you're talking about?"

"Well, that's another development that Feingold and I came up with. It's a gene-splicing technique that greatly accelerated growth and maturation. We replaced the gene that regulates growth-rate with one from another organism, that had a much faster rate."

"How the hell did you do that?"

"We destroyed the old gene, with X-rays, and inserted the replacement gene on the appropriate chromosome."

"Where did the replacement gene come from?"

"From — another organism."

"What organism, Harry?"

"Well, it's not very glamorous. But it works . . ."

"I'm waiting."

"OK. It comes from a rabbit. Their gestation period is 31 days, they mature in a few months, and they're readily available.

"And that works? I mean, it doesn't hurt them?"

"That's right. Gene-splicing frequently combines genes from different species. It's called transgenics, and it's been used since the 1980's."

"So she looks like she's about 28, but she grew to that age in six months?"

"Yes."

## A.N.G.E.L.S., Inc.

"Wait a minute, Harry. What keeps her from continuing to age at the accelerated rate? I mean, is she going to look like she's eighty — next year?"

"No," Harry chuckled, "although that's a very good question. We programmed the quick-maturation gene to turn itself off at the end of the incubation process."

"How did you do that?"

"Telomeric manipulation."

"Telo — what? What the hell is that?"

"We shortened the telomeres in the quick-maturation gene . . . Jack, I can't give you a complete course in recombinant DNA in one telephone call. But let me ask you a question."

"What?"

"You met Maria two years ago, right?"

"Yeah, that's about right."

"Does she look or act any different to you today?"

"No," he said thoughtfully, "she seems about the same."

"OK, Jack. Now, a couple of other *good* things about Maria and Stephanie. They've got terrific vision and hearing. And they can solve complex math problems, mentally, without pencil and paper."

"More gene-splicing?"

"Yes."

"Anything else?"

"Yes. One negative thing. Maria mentioned it yesterday. They can't have children. Unfortunately, one of the key genes required for fertility got turned off with the quick-growth gene. I didn't know how to fix it, and Feingold didn't leave any notes on the subject."

Jack remained silent for several seconds.

"Jack?"

"Still here. Just mulling over what you've told me."

"Anything else I can help you with, Jack?"

"No, I guess not. Steph's OK now?"

"Well, *physically*, she's OK."

"Physically?"

"You want the truth, buddy?"

"Yes, I do."

"She's been crying ever since Maria told her you didn't want to talk to her."

"She's crying?'

"What can I say, pal? They learn quick. She thought you were quite a guy, and she started to fall for you — that fast. Now you don't want to see her, or even talk to her. So she's hurt."

Jack thought of Stephanie's beautiful face in tears. Guilt washed over him. But it did not assuage his disappointment about their deception. Most importantly, he still felt uncertain of his ability to accept the facts of her origin. "Harry, please tell her I'm sorry, but I need more time to think this through."

"OK, Jack. I'll tell her. I hope we'll hear from you soon." He hung up.

Jack decided that he needed to get out, be around people, and think about something else. He'd come back to this later, with a fresh perspective. He still wore his bathing suit, and it itched. He headed for the shower, and stopped cold. A pretty blue bikini hung on the faucet. The image of that beautiful, happy girl rushed back into his thoughts, and he felt a stab of remorse as he thought of her crying over him. "Damn," he swore.

He yanked a drawer open, tossed her bikini in, and shoved the drawer closed. He turned the radio on, loud, to fill the house with sound, and stepped into the shower. As the water washed the salt off his skin, he hoped it would also wash away the strange combination of emotions confronting him.

After his shower, he did feel a little better. He stepped out and toweled himself briskly. He started to think about getting some food. As he quickly threw on some clothes, the radio disk-jockey said, "And now, from the sound-track of 'Sleepless in Seattle,' here's Celine Dion with 'When I Fall in Love'."

"Damn," he swore again and punched the radio's OFF button. He jumped into his car and drove to the Rusty Crab, a popular seafood shanty with a sawdust-covered floor. He drank two beers and wolfed down a plate of barbecued shrimp. The image of Stephanie's face repeatedly crept into his mind, but each time he tried to think of something else.

He went to a movie, a Schwarzenegger "shoot-em-up", to get a couple of hours of welcome escape from his thoughts. Then he drove to Charlie's Wharf and ordered a Scotch. He looked around, but didn't see anybody he knew. Mostly tourists. Disgusted, he drank up and went home where he tossed restlessly on the mattress for two hours before falling asleep.

The next day, work kept him busy and that helped. He thought of Stephanie several times, but forced her from his mind. During his lunch-hour, he drove home, grabbed her bikini and headed for the post office. He bought a large, padded envelope, printed her name and Harry's address on the outside, and decisively pushed it across the counter to the postal clerk. Back at work, he thought of her a couple of times that afternoon, but quickly drove her image from his mind. He had made his decision.

Three days later, when he got home from work, a letter from Stephanie lay in his mailbox. She had enclosed the pictures of them at the beach. In one, she stood beside him with her head on his shoulder. Her beautiful face seemed to glow with pure happiness. Strong feelings rushed back to him again. The letter, written in a delicate feminine hand, read:

Dear Jack,

Thank you for returning my bathing suit.

I apologize for misrepresenting my background. It was foolish of me not to be honest with you from the start.

I'm enclosing copies of the pictures, taken during happier moments.

I think of you often. You're a fine and very special man. I wish things could have been different. I truly believe they might have been. I wish you all the happiness in the world.

               Fondly,
               Stephanie

Jack sat in his living room, re-read her letter, and stared at her pictures for a long time. Then he picked up the phone.

# CHAPTER 8

Harry answered the phone.
"Harry. Jack. Can I speak to Stephanie, please?"
"You bet! Hold on," and he dropped the phone.
Stephanie picked it up in a few seconds, "Jack! Oh, I'm so glad to hear from you. How are you?"
"Well, I'm feeling lots of things, Steph. I'm feeling kind of foolish, and embarrassed, I guess, about my reaction to your — situation. And I feel very badly that I mailed your bathing suit without even enclosing a note. I just didn't know what to write . . . "
"Jack."
"Yes?"
"Let's get past embarrassed. What else?"
"I want to see you again."

He heard her sigh, and realized that she must have been holding her breath. "Oh, Jack. I want that *very* much."

"Good. When shall we . . . ?"

"Right now, Jack?"

"I'll be there in half an hour."

When he pulled into Harry's driveway, the door swung open and she ran to him. She threw her arms around his neck, and kissed him for a long time. Then, keeping her arms around him, she pulled her head back a little, looked deep into his eyes, and said, "I'm so glad to see you, Jack."

He gazed at her exquisite face and thought, *How beautiful she is. How genuine in her feelings. So sweet. I can't believe I almost let her get away.*

He took her to dinner at a seafood restaurant on the San Clemente pier. They took an outside table and watched the sun as it began to set behind Catalina Island. "Like a postcard, isn't it?" he said. "My favorite time of the day."

"It's unbelievable, Jack." She gazed at the magnificent sunset, the red and gold clouds darkening as the sun disappeared behind the island. Then she sang softly, "Twenty-six miles across the sea. Sunny, sunny Catalina, that's the place for me."

"Have you ever been to Catalina, Steph?"

"No. Not yet. But I'd like to . . . "

"Maybe we could go some time. It's a skin diver's paradise. The water is crystal clear. Visibility sometimes one hundred feet."

"Wow! That must take your breath away. What else have they got besides skin-diving?" She looked at him over the top of her wine glass, as she had the first night he met her.

"Well, Avalon, is a tourist haven. Restaurants, gift shops, glass-bottom boat rides. It's a popular spot for honeymooners."

She broke eye-contact suddenly and looked at the table. After a moment, she cleared her throat and said, "Speaking of that — honeymooners, that is — you know that I'm — that I've never been intimate, with a man."

He reached out and covered her hand with his. "I know, Steph. And I'm in no hurry. We'll cross that bridge, when the time is right."

"Whew." She blew out a breath. "I'm glad that's out in the open." Then looking at him seriously for a moment longer, her face broke into a grin. "Know what else?"

"No. What?" he asked, smiling back at her.

"My belly-button's fake."

"What?"

"I didn't need a real one. No umbilical cord. So Maria made me one, surgically. You didn't notice the difference at the beach the other day, did you?"

"No I didn't," he said slowly. He thought about adding, "I'll have to inspect it at close range, sometime." But decided to steer clear of any innuendoes. Instead, he picked up his menu and said, "We better order soon. It gets cold at night out here, even in July."

\* \* \* \* \* \*

After dinner, he took her dancing, slow-dancing, in the lounge of a luxurious hotel in Dana Point. "You remembered," she smiled, as he took her in his arms.

She moved with the same grace that he had seen when she walked, or ran, or swam in the ocean. The soft lights of the dance floor made her even more beautiful. They danced for hours. The soft warmth of her body against him, the clean, sweet smell of her hair, the musical sound of her laugh, all filled him with great happiness. He kissed her several times, and each time she responded with a tenderness that spoke to his heart.

Finally, the combo played their little, "time-to-go" ditty, and the leader said, "Goodnight, folks."

As they walked to his car, she looked at him. "I don't want this night to end, Jack."

"Neither do I, Steph."

"Take me home with you, Jack?"

His heart leapt, "Yes, Steph. That would make me very happy."

After they got into the car, she said, "I guess I should call Harry and Maria, so they won't worry."

"Yes, I think you should." He opened the glove box and handed her the cellular phone.

A few seconds later, she said, "Hi, Maria. It's me. We're going to Jack's . . . I don't know. It's up to him. We've been dancing . . . Perfect . . . Thank you, Maria. I'll tell him . . . OK, Goodnight."

Putting the phone back in the glove box, she said, "Harry and Maria send their love."

When they got to Jack's place, she suggested some music, and started looking through his CD's. He went into the kitchen to heat a pot of water. A few minutes later, he heard Celine Dion's voice, singing "The Power of Love." *You remembered, too,* he thought.

When the water started to boil, he poured it into two brandy snifters and swished it around. Then he dumped out the water and poured generous shots of Drambuie into each snifter.

He carried the glasses into the living room and found Stephanie curled up on the couch, with her legs under her. She had dimmed the lights, and her skin had a soft, warm glow. He sat beside her, and handed her one of the snifters, "Be careful, the glass is hot."

She savored the fumes of the Drambuie for a moment, then sipped the sweet liqueur. "Oh, my. That will warm the cockles of my heart," she laughed.

They drank their Drambuie, listened to the romantic music, and kissed. They danced again, and kissed almost continually while they danced. Their kisses became more passionate. Then, looking into his eyes, she said softly, "I know you'll be gentle . . . " She took his hand and led him into the bedroom.

\* \* \* \* \* \*

He took the next day, a Friday, off from work. That gave them a three-day weekend, and it seemed like a short honeymoon. They went to the beach every day, basked in the warm sun and swam. He barbecued steaks at night, and they ate them with Cabernet Sauvignon. And she made breakfast for them in the morning. He took her shopping for some clothes. They went to the theater and he took her dancing again. And they made beautiful, sweet, tender love. He had never known a more sensuous, more loving woman.

Sunday morning, he awoke to find her lying beside him, propped up on one elbow, looking at him. The morning sun streamed in through the tiny window behind her. Her blonde hair, slightly disheveled, caught the warm, golden rays like a halo around her face. "You look like an angel, Steph." She continued to gaze at him with a warm, loving smile. "Have you been watching me sleep?"

She nodded and caressed his cheek lightly with her finger-tips. "I'm falling in love with you, Jack."

He felt a great surge of warmth, "I love you, too, Steph." She bent her head and kissed him with exquisite tenderness. After a moment, he could taste salt on her lips, and he knew that she had been moved to tears.

When she pulled back, she wiped away the tears with the back of her hand, "I told you I love movies where I can have a good cry." They laughed together. And then they made love.

\* \* \* \* \* \*

Later that morning, he sat in the tiny kitchen and sipped his coffee as he watched her make an omelet. He felt great happiness and contentment. "Steph, would you like to move in with me?"

She dropped the spatula and rushed to him, "Oh, sweetheart! Yes!" She leapt into his arms and he held her for a moment. Suddenly, she yelped, "Yipes! The eggs!" and rushed back to the stove. As she stood with her back to him, she wiped her cheeks with the back of her hand.

He walked up behind her, wrapped his arms around her slim waist and nuzzled her neck. "You are the sweetest, most tender woman I've ever known, Steph. And I love you very much."

"I know, Sweetheart, but if you keep nuzzling my neck like that, you're going to get more than an omelet for breakfast."

After breakfast, she called Maria and told her the news. Maria and Harry were both delighted. Steph told them that she'd come over the next day to pick up her things.

\* \* \* \* \* \*

Monday morning, Jack had Stephanie drop him at work. "If Maria's free, ask her to go shopping with you. You still need some more clothes." He handed her his VISA card.

"How can I sign on your card, Honey?"

"I'll call the Credit Union this morning, and have them add your name to the account."

"That's very generous, Jack. Thank you."

"Well, Honey," he drawled, "like it says in the song, 'You are my Lady', now."

She sang the next line softly, "And you are my man." She gave him a very sweet kiss. "I'll pick you up at five, Sweetheart." She drove off, waving gaily at him.

For the next few weeks, they were still on a "honeymoon". Jack loved coming home to the smell of her cooking. On their second weekend together, he took her to Catalina Island. They sailed on a large catamaran, and stayed at a bed-and-breakfast inn called The Pelican House. Too modern to be charming, Jack called it "L.A.-plastic-apartment decor". But it only had two guest rooms, and they picked a weekend when the other room sat vacant. That gave them exclusive use of the Jacuzzi, a definite plus for honeymooners. They swam, and snorkeled in the clear water. They basked in the sun, ate good seafood, and made love, with great passion at times, and with gentle tenderness at others.

Their second week together, Jack wanted Stephanie to get a driver's license. She had no ID. He called Harry, who said that he had made a birth certificate for Maria. That had been enough for the DMV.

"How the hell did you do that?"

"Oh," he chuckled, "it's wonderful what you can do with a desk-top publishing program and a little imagination. I'll make one for Steph. Pick a small town, out of state. I don't think they bother to check. As long as she passes the written and the driving test, they'll be happy to take your twelve bucks."

"OK," Jack said, "let's keep her a Hawaiian, any city but Honolulu. How about Lahaina, that's on Maui." He turned to Steph, "Honey, what's the population of Lahaina, Hawaii?"

In less than one second, she answered, "9,073 in the 1990 census, but it was only 6,095 in the 1980 census. At that rate of growth, it's probably about 10,500 now."

# A.N.G.E.L.S., Inc. 81

Jack stared at her in disbelief for several seconds. Then he turned back to the phone, "OK, let's use Lahaina, Harry."

"OK, I'll Fax it to you later today."

After they hung up, Jack looked at her, "Sweetheart, you are a wonder. How did you find that so fast?"

"Oh, honey, that was easy. The population stat's are in 'The World Almanac'. That's the third book Harry's computer read to us."

"What're the first two?"

"Well, the first one was 'Webster's Unabridged Dictionary'."

"What's the second one, Steph?"

"The Bible."

"The Bible?"

"Yes, darling. Many people feel it's the most important book in the world. I do, too."

"Now I know why I thought you were an angel that morning."

"Oh, you are the silliest man I ever saw," she laughed gently.

After a few weeks of living together, they began to settle into a routine. She got her driver's license without any problem, and he bought her a car. Weekdays, while he worked at the office, she spent a lot of time with Maria. They shopped, and went to the beach, and just talked for hours.

Stephanie became interested in business, especially marketing, because she wanted to intelligently discuss Jack's work with him. Maria, had the equivalent of a Ph.D. in biology, and had also learned everything she could about artificial intelligence, Harry's field. The women shared their knowledge, and delighted in quizzing each other.

The four of them got together often. They took turns having each other for dinner on weekends, and often went out for dinner and a movie during the week.

Jack's love for Stephanie continued to grow. After living with her for a few months, he realized they were as close as any married couple he knew. He never tired of her. "You're fun to be with, Sweetheart," he said. "Always happy. Always focusing on the positive." She had a wonderful sense of humor. They became good friends, as well as lovers. They shared the joy of swimming, running, and just reading quietly together.

On their first Christmas, they had lived together for five months. They sat at a small tree in the living room, drank eggnog laced with a little bourbon, and listened to Christmas carols. He pulled a small package out of his pocket and handed it to her. She quickly peeled away the wrapping paper and saw a small, velvet-covered box. Her hands trembled a little as she lifted the lid. And she gasped when she saw the diamond ring.

Before she could speak, he said, "I love you very much, Steph. I want to spend the rest of my life with you. Will you marry me?"

She flew into his arms, and the tears started before she could say, "Yes, darling. With all my heart, yes."

# CHAPTER 9

Jack and Stephanie joined Harry and Maria for a late dinner and gift exchange that night. When Stephanie showed them her ring, Maria leaped out of her chair and hugged her. The two women laughed with tears in their eyes. "I'm *so happy* for you," Maria exclaimed, as she looked at the ring, then hugged Stephanie again.

Harry beamed and pumped Jack's hand. "You know, Maria and I have also been talking about marriage, maybe we should make it a double wedding."

Maria, overhearing Harry's comment, rushed to him, threw her arms around his neck, and yelped, "*I do!*"

They all laughed. Then the women started making serious plans for a double wedding. "OK, Sis," Maria said, "we'll be each other's Maid of Honor, and the guys will be each other's Best Man."

"Yes," Stephanie replied. "Now, what kind of dresses should we get?"

Harry and Jack went into the kitchen, in search of champagne. When they returned to the dining room, Stephanie asked, "How's Las Vegas sound to you guys?"

"On New Year's Eve," Maria added.

"That's only a week away," Harry commented.

"Well, I know my family couldn't come all the way from Florida," Jack offered. "Dad's retirement pension is nothin' to get all glassy-eyed about."

Harry just looked at Maria with a little smile. They all knew his parents had died in a plane crash several years before, and he had no brothers or sisters. Stephanie and Maria, of course, had no relatives.

"OK," Jack said, "sounds like it's Vegas on New Year's. Now, hotel reservations could be a problem on such short notice, but I've got a friend in marketing at Disneyland who could get front-row seats to a coronation."

\* \* \* \* \* \*

When their plane arrived at McCarran Airport in Las Vegas, they spotted a uniformed limo-chauffeur holding a sign: "Hanley-Washburn". The driver handled their baggage while they relaxed with drinks and toasts to each other in the limo.

Jack's friend got them a penthouse suite at the Tropicana. He had also arranged round-trip air fares, limo service for their entire stay, iced champagne waiting in the sitting room of their suite, and a dozen roses in each bedroom.

Jack kidded Harry that if he ever made another Maria or Stephanie, he'd have to give her to his friend. Stephanie and Jack laughed at that. But Jack noticed that Harry and Maria exchanged a quick glance, and did not laugh.

After they got settled in their suite, they went to City Hall and got the marriage licenses. "This has to be the only government office in the world that's open in the middle of the night," commented Harry.

From there, they rode to one of the little chapels on the Strip. They had to sit in a waiting room for about a half-hour. "The wedding business in Vegas is doing very well," Jack observed. "I wonder who handles their marketing?"

"Hormones," chuckled Harry, "Horny-mones!" The limo had a well-stocked bar, and the two men began to feel mellow. They pretended they were going to "escape" from the wedding.

"OK, Harry, you create a diversion," Jack said in a stage whisper. "I'll sneak out and get the car. When I honk, run like hell!" Stephanie and Maria smiled patiently at their antics.

But when they got in front of the Justice of the Peace to say their vows, the men behaved with proper decorum. Jack had slipped a tape cassette to the J.P., and asked him to have it played during the ceremony. When Stephanie heard Doris Day's voice singing "When I Fall in Love", her eyes filled with tears. She gave Jack a radiant smile and silently mouthed, "Thank you, darling."

For their reception, they had a gourmet dinner for four served in their suite. Jack played tapes of their favorite songs. They ate lobster, drank champagne, and danced. Finally, as Jack and Stephanie danced to "You are the Wind Beneath my Wings" for the fourth consecutive time, Harry and Maria joined them. The men shook hands warmly. Maria hugged Stephanie and said quietly, "Goodnight, Mrs. Hanley."

Harry and Maria went into their room, and closed the door. Stephanie and Jack danced awhile longer. As the song ended, she looked at him tenderly, "And now, Mr. Hanley, your wife would like to be loved."

He bent down, lifted her into his arms and carried her into the bedroom, kissing her all the way.

\* \* \* \* \* \*

The next morning, Jack awoke to the smell of coffee. Stephanie sat beside him, gently blowing on a steaming cup. As his eyes opened, she smiled and asked, "Want some coffee, honey?"

"Why, thank you, Mrs. Hanley." He took a sip from her cup.

"Oh, I love my new name," she said, glowing. They sat in bed together, quietly sharing their coffee.

They heard a rap on the door. "Oh, that's room service with breakfast." She jumped out of bed, threw on a robe and let the waiter in.

Ten minutes later, the four of them ate Eggs Benedict in the sitting room. After breakfast, Jack pushed his chair back, stretched his legs and said to Harry, "This is not too hard to take, ol' buddy."

"Yes, indeed. I could get used to this real easy," Harry agreed.

Maria said, "Well, that might be easier than you think, Stud Muffins."

"Stud Muffins?" Jack grinned at Harry.

"What can I say?" Harry hit a pose. "Some guys got it . . ."

Stephanie ignored the mens' kidding and looked closely at Maria, "What do you mean, 'easier than you think'?"

Maria asked Stephanie, "Have you read 'The Eudaemonic Pie'?"

"No. What's that?"

"It's a book. Supposed to be a true story about a bunch of grad students at U.C. Santa Cruz. Physicists and computer science types. They used computers and radios, built into their shoes, to beat roulette wheels."

Harry sat up in his chair, "How's that?"

Maria became more animated, "One guy stood near the wheel and stared at a fixed point near its edge. He pressed a switch, with his toe, every time the Double Zero went by. With three data points, the computer in his shoe could calculate the speed of the wheel. Then he did the same thing for the ball. The computer calculated its speed and deceleration. Then it predicted which octant of the wheel the ball would land in."

"What the hell is an octant?" Jack yawned.

"One eighth of the wheel." Harry stared intently at Maria.

Maria nodded, "There are 38 numbers on a roulette wheel. But the payoff is only 35-to-1, which is where the house has its edge . . ."

"And," interrupted Harry, "if you can predict the octant where the ball is going to land . . ."

Stephanie jumped in, "You could bet those four or five numbers, win 35-times your bet, and clear about 30!"

"Why are you guys getting so excited?" Jack asked, still logy from too much breakfast. "We haven't got computers or radios."

"We sure as hell have." Harry looked at Maria and Stephanie.

Maria smiled, "I could watch the wheel, and as soon as I've got the probable octant, I could signal Steph . . ."

"Then," Stephanie blurted "I could bet the four or five numbers in that octant before the dealer calls 'all bets down'."

"I don't know, you guys," Jack said skeptically. "They've got signs all over the place saying that it's against the law to use computers."

Stephanie took a breath, swelling her chest, "Do I really look like a computer to you, Lover Buns?"

Over the laughter, Harry said, "Tell you what, let's go downstairs and see if it would work. I mean, we won't really gamble. Just let Maria study the wheel, send messages to Steph, and see if they'd make any money. What do you say, *Lover Buns*?"

Jack answered carefully, "I say, as long as we're not really rippin' anybody off, I guess we don't have to worry about getting our knees broken."

"OK," said Maria as she and Stephanie jumped up. "Let's get dressed. See you here in — what? Twenty minutes?"

"Fifteen," yelled Stephanie over her shoulder as she hurried into the bedroom.

Thirty minutes later, Jack, shaved, showered and dressed, walked calmly into the sitting room. The others waited anxiously for him. As soon as he entered, they jumped up and headed for the casino. Jack thought Stephanie and Maria seemed as excited as a couple of teen-age girls going to a prom. Harry also seemed intrigued by the idea. Jack thought he must be missing something. He did not understand why they were so excited.

When they arrived at the casino, the girls hurried to the nearest roulette wheel. They studied the wheel for a moment, and talked quietly. Harry turned to Jack, "They're dividing the wheel into octants, memorizing the numbers in each, and setting up a code."

Then Stephanie walked down to the end of the table where the players placed their bets. Maria stayed near the wheel. Harry and Jack just stood and watched.

Maria chewed a piece of gum, and Jack noticed that periodically she stopped chewing for a moment. Then she'd quickly chew a few times, and then pause again. After watching her do that several times, Jack realized that she must be clicking her teeth, just loudly enough for Stephanie to hear it. The number of clicks probably identified the octant.

After an hour, Jack felt bored. But the girls concentrated intently on their "game", and Harry seemed content to let them play until they were satisfied. Finally, Maria said, "OK, let's go," and they all walked away from the table.

"Well," Jack asked, "how would you have done?"

Stephanie just shook her head, and he could see that she held back laughter. When the four of them were alone in the elevator, both girls erupted.

"Over $100,000!" Maria yelped.

"$115,000, to be exact!" Stephanie squealed, her face flushed. "That's with $100 bet on each number."

Maria said, "We decided it was simpler to use quadrants instead of octants. That way we only needed four codes."

"One, two, three, or four tooth-clicks?" Jack asked.

"Very good, Lover Buns," Stephanie exclaimed. "Anyway, that meant I'd have to bet ten numbers each time, risking $1,000."

"Then," Maria interjected, "with a payoff of $3500 on the winner, we'd get a profit of $2500 on each spin."

"We played 60 spins, and won 50, for $125,000," Stephanie blurted. "The 10 spins we lost means we would have cleared $115,000." She and Maria hugged each other, and laughed like two schoolgirls with a wonderful, secret joke.

Jack glanced at Harry, and could tell from the look on his face that he wanted to go for it. "OK guys, I like the idea of you two Wonderwomen making 100-grand an hour, as long as you keep your clothes on. But if we're going to try this, we need to be careful. We shouldn't take that kind of money out of any one casino."

# A.N.G.E.L.S., Inc.

"Makes sense," Harry nodded. "Let's say, $10,000 tops, out of any one place."

"One other thing," Jack said, "let's not play here, at the Tropicana."

"Ah, so," Harry said with a Chinese accent. "The wise fox doth not despoil its own nest."

The girls bubbled with exuberance. "OK!" Maria exclaimed. "Let's go despoil a few nests!"

"Yeah! Come on, Honey!" urged Stephanie, grabbing Jack's arm.

The elevator door opened on their penthouse floor. Jack hesitated a moment, then said, "Oh, what the hell. So we'll be a couple of kept gentlemen of leisure, Stud Muffins," and he punched the "Lobby" button.

Jack found the girls' enthusiasm contagious. By the time they had giggled all the way to the Lobby, Jack had caught their excitement.

Jack told the limo driver to take them to Caesar's Palace. They headed for the nearest roulette table. Maria worked the wheel, and Stephanie placed the bets, putting a $100 chip on each of ten numbers, every play.

On their first five plays, they won four, for a profit of $9,000. Since that fell under their $10,000 limit, they played one more spin, and won. They were $11,500 ahead.

A man in a tuxedo, the Pit Boss, walked over to the Wheel-man and they exchanged a few words. The Pit Boss stood solemnly and watched, lightly bumping a knuckle to his lips. Maria, aware of his interest, stopped chewing her gum. Stephanie deliberately lost $300 apiece on the next five spins.

The Pit Boss ambled off. Stephanie picked up her chips, tipped the Wheel-man $100 and walked to the cashier's cage. She came back in a few minutes, and they all walked out together.

In the limo, she passed around two $5,000 cashier's checks, one made payable to Stephanie Hanley, and the other to Maria Washburn. The girls laughed uncontrollably, their faces flushed with excitement.

"Hey!" Jack pretended to pout, "I thought Stud Muffins and I were going to be kept gentlemen?"

"OK, Lover Buns," Stephanie snuggled against him. "I'll get the next two checks in your names."

For the next few hours, they methodically worked their way down the Strip. They visited a dozen major hotel-casinos, following their plan, taking about $10,000 from each. After the third casino, Stephanie worked the wheel for awhile, and Maria laid down the bets.

After the sixth casino, they realized that Harry and Jack could place the bets, if the girls could give them some kind of signals. Since they needed only four codes, nose-scratches, eye blinks, and coughs, worked fine. They became creative and used each signal only once, in each casino.

Jack had trouble remembering which 10 numbers were in each quadrant. The girls had nearly perfect recall. And Harry, being a computer scientist, also had a good memory for numbers. But Jack's imperfect betting made them less obvious. It usually took him a few more spins to hit the $10,000 limit.

When he had it reasonably well mastered, they broke up into two teams. Harry and Maria worked one wheel, while Stephanie and Jack worked another. That meant they took only $5,000 from each wheel. It also meant they hit their $10,000-limit in about half the time.

When they stopped for lunch, they had a stack of 24 cashier's checks, of approximately $5,000 each. Maria quickly calculated the exact total, $122,600. Jack had become as excited as Harry and the girls. He told Stephanie that he'd like to buy them a house. That brought tears to her eyes.

After lunch, Stephanie exclaimed, "OK, troops, back to work!"

"So many casinos, so little time," laughed Maria. After lunch, they hit another dozen casinos. Their cashier's checks totaled over $200,000.

While making that kind of money in one day thrilled them, they also felt tired. The game required a lot of concentration. They had to remember all the numbers in each quadrant, and the codes. They also had to be alert for the Pit-boss, or anyone else who appeared to be watching them. When that happened, they would immediately go "off-game". The girls would stop giving real signals, and would make a lot of random movements, *noise* Harry called it. They would let the house's built-in advantage beat them for several spins, while they reduced their bets.

They decided to quit for the day. All banks were closed for New Year's Day. They went back to the Tropicana and got a safe-deposit box. Stephanie and Jack counted out the checks that were in their names. They totaled $107,800. Harry and Maria had the same.

They put the checks in the deposit box and went up to their suite.

About two hours later, the phone beside Jack rang. He picked it up, and Harry asked, "You alive in there, Hanley?"

"Just barely, Pal," he chuckled. "All this gamblin' excitement got my wife into a very marital mood." He turned to Stephanie, and she smiled up at him contentedly.

"Yeah. Maria too. Tough duty, ain't it, Buddy?" he laughed lazily. "You guys want to catch the eight o'clock dinner show? It's a 'Follies' kind of extravaganza."

Jack asked his wife, "Want to eat and see the 'Follies' show, honey?"

"OK," she grinned, "as long as I get to reap the rewards if you get your hormones jangled, lookin' at all those half-naked showgirls."

"Sounds good, Harry. Meet you at the door, in thirty minutes."

\* \* \* \* \* \*

The next morning, after breakfast, they headed for the casinos in the downtown section of Vegas. As before, they split into two teams, taking only $10,000 from each casino. Jack had the quadrants memorized and frequently made his $5,000 profit on the first two spins of the wheel.

After a few casinos, they found that they spent more time traveling from one place to another than they did at the wheels. They decided to let each team take

$10,000 per wheel, which meant they took $20,000 per casino. At lunch, they counted their cashier's checks. They had nearly $160,000.

"Jack," Harry said, "we're running out of casinos. How do you feel about going back to some of the places we hit yesterday?"

"I don't know, Harry," he said. "I'd love to stay with it until Steph and I could buy a house like yours, for cash." Then, he nodded, "Sure. Why not?"

After lunch, they headed back to the Strip, going over the same ground they had covered the previous day. By 3:00PM, they had visited eight more casinos, bringing their second day's winnings to over $300,000.

The four of them stood at the Cashier's window, in one of the newest, most opulent casinos. As Stephanie and Maria reached for the $10,000 checks, they were all suddenly surrounded by six men. Two wore tuxedoes, and the other four were armed, uniformed guards.

One of the men wearing a tuxedo, spoke no louder than necessary for them to hear, "OK, folks, please come with us."

# CHAPTER 10

"Hey!" Jack yelled. "What the *hell* is this?" He felt strong hands grip both of his arms. He instinctively started to resist, and felt both of his wrists immediately gripped as well. He tried to twist free, but the guards on either side lifted enough of his weight to prevent him from getting traction on the floor.

One of the guards said, "You are coming with us, Sir. The easy way, or the hard way. It's up to you."

Two of the other men had grabbed Harry's arms. Another had grasped Maria's wrist, and the fourth guard reached for Stephanie. She easily twisted free from his grasp. The man grabbed at her again, and in the scuffle, he accidentally struck her chest.

Stephanie grasped her breast in pain and yelled, "You filthy pig!"

Jack nearly went berserk with rage. The men on either side held him firmly, but Jack had played football for ten years, nearly 100 games, carrying the ball over

1,000 times. For years, big, mean people had grabbed at him, tried to tackle him, hurt him, make him fumble, and even put him out of the game. He reacted instinctively.

He twisted to his left, then back to his right, then left again. He got solid footing and dragged the two men, desperately clinging to his arms, over to the guard who had hurt his wife. Jack pulled his left leg up, almost to his chest, then kicked down with all of his strength. The sharp edge of his shoe slammed into the guard's knee. The man screamed in agony and dropped like he had been shot.

Jack continued to twist, and the guard holding his left arm lost his grip. The guard on Jack's right tried to bend his arm up behind his back. But with his left arm free and both feet on solid ground, Jack swung around and smashed his fist into the man's face. A torrent of blood gushed from the badly broken nose. Jack then spun back to his left, anticipating an attack from behind.

He was too late. The blackjack hit him squarely on the forehead. He heard a very loud noise, and felt a lot of pain. He heard his wife scream his name as he lost consciousness.

When he came out of it, he lay on a table in some kind of hospital. Stephanie, with a worried look on her face, gently held an ice-pack to his forehead. "Jack! Are you OK, Honey?"

"My head hurts like hell. What did that bastard hit me with?"

A man's voice to his right said, "I wish he'd hit you with a fuckin' pipe, you prick."

## A.N.G.E.L.S., Inc.

Jack turned to his right, and saw the guard he had kicked. He also lay on a gurney, with an ice pack on his knee. "As I recall, you hit my wife in the chest. . ."

"I'd like to take you out behind the hotel and hit *your* fuckin' chest, for about five minutes."

"Anytime you want to take off that cap pistol, I'll be glad to kick your ass. And watch your filthy mouth in front of my wife, or we'll do it right here."

A man in a neat, brown suit with a stethoscope draped around his neck, walked in. "OK, boys. You've done enough damage for one day."

Another man came in, "The ambulance is back. The E.R. Doc said Edmundson's nose is broke all right, three places."

"OK, tell him this one's cartilage, for sure. Medial meniscus. Possible ligament damage, too. Anterior and posterior crucials. He should have an orthopedist look at him."

The attendant said "OK, Doc," and wheeled the guard out.

The man in the brown suit turned to Jack. "What's your name?"

"Hanley. Jack Hanley. Who are you?"

"I'm a doctor, and I'm trying to assess how bad that bump on your head is. Do you recognize this lady?"

"Yes. She's my wife, Stephanie."

"Good. Do you know where you are?"

"Last I knew we were in the Hotel Parthenon, in Las Vegas."

"You still are. This is our infirmary. Do you know what day this is?"

"Monday. Day after New Year's. January second."

"Where do you live?"

"520 West Balboa Boulevard, Newport Beach, California."

"Where do you work?"

"Global Nutrition, 3300 Harbor Boulevard, Costa Mesa, California."

"OK. Sounds like you're all right. Slight concussion. Your head will probably hurt for a day or so. Aspirin will help. If it persists beyond two days, you should see a doctor again."

"Can I go now?" Jack tried to sit up, then realized that his wrists and ankles were strapped to the gurney.

"Sorry, Mr. Hanley, but you are in some pretty serious trouble."

"What kind of trouble?"

"You put two men in the hospital, for one thing. One man has a badly damaged knee, and the other has a broken nose. They'll probably both file charges against you."

"So, am I going to be arrested?"

"I don't know. The Casino Security Director wants to talk to you, as soon as I release you."

He looked over Jack's head "OK, fellas, he's all yours."

Two more uniformed guards came into Jack's field of vision. One looked like an ex-boxer. His ears and nose were disfigured, and he had many scars around his eyes. The other, an Asian, looked like he was made out of piano wire. The look on his face told Jack that he would be the more dangerous of the two.

The ex-boxer said, "Listen. I'm gonna take these straps off, one at a time, and I'm gonna 'cuff you, behind your back. If you try anything funny, my partner is gonna put you in the hospital, for a long time. You understand?" The Asian moved closer to the gurney and stared coldly at his Adam's apple. Jack knew that's where he'd be hit, probably with a Karate chop, if he flinched.

"OK," Jack said agreeably.

"Good." The guard carefully unfastened the strap on Jack's left wrist. "Slide your left arm under your back, far as you can — farther. OK, now roll to your left." Jack felt handcuffs being clamped on his wrists. The guard released the other straps. "OK, sit up. Come with us." Turning to Stephanie, he said, "You come too, Missus."

Each guard gripped Jack firmly by an arm, his wrists handcuffed behind his back. He let them lead him out of the infirmary and down a very plain tile hallway. He guessed they were in a part of the hotel not ordinarily accessible to the guests.

They walked a short distance and the Asian opened a door marked "Security". A uniformed, female guard sat at a gray metal desk, in a nearly-empty room. "Take him right in," she said, staring at Jack without expression. "Cappie's waitin' for him."

The ex-boxer opened an unmarked door and led Jack into another very Spartan office. A man, about fifty, sat behind a plain metal desk A little overweight, he looked like an ex-cop. Wearing a blue shirt, open at the neck, with his tie loosened, he looked tired and unhappy. He smoked a cigarette, and the smoke made his eyes water.

Harry and Maria sat on gray metal chairs against a wall. A uniformed female guard, who looked like a WAC drill sergeant, stood next to Maria. A young, male guard stood beside Harry. Fresh out of the Marines, Jack thought. Trained for three years, how to kill with his bare hands.

Maria looked at Jack with concern, "Are you OK, Jack?"

"I'm fine. You guys OK?"

"So far, so good," Harry said cautiously.

The man behind the desk motioned to the two guards holding Jack, indicating a chair on the wall opposite Harry and Maria. The guards led him to the chair, and sat him down, with his cuffed hands behind the back of the chair. Stephanie sat in a chair as close to him as she could, but his guards stayed on either side of him.

"Mr. Hanley," said the man behind the desk, "my name is Anthony Capodilupo. I am in charge of Casino Security. And you are in very serious trouble."

"Oh really? What kind of trouble?"

"First, we have reason to believe that you and your friends have defrauded the casino, by using computers, which is against Nevada State Law. Second, you have committed assault and battery against two security officers, while they were performing their lawful duties. They are both sworn constables, by the way, which makes your attack a felony."

"I was defending myself and my wife. We were in the process of collecting a large sum of money, when we were accosted by a group of men, who used force to unlawfully detain us. One of them struck my wife's breast. I reacted the way any man would, under those circumstances.

"We have no computers, and I'm sure you knew that, when you sent your thugs to harass us. Since we had not violated the Nevada State Gaming Laws, their action was clearly unlawful."

"Are you an attorney, Mr. Hanley?"

"No, but I assure you that I shall have one here in a very short time, and that he will sue you for *my* injury. And, by the way, a black-jack is an illegal weapon, which makes *that* a felony, and makes *you*, as the Security Manager, subject to criminal charges as well. Finally, I would like to leave now, with my wife and friends. If you do not immediately release us, I will call the Las Vegas Police, and have you arrested for kidnapping."

The ex-boxer beside Jack snorted.

"I'm afraid that's not very realistic, Mr. Hanley," Capodilupo smiled. "The fact is, you are being lawfully detained for investigation, in much the same way as common shoplifters. Now, I would like you to explain how you were able to win $10,000 here yesterday, and $20,000 more today, in just a few spins of a roulette wheel." He looked very hard at Jack as he mashed his cigarette butt in an ashtray.

Jack smiled at him, "Just lucky, Mr. Capodilupo."

"OK, let's stop playing games, Mr. Hanley. For the past twenty-four hours, your pictures, and reports of your winnings, have been faxed back-and-forth between casino security offices throughout this city. Videotapes of your Modus Operandi have been reviewed by experts. It's clear that your wives have been using computers to predict quadrants on roulette wheels, and that you have made over $500,000 illegally."

"Mr. Capodilupo, you and I both know that if these ladies had been using computers, we would not be having this conversation."

"What is that supposed to mean?"

"It means we'd be under arrest, and in the custody of the Las Vegas Police. But you haven't called them, because you *know* that we're not using computers."

"We haven't conducted a body search — yet."

"I know you haven't. And I know you're not going to."

"Oh, really?"

"That's right. For two reasons. First, you don't need to. You already know we don't have any computers on us. We've had more metal detectors passed over us in the past twenty-four hours than visitors to a state prison. And second, you're too smart to authorize a body search, especially of a female, against her wishes. Nobody does that today, except the police, and even then, only after an arrest."

That stopped him cold. After a moment, he slowly smiled. "Are you sure you're not an attorney?"

"Not guilty," Jack smiled back.

"How did you know you were being checked with metal detectors?"

Jack looked him squarely in the eyes, "Mr. Capodilupo. I'll tell you how we knew we were being checked with metal detectors — and I'll even tell you how we beat the wheels, if you'll agree to my terms."

Capodilupo sat forward in his chair, and tried to freeze his face, to mask his interest. "What terms do you have in mind, Mr. Hanley?"

Jack knew that he had him. "First, I want these handcuffs off. Second, I want you to release the four of us as soon as I've explained our method. Third, I want your guarantee that we can keep the money we've won. Fourth, I want your guarantee that we will not be interfered with, in returning to our hotel, in leaving Las Vegas today, or at any time in the future, provided we do not use our method here again. Fifth, I want your guarantee that I will not be charged for the altercation with your security guards today. And finally, I want all of this in writing, and I want it faxed to my attorney in California. When he tells me he has it, I'll explain our method to you."

Capodilupo thought for several moments, and said, "I cannot give you all of these guarantees. I will have to speak to our Corporate Attorney. He can deal with anything concerning our casino, and our employees. But, neither he nor I can speak for the other twenty-two casinos you have — uh — visited."

Jack felt pleased that they had only "visited", not "defrauded", the other casinos. "Then you give us security until we're on the plane."

Capodilupo pulled a phone out of his drawer and punched a few digits. After a moment he said, "This is Cappie. Can I speak to Mr. Carter? It's about the roulette whiz-kids."

After another moment, he said, "Hello, John. They've agreed to tell us their method, if we let 'em keep the money, file no charges on the injured guards, and protect them from harassment by other casinos 'till they're on the plane. They want it all in writing, faxed to an attorney in California."

After listening for a moment, Capodilupo said, "In all, over 500-grand, from over twenty casinos. Just from us, 30K." After another long pause, "OK, John," and he hung up.

Capodilupo looked at Jack, "That was our Corporate Counsel. He's preparing the letter, and we'll give you protection until your flight leaves — provided, of course, that your explanation is satisfactory." He looked at the ex-boxer, "OK, uncuff him. Then you guys can all go back to your shifts."

After the handcuffs were removed and the four guards had left, Capidolupo asked, "While we're waiting, would you like some coffee?"

"I'm sure we'd all love some," Jack said. "Thank you very much."

Capodilupo pressed a button on his phone, "Ginnie, please bring in five coffees."

The female security guard came in with five Styrofoam cups on a tray. They drank the strong, hot coffee gratefully, and relaxed for the first time, it seemed, in hours.

Thirty minutes later, Ginnie brought a sheet of paper to Capodilupo. He read it, and handed it to Jack. Printed on the Parthenon's letterhead, it had been signed by John Carter, J.D., Corporate Counsel. He had weasel-worded everywhere he could, to protect his company, but it looked like they were going to be out of there, with their winnings.

"OK." Jack handed the letter back to Capodilupo.

Capodilupo handed it to Ginnie, "Fax this to Mr. Hanley's attorney. And ask him to call me after he's got it."

She looked at Jack, "You got a number?"

"Nope. But it's Myron Goldsberry, on Seventeenth Street, in Tustin, California." She turned and went out.

Ten minutes later, Capodilupo's phone buzzed. He picked it up, listened for a moment, then said, "He's right here." He handed the phone to Jack.

"Myron?"

"Jesus H. Christ, Hanley! What the hell is this fax I just got from Vegas?"

"Read it to me, Myron. I want to confirm it's the same one I've been shown."

The attorney read it to Jack.

"OK, that's it. Just file it Myron. I'll explain the details when we get home."

"Wait! You guys really win half-a-million-dollars?"

"Yeah, just about."

"And you put two security guards in the hospital?"

"Yes."

"And they're letting you go? No charges?"

"That's right."

"You are one lucky son-of-a-bitch, Hanley. You know that?"

"Yes. I know, Myron. I'll call you when we get back." He handed the phone back to Capodilupo.

He hung up the phone, and looked straight into Jack's eyes, "OK, how'd you do it?"

"Do you know who was the greatest hitter in baseball history?"

"What the hell has that got to do with roulette?"

"Bear with me."

"All right," said Capodilupo, with a guarded look, "Babe Ruth."

"Nope. He hit a lot of home runs, but his batting average was never that great."

"So?" asked Capodilupo impatiently.

"Most experts agree Ted Williams was the greatest hitter. He hit over .400 — the only man in modern baseball to do that. And he faced guys like Bob Feller, and Bob Lemon, who could throw over 90 miles-per-hour."

"So? What the hell . . . " sputtered Capodilupo.

"He could *see* the *ball*!"

Capodilupo looked at him, still puzzled.

"Ted Williams had 20:10 vision. He could read print at 20 feet, that a normal person couldn't read further than 10 feet away. Williams often said that he could see the ball, and he only swung at the good ones."

"Wonderful. But, I still don't see what that's got to do with . . . "

"My wife, and her sister," he nodded toward Maria, "both have extraordinary vision. They can see the ball, and the numbers on the wheel, while it's spinning. And they can predict, accurately, where the ball will land."

Capodilupo squinted hard at him, "So they can see the ball. That's not good enough. To predict where it will land, they need to do so much calculation — there's *got* to be a computer."

"Nope. They do the calculations in their heads. They've had all the math and physics they need. They've memorized the formulas, and they can handle the math mentally."

"I don't buy it. Nobody can do that. Not in the time they did it. We're not talking simple arithmetic here."

"You're right," Stephanie said.

Capodilupo turned and looked at her expectantly.

Meeting his gaze steadily, he continued, "It's differential calculus."

"You're telling me you can do calculus, *in your head*?"

Maria chimed in, "The first derivative of velocity is acceleration. The problem involves the deceleration, negative acceleration, of a ball."

Capidolupo looked from Stephanie to Maria, then back to Stephanie, searching their faces. "Sorry, ladies. I still don't believe it."

Wanna bet?" asked Stephanie, smiling coyly at him.

Capodilupo tipped his head, and smiled at her, "You've already got all the money you're ever going to take out of this town, Mrs. Hanley. But I *would* like a demonstration, at close range. And I'd appreciate it if you'd keep both hands on the rail of the table, and remove your shoes, while you play."

"For a half-million-dollars, Mr. Capodilupo, I'll do it in my bikini," she fluttered her eyelashes at him.

He laughed, picked up the phone, and punched a few numbers. After a moment he said, "Jimmie? This is Cappie. I want the roulette whiz-kids to give us a demo. Rope off a table. And I want three video cameras . . . No. Set 'em up right on the floor, close range. The overhead cameras didn't spot anything before." He hung up, pulled himself out of his chair, and grabbed his coat off a coat tree. "OK folks, let's do it."

# CHAPTER 11

Capodilupo led the four of them out of his office and down the plain, tiled corridor. He stopped at a door with a full-length mirror, buttoned his coat, and adjusted his tie. He opened the door, and the sudden din of the gambling casino assailed their ears.

He led the way briskly to a roulette table, where two guards attached yellow ropes to heavy chrome posts. Three men arrived, each carrying a video camera and tripod. The cameras were ready in a few minutes. A contingent of uniformed guards kept the curious customers outside the ropes.

Capodilupo gestured to the wheel, "OK, Mrs. Hanley. It's all yours."

Stephanie walked confidently to her position near the wheel. She turned to Capodilupo, "Quadrant One will be from zero to six; Quadrant Two will be 18 to 27; Quadrant Three will be double-zero to five; and Quadrant Four will be 17 to 28. OK?"

"Same as before," he nodded.

"Why, Mr. Capodilupo, you've been watching my TV show," she smiled as she slipped off her shoes and handed them to him.

The wheel-man spun the wheel and fired the ball. It flew around the track at high speed. Stephanie laid both of her hands on the table rail and concentrated on the wheel. In about five seconds, she said simply, "Quadrant Three."

Jack had the wheel memorized by then. He knew that meant the series of ten numbers: 00, 1, 13, 26, 24, 3, 15, 34, 22, and 5. The wheel-man had thrown the ball so hard, it took a long time to slow down. Finally, it fell out of its track, bounced a few times, and settled into a pocket. The wheel-man announced: "Three, Red."

Jack knew that was right in the middle of Quadrant Three. The wheel-man picked up the ball, spun the wheel and threw the hard, metal sphere again. Stephanie gave her prediction within five seconds, "Quadrant Four."

Jack knew that meant the series of nine numbers: 17, 32, 20, 7, 11, 30, 26, 9, and 28. "Twenty-six, Black," said the wheel-man.

Stephanie was two-for-two. As they continued to play, Capodilupo stalked around the table, watching from every possible angle. He directed the three camera-men to get close-ups of her hands, feet and face. He talked to some of the older men wearing tuxedos: pit bosses, and the floor boss. Seasoned casino-men who had seen it all. He motioned to a female guard to pass a metal detector around Steph. After making a thorough search, she shook her head.

The crowd around the roped-off table was five deep, and buzzing. A young man asked Jack, "What's goin' on?"

"They're making a movie."

"No kiddin'? Who's the actress?"

"Helen Lockhart."

"I *told* you that was her!" he said to his companion.

That piece of mis-information made its way like wild-fire around the table. Stephanie was nine-for-ten, and Capodilupo had all but stood on his head, trying to see something that the four of them knew was not there.

A man about forty years old asked Jack, "Are they really making a movie? That's not Lockhart — is it?."

Jack looked at him, "No. That's my wife."

"What's the deal?"

"We've been lucky, and they think she's been using a computer. So she's giving a little demo to the casino management."

"No foolin'? How lucky?"

"Five-hundred-grand."

"Jesus! Are you kiddin?"

"Nope."

He stuck out his hand, "I'm Nort Quinlan, with the L. A. Times. This sounds like a story. Do you mind?"

"Why not?" Jack took his hand. "I'm Jack Hanley. That's my wife Stephanie."

"Glad to meet you, Jack." He pulled out a pen, and started making notes on a Keno card. "How does she do it?"

"She's got terrific eyes. She can see the ball, and read the numbers on the wheel, while they're moving, fast. She knows the physics of the problem, and she's got unbelievable math skills. She can compute the deceleration of the ball, and predict when it will come out of the track, and which quadrant it will land in."

"What's a quadrant?" asked Quinlan, as he scribbled furiously. "One-fourth of the wheel?"

"You got it."

Harry and Maria noticed the man taking notes, and moved closer. "A gentleman of the press?" asked Harry.

"This is Nort Quinlan, L. A. Times. Nort, these are my friends, Harry and Maria Washburn." They shook hands and exchanged greetings. "Maria and Stephanie are sisters," Jack continued. "They're both roulette whiz-kids."

"Roulette whiz-kids?"

"That's what the casino calls 'em."

"I love it!" Quinlan, wrote it down. Then he turned to Maria, "And you can do this too? I mean, predict the quadrants?"

"Yes," she said, "we've been doing it for about a day and a half."

"How long you been married?"

Glancing at his watch, Harry said, "About forty-two hours."

"Wow! You're newly-weds. On your honeymoon! How about you, Jack?"

"Same. Double-wedding. New Year's Eve."

"Oh my God! What a story," Quinlan wrote furiously on the other side of his Keno card.

Capodilupo and Stephanie walked over. "How'd you do, Honey?" Jack asked.

"Forty-six out of fifty," Stephanie said smiling.

Capodilupo said, "OK, I gotta tell you, I can't believe it. I've been watchin' her for over ninety minutes. I've seen her do it fifty times, and I just can't believe any human being can do that."

"Well, believe it," Stephanie smiled at him, "I'm not using a computer, honest."

He smiled back at her, "I know, Mrs. Hanley. There's no way you could be using a computer."

He turned to Jack, "Well, a deal's a deal. No computer, so, you guys can go. I'll have two of my men stay with you 'till you're on the plane. They got radios and they'll call me if you get hassled by another casino's people. I'll straighten it out."

He shook hands with Jack and Harry. "Listen. I'm not going to have the pleasure of seeing you guys in Vegas again, right?"

Jack smiled, "A deal's a deal, Mr. Capodilupo."

The security director turned to Stephanie, and looked down at her, almost like a stern father. "And I want you to promise me, Mrs. Hanley, that you won't teach anybody else how to do this."

She looked up at him and said solemnly, "I promise." Then she stepped forward quickly and kissed his cheek. "Bye, Cappie. And thanks."

Capodilupo looked at her, smiled broadly, and then looked at Jack. "Oh, you are the luckiest son-of-a . . ." He turned and walked away.

As Jack watched him go, he could hear the man continue to mutter to himself. Jack wondered if they had really heard the end of their Vegas adventure. Then the four of them walked out, Maria arm-in-arm with Harry, and Stephanie clinging to Jack. Two uniformed guards followed them, and Quinlan tagged along.

When they got to the limo, the reporter asked if he could take a picture. They agreed, and he pulled a small camera out of his pocket and took several fast shots. Then he thanked them, and pulled a cellular phone out of another pocket. The two guards got in front with the driver. The "whiz-kids" and their husbands got in back and popped open some champagne.

When they arrived at the Tropicana, they emptied their safe-deposit box, packed their clothes, and checked out.

At McCarran Airport, they gave the limo driver an extravagant tip. The guards stayed with them until they walked through the "Passengers Only" gate.

They had a bumpy flight back, but none of them minded as they had up-graded their seats to first-class, and were drinking the airline's best liquor.

\* \* \* \* \* \*

The next morning, Jack awoke to the smell of coffee. He rolled over and saw Stephanie reading the paper in bed beside him.

"Good morning, Sweetheart," she said. "You take a great picture." She turned the paper so he could see what she read. They were on the front page of the "Life Style" Section. The picture was eye-catching. Both women were photogenic, and their faces radiated excitement. They looked like movie stars.

The headline read: "Whiz-kids Win $500,000 in Vegas." The sub-head read: "Sisters Beat Roulette Wheels. Claim Super Vision and Math Skills Help Them to Pick Winners."

Stephanie kissed him, handed him a cup of coffee, and read aloud: "Newly-wed sisters, Stephanie Hanley, and Maria Washburn gave their husbands wedding presents of over $250,000 each, after playing roulette in Las Vegas on their honeymoon. The couples, married on New Year's Eve, won a total of over a half-million-dollars."

Stephanie read the rest of the article to her husband. When she had finished, Jack said, "Well, *thank you*, Sweetheart."

"For what, Honey?"

"Well, it says in the paper that you're giving me a $250,000 wedding present."

"So it does." She smiled, fluttering her eyelashes. "Wanna negotiate?"

He put his cup on the bedside table, smiled back at her and started to say, "Negotiating is good . . ." But she was already in his arms.

# CHAPTER 12

Capidolupo watched the videotape of the Hanley woman's demonstration for the fourth time. Something vaguely bothered him, but he could not put his finger on it. He had been a cop for twenty-five years, a good cop. Since leaving LAPD, he had quickly risen to command the security department of one of the top hotel/casinos in Las Vegas.

For thirty-five years, he prided himself on being able to tell when something just did not *smell* right. He could tell when most people were lying, easily. And he could sense, maybe through body language, or facial expression, or maybe even some form of extra-sensory perception, when a person was about to do something. He had been taken by surprise very few times in his career. He seemed to know when a *perp* would run, throw a punch, or even go for a weapon. He had only been hit a few times, because he had set himself to duck, and throw a counter, before the perp threw his punch. He had been shot at three times, but never hit, because he dove for cover ahead of the shot. In each case, he had then returned fire with deadly accuracy.

The intercom on his desk buzzed. "Yeah, Ginnie?"

"Cappie, come here quick! There's a thing on the news about one of the Whiz Kids."

Capodilupo jumped out of his chair and hustled through the door to the outer office. Ginnie pointed at the TV.

A young, blonde, athletic man said, ". . . like a porpoise out to those kids. She was pulling further away from me the whole time."

The camera shifted to the television reporter interviewing the young man. "We've been talking to Scott Klein, the California State University Champion, in the grueling 1650-yard free-style. Klein, who spends his summers life-guarding here in Newport Beach, says he's sure that it was Stephanie Hanley who helped him save six children caught in a rip-tide last summer. This is Jeff Lund, live from Newport Beach. Back to you, Jennifer."

The picture changed to an earnest, female anchor who said, "Thank you, Jeff . . . Jeff, do we know if she's a competition swimmer herself? It sounds like she should be in the Olympics."

The picture changed back to the field reporter, standing in front of a lifeguard tower with Scott Klein. "Yes, Jennifer, I understand that she swam for the University of Hawaii, and also life-guarded several summers in Honolulu."

"Thank you, Jeff." The picture changed back to the anchor-woman. "Stephanie Hanley has been in the news the last few days, as she and her sister won over $500,000 in Las Vegas recently. In fact, they're being called the 'Roulette Whiz Kids', because of their ability to predict where a roulette ball is going to land.

"Also in Orange County today, the District Attorney said he would seek indictments against two former County Supervisors . . . "

Cappie rushed back into his office, flipped through his Cardex file and dialed a number. A moment later, he heard a business-like female voice, "County Clerk's Office. Helen Llorente speaking. How may I help you?"

"Helen. Cappie, at the Parthenon. How ya' doin', Doll?"

"Cappie! I'm good. How're *you* doin'? You guys got touched by the 'Roulette Whiz Kids', didn't you? They clean you out?" she teased.

"Yeah, they took us for thirty-grand. I may have to cut back on my lunches for a week," he chuckled. Then his tone turned more serious, "I need a favor, Doll. Matter of fact, it's about the 'Whiz kids'. They got married here New Year's Eve. I need copies of their marriage licenses. Would you fax 'em to me?"

"You got it, Cappie."

"Thanks, Doll."

After they rang off, he called Ginnie on the interphone. "There'll be a couple of faxes, wedding licenses, comin' in. Bring 'em to me right away. Also, send two tickets for Saturday night's show to Helen Llorente in the City Clerk's office."

Ten minutes later, Ginnie brought in the faxes. He looked at Stephanie's first. It showed Stephanie Winthrop, born in Lahaina, Hawaii, March 8, 1980.

Cappie flipped through his Cardex again, then dialed a number. A moment later, he heard a woman say, "Hyatt Regency, Waikiki."

"Tell me, is Takehara still Director of Security?"

"Yes, sir."

"Would you put me through to him, please? My name's Capodilupo."

After a moment, he heard Takehara's voice, "Cappie. What's up? You still in Vegas?"

"Yeah, still here. At the Parthenon. Pay's terrific, but Rosie hates it. She wants us to get a motor home and really retire for good. I don't know. We'll see. How you doin', Tee?"

"You know, Cappie. Every day's the same. Weather's perfect. No earthquakes. My only problem is tryin' to keep the hookers out of the lobby."

"No foolin'?"

"You better believe it, Cappie. All these kids come over from the mainland, lookin' for paradise. They find out jobs are tough to come by, so they wind up sellin' it."

"Jesus. Thought we had 'em all in Vegas." He paused briefly, then got down to business. "Tee, I need a favor."

"You name it, Cappie."

"You read about those two women that won half-a-mil' here, over New Year's?"

"Sure, Cappie. We even got television, now."

Capodilupo laughed with him. "One of 'em was born in Lahaina. Maiden name was Winthrop. Stephanie Winthrop. March 8, 1980. She went to the University of Hawaii, and was a competition swimmer. Lifeguarded summers in Honolulu. Find out anything you can for me, will ya, Tee?"

"I'll get right on it for you, Cappie. But I thought you guys figured they weren't using computers."

"Yeah, we couldn't find diddly squat. But I just got a feelin', Tee. Somethin' ain't kosher. Call as soon as you get somethin'? You still got my number at the Parthenon?"

"Yup. I'll make some calls. Get back to you today or tomorrow."

Cappie jumped up and strode into the outer office. He got a cup of coffee, and paced back and forth between his and Ginnie's offices. He could not sit still. His mind scanned for that undefinable something that just did not fit . He turned on the video of Stephanie again. He paced around his office, watching the TV. It's gotta be there, he thought. He just could not pull it out.

"Ginnie, page me if Takehara calls from Hawaii." He walked out to the casino, prowled the roulette wheels, and watched one as it spun. The ball fell out of its track, bounced several times, and settled into a slot. He went into the coffee shop, ordered a burger, fries, and coffee. After he ate, he wandered back toward his office. Just as he reached for the knob, his pager went off. He opened the door. Ginnie had a phone to her ear. She nodded to Cappie, "He just walked in, Mr. Takehara."

He dashed into his office and grabbed the phone. "Tee, whadaya got?"

"She wasn't born in Lahaina, Cappie. Not on March 8, 1980, or within ten years either way, of that date."

"No foolin'?"

"Right, Cappie. And there's no record of her ever being employed by Honolulu City/County, as a lifeguard or anything else. Never had an employee by that name."

"How about the University of Hawaii?"

"Never enrolled, at either campus, Honolulu or Hilo. I also checked Hawaii Pacific University. Not there either."

"I *knew* somethin' was fishy about that broad! Thanks a million, Tee. Remember, you guys come to the mainland, drop by and see us in Vegas. OK?" They said their good-byes and hung up. Cappie said out loud, "OK, Maria, let's see if you check out."

He looked at Maria's and Harry's marriage license. It showed Maria Winthrop, born in Newburyport, Massachusetts, on June 10, 1978. Cappie reached for his Cardex again, and dialed a number. This time, he called a Boston Police detective, named Peter Murphy. Murph' had worked the "Boston Strangler" case. Cappie had contacted him when he had been working on the "Hillside Strangler" case for LAPD. Cappie needed a psychological profile of his suspect, and Murph' had helped him. They had stayed in touch ever since.

## A.N.G.E.L.S., Inc.

Murph' called Cappie back within half-an-hour and gave him the expected answer: Maria Winthrop had not been born in Newburyport, Mass.

"Two 'Whiz-Kids'," Cappie muttered, "and both of them gave bogus birth records when they got married. They both can predict where a roulette ball will land. And one of them outswam a champion."

He strode into his assistant's office and thrust the wedding licenses at her. "Ginnie. Get me some TRWs."

Sensing her boss's urgency, she turned her chair quickly to her computer. "OK, Cappie. I'll get right on it." She began hitting keys on her keyboard. "You want sheets on all four of 'em?"

"Well, you can try," he said, looking over her shoulder. "But I'll bet you won't find anything on the women."

Ginnie quickly keyed in Stephanie's name and address. In a few moments, the screen flashed the message: "No TRW Credit Data record found."

"You got *that* right, Boss."

Cappie just nodded and breathed out sharply, as Ginnie keyed in the query for Maria. Within another few moments, they again saw the "No record found" response.

"OK. So much for the phantoms," Cappie said grimly. "Now let's see if the guys are real."

Ginnie keyed in Jack's name and address. The system immediately responded with a *hit*.

"Bingo," Ginnie announced, as she sent the report to her printer.

Cappie grabbed the page as soon as it was free and quickly scanned it. "I'll be damned. Hanley's a VP at a vitamin company." Thinking of his two injured guards, he reflected, "I woulda thought he was Karate instructor, or somethin'."

"Got a hit for Washburn," his assistant stated.

Cappie pulled the page out of the printer. "Holy *shit*! Washburn's a college professor. Works for UCI." Cappie paced in front of his assistant's desk. "I wonder what the hell he teaches . . . "

"That's easy, Boss."

"Huh? How's that?"

"All colleges got their catalogs on the Internet. It's like free adver . . .

"And they got their faculty listed in the catalog!" Cappie interjected.

"You got it."

"Can you bring it up?"

"Sure. Might take a few minutes."

"OK. Bring it to me as soon as you got it." Cappie strode into his office, clutching the TRW reports on Jack and Harry. Seated at his desk, he flipped through his Cardex one more time, and dialed a Los Angeles police detective named Stuart Bertram. Stu' and Cappie had partnered on LAPD Vice, for eight years.

Cappie heard his friend's voice as he answered, "Homicide. Bertram."

"Stu. Cappie. I need a coupla DMV checks."

"OK, Cappie. Shoot."

"First guy's Hanley, Jack . . . " Cappie scanned the TRW form, and spotting Jack's California driver's license number, he continued, "CDL: C1616398."

"OK, Hold on." Within moments, Bertram reported, "No wants or warrants. He's had a coupla tickets — speeding. No accidents, last three years. Drives a 2002, red Nissan 680-Z. You need the plate number?"

"Naw. Second guy is Washburn, Harry, CDL: N0937612."

Again, in just a few moments, Bertram replied, "He's even cleaner than the first guy. Not even a ticket. He drives a '99 Volvo."

"That figures. He's a college prof . . . "

"Hold it, Cappie! There's an NCIC flag on Hanley."

"NCIC? Jesus! Can you pull it up?"

"Yup. Hold on."

While Cappie waited for his friend's report from the FBI's National Crime Information Center, he fidgeted in his chair. He thought out loud, "What the hell kind of scam did you do, Mister Vitamin VP?"

"OK, Cappie, it's comin' up . . . No felony arrests or convicts. No misdemeanor arrests or convicts . . . "

"Well, why the hell is he in the Fed's database?"

"Hold on, Cappie. Here it is. Shit! He ain't no *bad* guy, Cappie. He's a friggin' hero!"

"Whadaya mean? Hero?"

Bertram read the FBI file to Cappie, "Item one: Saddleback College, Mission Viejo, California. Campus PD reports subject assisted on felony arrest (mugging), 4-10-88. Perp suffered broken jaw, nose, two ribs."

"That sounds like my guy, all right."

"Item two: Newport Beach, California, PD reports subject assisted on felony arrest (attempt rape), 7-14-04. Perp #1 suffered broken teeth, nose. Perp #2 suffered broken cheek bone, rib." Bertram concluded, "Summary: Strong moral beliefs. Will not hesitate to assist victims. If confronted, will use force. No record of martial arts training, but above-average skill in hand combat."

"They got *that* right, Stu."

"How's that?"

"He put two of my guys in the hospital."

"No foolin' ?"

"Yeah. Well, thanks a million, Stu. You and Betty come to Vegas. Let me know. Rosie and I'll show you guys the town."

After they said their good-byes, Cappie walked back into Ginnie's office.

She handed him a sheet of paper. "Here's the UCI catalog page with Washburn's degrees. He's got his own Web page, too. I'm printin' it now."

Reading the page, Cappie saw that Harry received an A.A. from Saddleback College, Mission Viejo, CA, in 1988. "Ah, that's how he knows Hanley," he said out loud. Reading on, he saw that Harry also had a B.S. from the University of California, San Diego, 1990; an M.S. from Massachusetts Institute of Technology, Cambridge, Mass., 1991; and a Ph.D. from Carnegie-Mellon University, Pittsburgh, PA,

1994. He saw that all of Harry's degrees were in Computer Science.

Just as Cappie finished reading the catalog page, Ginnie slowly walked toward him, studying a page she had just taken from her printer. "Wait'll you see *this*, Boss," she said thoughtfully, as she handed him the paper.

Cappie quickly scanned the page. Harry's Master's Thesis at M.I.T. was titled: Expert Decision Systems: Applications in Humanistic Behavioral Environments. "Humanistic behavior," he mused out loud. Then quickly reading on, he saw Harry's Ph.D. Dissertation at Carnegie-Mellon involved ALVINN, an Autonomous Land Vehicle in a Neural Network. "An autonomous land vehicle . . . ?"

"That's a computer-controlled, driverless car," Ginnie said proudly. "I read about it in a computer magazine a while ago."

Finishing Harry's Web page, Cappie read that he had published extensively in the areas of neural networks, massively parallel processing, natural language translation, and robotics. "Robotics?" Cappie looked at Ginnie quizzically.

"Read about the Stanford thing, Cappie."

Cappie read aloud the last entry on Harry's Web page. "Speaker, Artificial Intelligence Symposium, Stanford University, 1998. Topic: 'Intelligent Robots: Was Asimov Right?' — Who the hell is Asimov?"

"Isaac Asimov," Ginnie said slowly, "is one of my favorite Sci-Fi authors. Right up there with Bradbury and Heinlein. He wrote about robots — intelligent robots — and the social implications thereof."

"Bingo!" Cappie yelled. Grabbing his assistant by the arms, he exclaimed, "Great job, Ginnie." Then staring at Harry's Web page again, he continued thoughtfully, "I think, Dr. Washburn, Asimov *was* right, and *you* did it!" And in that instant, the thing that had been bugging him about Stephanie, clicked. He rushed into his office, turned on the VCR, and waited impatiently for the picture to come on.

Finally, Stephanie's image appeared on the screen. She announced: "Quadrant Four." Cappie backed up the tape until he saw her chest swell slightly. She had inhaled just before she called the quadrant. He pressed the "Play" button, and started his stop-watch. He studied her chest. She did not inhale again until the ball landed in its slot. Cappie checked his watch. One minute, twenty-eight seconds had elapsed! "And *you*, little Robo-Doll," Cappie said to Stephanie's image, "forgot to breathe!"

# CHAPTER 13

Cappie watched the entire tape again. He found several places where Stephanie did not breathe for more than two minutes. Cappie picked up his phone and punched a few numbers. A breathy voice answered, "Corporate Council's Office."

"Gwen. This is Cappie. Please tell Mr. Carter I need to see him as soon as possible. It's about the Hanley and Washburn women."

"Hold on, Cappie. I'll check". After a moment, she announced, "He can see you, for a few minutes, right now."

"Thanks, Gwen. I'll be right there." Cappie grabbed his file labeled "Hanley/Washburn" and headed for the door. He hustled down the tiled hall to the elevator, and punched the button marked "15th Floor - Executive Offices." When the elevator door opened, he walked briskly down the mahogany-paneled hall, on plush, maroon carpeting. He opened the glass door with gold letters "John H. Carter, Corporate Counsel."

Gwen, Carter's well-endowed, blonde receptionist greeted him. Cappie knew that she had been a showgirl, a *mannequin*, not a dancer. He also knew that she could not type her own name. But, at a company party after he had put away too much Scotch, Carter had told him, "She gives great telephone." Since Carter also had a staff of real secretaries, he allowed himself this perk.

"Go right in, Cappie," Gwen smiled at him. "He's waiting for you."

Cappie went through the mahogany door. Carter sat behind his imposing teak desk. At his back, floor-to-ceiling, wall-to-wall glass afforded a commanding view of the Las Vegas Strip. The wall to Carter's right held three framed degrees. The largest one proclaimed that he held a Doctorate in Jurisprudence from Harvard, Carter's ticket to this job.

John Carter had a thin, hawkish face. At 39, he had lost much of his hair, but he had the remainder professionally styled, every week. Dull gray eyes peered through gold-rimmed glasses, giving him a dour expression. He treated anyone he considered beneath his position in a condescending manner.

He wore a three-piece, navy-blue suit and an understated power tie: narrow, red stripes on a dark blue background. He did not stand up, and he did not invite his visitor to sit. He continued to hold a piece of paper he had been reading. "What's up, Cappie?"

Capodilupo sat in one of the two leather chairs in front of the attorney's desk. "John, I've got somethin' to tell you about those two broads, the 'Roulette Whiz Kids', that's probably gonna make you think I'm nuts."

"What?" asked Carter, still looking at his paper.

"They both gave phony birthplaces on their marriage licenses. Also, the Hanley woman said she went to the University of Hawaii, and life-guarded in Honolulu. That's bogus too."

"So? They're illegal aliens?"

"That's not all. One of 'em is married to a Computer Scientist. He's got a Master's from M.I.T., and a Ph.D. from Carnegie-Mellon. He's into Neural Networks, computers that learn. At Carnegie-Mellon he worked on a computer-controlled car."

Carter furrowed his brow. "No human driver?"

"That's right. And he spoke a couple of years ago at an Artificial Intelligence Convention. His topic was intelligent robots — imitating humans."

Carter put down the paper. Cappie had caught his attention.

"Did you see the thing on TV about the Hanley woman, yesterday?" Cappie asked.

"No."

"Last summer, she helped a lifeguard save a bunch of kids caught in a rip tide."

"So?"

"She out-swam the guard. He said so himself, on TV. And he's some kind of long-distance champion."

Carter got up, and walked around the desk, with his finger on his nose. "So you're saying we have two women who can predict where a roulette ball is going to land. One of them also out-swims a champion swimmer. They both give false birth data on their marriage licenses. One of them is married to a computer scientist who is an expert on robots . . . So, what are you saying? You think they're *robots*? Jesus, Cappie."

"That's not all. I got ninety minutes of videotape of the Hanley broad, taken by three cameras at close range . . . "

"And?"

"She doesn't breathe. Normally, I mean. She holds her breath for two minutes."

"So? Lots of skin-divers can hold their breath that long."

"Yeah, sure. But they only do that when they're underwater."

"Well, if she's a robot, why would she need to breathe at all?"

"I don't know, John. Maybe she's been programmed to look like she's breathing."

"So you're saying she *forgot* her programming, because she got excited or something?" Carter shook his head. "I don't think so, Cappie. I'm not an expert on computer technology, but I've always been led to believe that computers follow their programming, exactly."

"I don't know much about computers myself, John. And I don't know a damn thing about robots." Cappie studied his palms, then looked up. "But I do know people. And this Hanley broad, as beautiful as she is, is not a normal woman. I'd bet my pension on it."

# A.N.G.E.L.S., Inc. 135

"Another thing, Cappie. Didn't you say you passed metal detectors all over them? If the women were robots, wouldn't the detectors go off the scale?"

"We practically stuck the detector up the Hanley woman's ass when she was doin' her demo. We got zip on the meter."

"Well," said Carter, returning to the paper he had been holding, "it sounds like there's no metal in her body."

"Maybe she's made of plastics."

"OK. Let's just say for a minute that they are robots, and I'm not convinced that they are. What of it? Are you suggesting that we try to recover the money they won, because they're not humans? It was only $30,000, wasn't it?"

"You're right, it was only 30K. And I have absolutely no idea what we should do, if anything. But I think it's a hell of a scam, and I had to tell somebody what I found out, and what I think. And since you're my boss, I figured I should tell you." Cappie stood up and walked toward the door.

"Cappie, I didn't mean to discount your research, or your analysis. You could very well be correct. I'm going to give this some thought, to see if there's some way we could — utilize this. In the meantime, please don't divulge your findings, or your opinion, to anyone else . . . Oh, and Cappie, is that your file on the matter?" He pointed to the folder Cappie held.

"Yes. I've got copies of their marriage licenses here. I've also got TRW reports on the two men, a couple of Web pages on Washburn's computer background, a newspaper article on the 'Whiz kids' roulette caper, and a couple of pages of my own notes."

"Good. Ask Gwen to make a copy for me."

"OK, John."

"I'll let you know what I decide." Carter turned back to the paper he had been reading.

Cappie went out, and asked Gwen to copy the file. Apparently she also "gave great copy machine", as she returned the file to him in a few moments, and rewarded him with a smile.

\* \* \* \* \* \*

Later that day, Carter studied Cappie's file. Still skeptical, but curious, he buzzed Gwen on the interphone. "Call Harvard University. Get Professor John Siemans of the Graduate School of Business for me."

A few minutes later, she buzzed him back. "Professor Siemans on Line One."

"Professor Siemans. My name is John Carter.

"Yes, Mr. Carter. How can I help you?"

"Well, Sir, you probably don't remember me, but I took a class from you about ten years ago."

"I see. And what can I do for you today?"

"I'm an attorney now, Professor, and I'm interested in a case regarding a man who studied computer science at M.I.T. Got his Master's degree there."

"M.I.T. . . ?"

"Yes," Carter said quickly. "He studied artificial intelligence. As I recall, you taught courses in expert systems."

"That's correct. For business decision-making."

"That's a form of artificial intelligence, is it not?"

"Certainly."

"Could you recommend someone at M.I.T. whom I might speak to, about this former student?"

"Well, if he was a grad student, involved in expert systems, Paul Winthrop probably would have known him."

Carter froze. Then he quickly leafed through the papers in Cappie's file and stared at the two marriage licenses. Stephanie and Maria had given their maiden names as Winthrop.

"Mr. Carter? Are you still there?"

"Oh, sorry, Professor. I was distracted for a moment. Did you say Winthrop?"

"Yes. Paul Winthrop. He's the Director of the Artificial Intelligence Laboratory at M.I.T. He'd be aware of all graduate research projects in the lab."

"Really? Well, I thank you very much, Professor. This has been very helpful."

After they rang off, Carter told Gwen to get Winthrop for him. After a few minutes, she told him that Paul Winthrop was on the line.

"Professor Winthrop, my name is John Carter. Professor Siemans at Harvard suggested I call you."

"Yes?"

"I'm interested in a former student of yours. Harry Washburn. I understand he got a Master's degree in Artificial Intelligence at M.I.T. about ten years ago."

"I remember him well. Brilliant young man. Went on to do a Ph.D. at Carnegie-Mellon. I believe he's now teaching at the University of California, Irvine. What is your interest in him?"

"I wish to employ him — as a consultant. Can you tell me — is he an expert in robotics?"

"Oh yes," Winthrop chuckled, "he worked with Robert Bergman. They were both grad students then. They built little insect-like machines that could walk."

"Really? Walking robots?"

"Well, yes — in a rather rudimentary way. Bergman is now on staff here. He's working on a humanoid robot . . ."

A *humanoid* robot?"

"Yes. Both Bergman and Washburn have dreamed about that for years. I heard Harry give a talk on the possible emulation of human behavior by robots a couple of years ago. Interesting, but pretty 'blue sky', I'm afraid."

"The symposium at Stanford, where he spoke on, 'Was Asimov Right'?"

"Yes. Were you there?"

"No. But I've read about it. May I ask what you think, Professor? Was Asimov right?"

"Well, in my opinion, the humanoid robot is still science fiction, Mr. Carter. We're a long way from that. Although I must admit that the rate of change in the entire field of computing is so great, it is virtually impossible to predict the future. If you had told me in 1965, that by 1977 private individuals would own computers in their homes, costing less than $1,000, I'd have laughed at you."

"Well, I guess very few people could have predicted that, Dr. Winthrop.

"Yes. But throughout the history of science, there have been individuals who have had some kind of extraordinary insight, that enables them to make a sort of quantum leap."

"You mean like Jones and Workman at Banana-Tree?"

"Yes, and Bob Doerr at Megasoft."

"Oh, yes. The world's richest man." Carter smiled. "Dr. Winthrop, is it possible to make a computer without metal parts?"

"Of course. If you use optical circuitry."

"Like fiber optic cables for telephone lines?"

"Exactly. Now you have light beams passing through fiber glass, instead of electrical signals moving along copper wires. It faster, cleaner — that is, no E.M.I. . . ."

"E.M.I.?"

"Electromagnetic interference."

"Ah. Such as might affect a metal detector?"

"Exactly."

"I see," said Carter thoughtfully. "Professor, do you know if Dr. Washburn has any experience with this technology?"

"Optical computer circuits? Not that I recall. At Carnegie-Mellon he worked on ALVINN . . ."

"The driverless car?"

"That's right. It uses neural networks. Electronic circuits that learn, in much the same way as the human brain."

"One more question, if I could, Professor. Dr. Washburn, and a friend of his, Jack Hanley, are married to sisters whose maiden names were Winthrop. Are they relatives of yours?"

That stopped the Professor cold. After a moment he replied evenly, "No, not that I know of, Mr. Carter."

"You've been very helpful, Dr. Winthrop. Thank you very much."

After they said their good-byes, Carter sat in the quiet of his office for thirty minutes. His mind raced through the details: a computer that could walk, using light beams instead of copper wires, and it could learn "in much the same way as a human." His thoughts kept returning to the extraordinary wealth of Bob Doerr, and he kept smiling.

# CHAPTER 14

At breakfast the following morning, Carter ignored his wife, as usual, while he read the newspaper and reviewed some work he had brought from the office. His wife, Norma, a plain woman of thirty-five, could not care less. She held the Fashion Section of the newspaper in front of her face, and thought of the tennis lesson she had scheduled for 10:00AM. She knew it would involve thirty minutes of tennis, and thirty minutes of sex with Brett, the tennis pro.

She had given herself to him the day after she found out about Gwen, six months earlier. What had started as a gesture of revenge had become a standing, weekly affair. She knew that Brett would never love her. Twenty-five and handsome, he would, no doubt, break it off some time. But she intended to enjoy it as long as it lasted. He was a thoughtful and exciting lover, and she ached with anticipation.

Carter dropped Cappie's file of papers on the table and picked up his coffee. He bent his head to take a sip, and something caught his eye. Cappie's papers had landed on the Sports Page. The newspaper photo of the "roulette whiz kids" partly covered a picture of a heavyweight boxer receiving a knock-out punch.

Carter said out loud, "Hmm, Dr. Washburn. If you've made a robot that out-swims a champion, can you make one that could out-box a champion?"

"What did you say, John?" asked his wife, as she reluctantly left the delicious fantasy she had been having about Brett.

"Oh, nothing, dear." He picked up the Sports Page and quickly skimmed the article, disregarding the fine points of boxing, looking instead for the financial details. The fight had been held at Caesar's Palace, walking distance from the Parthenon. People had paid $1,000 for ringside seats, and the cheapest seats had cost $100. Almost everyone who saw the fight stayed at Caesar's, as part of a package, and did much of their gambling there.

But, most important were the television and videotape markets. The fight had been shown live on pay-per-view cable channels across the country. Video cassettes would be sold to individual consumers within a week of the fight. And within a month, other cassettes would be sold to video rental stores. The revenue had been estimated at $100-million.

While Norma slipped back into her sexual fantasy with Brett, Carter enjoyed a fantasy of his own, about the thing that mattered most to him: money. Lots of it. And the power it could bring.

## A.N.G.E.L.S., Inc. 143

Being careful not to speak his thoughts aloud, he speculated. What if we *owned* the heavyweight champion of the world? And if he could fight several times each year, at the Parthenon . . . Why stop at just one fighter? Why not have the middleweight champ, the lightweight champ . . . How many are there? About ten? Christ! If we had a fight every month, the revenue could be over a *billion dollars per year*!

Carter grabbed the Sports Page and Cappie's file, tossed them into his briefcase, and leaned across the table to give his wife the obligatory good-bye kiss. Still into her fantasy, Norma unconsciously gave him a soft-lipped, open-mouthed kiss that surprised them both. For just an instant, Carter thought, how long has it been since we've made love? Maybe tonight . . . Then, as he felt the weight of the briefcase in his hand, the thought of what it contained and its potential pushed away any further thoughts of intimacy with his wife. He strode to the door and let it slam behind him.

Oh, you poor, stupid fool, Norma thought, as she headed upstairs for her shower. When I kiss Brett like that, he can't wait to . . .

As Carter drove to the Parthenon, he pulled his cellular phone out of the glove box and pressed the speed-dial key, followed by the number one. After a moment, he heard a breathy voice say, "Mr. Benito's Office. May I help you?" The voice belonged to Mae, Sollie's secretary. Like Gwen, she had been a showgirl, but she could also type. And she was Sollie Benito's personal property.

"Mae, this is John Carter. Could I please see Mr. Benito at his earliest convenience? I'm on my way to the office now. Should be there in about ten minutes."

"How much time do you need with him, Mr. Carter?"

"Only about ten or fifteen minutes."

"He should be in about 9:00AM. I can put you down for then. May I tell him what it's about?"

"I'd like to discuss a possible opportunity for us. It has to do with the 'roulette whiz-kids'."

"OK, Mr. Carter. I'll tell him."

"Thank you, Mae. I'll be there at 9:00." A few minutes later, Carter arrived at the Parthenon's parking garage. He drove down the ramp marked "Employees Only", and waited for the guard to open the gate at the foot of the ramp. As he drove by, the guard half-waved, half-saluted him. He parked in his private stall, grabbed his briefcase, and strode to the elevator.

As he arrived on the 15th floor, he checked his watch. 8:00AM. Right on time. He stepped through the door marked "Corporate Counsel".

When Gwen saw him, she smiled and breathed in, expanding her already impressive chest. "Good Morning, Mr. Carter."

With more important things on his mind, he just nodded and disappeared into his office.

In less than a minute she brought him a steaming cup of coffee, which she placed carefully on the sterling silver coaster on his desk. "Anything else — John?" In the privacy of his office, she called him "John".

"No. I've got a nine-o'clock with Sollie."

"OK," she smiled. She departed, closing his door quietly.

At 8:58AM, Carter walked briskly down the plush-carpeted hall to the door with large gold letters that read: "Salvatore D. Benito, Chairman/Chief Executive Officer". He opened the door and smiled at Mae. Even more beautiful than Gwen, she always wore her blouses low-cut, the way Sollie liked them. But Carter carefully avoided staring. She was his boss's private property.

Mae returned his smile. "Go right in, Mr. Carter."

Carter opened the door and walked in. Salvatore Benito slouched in his huge leather chair. He weighed nearly 300 pounds, and his bulk caused him to sweat, constantly. He looked much older than his fifty years, partly because of his obesity, and partly because his face was hardened from the things he had seen in his career.

Carter knew Benito's background. He had started his career as a street punk in East Boston. At twelve, he delivered bags of betting slips for a bookie. At sixteen, he killed a man who had tried to take a bag of cash he was delivering. That incident made his reputation. He threw the murder weapon, a .38 snub-nosed, off the Mystic River Bridge, and scrubbed his hands so hard they nearly bled, to get rid of any gunpowder residue. Most important of all, he kept his mouth shut. He didn't brag about "making his bones" to anyone. When his boss, the bookie, asked him, he admitted the killing. But he never told anyone else. That earned him a place in the big leagues of the Boston underworld.

By the time he reached his twenty-fifth birthday, the Boston Police estimated he had killed ten people. But they could never get an indictment, let alone a conviction, for first-degree murder against him. He did serve time for lesser charges twice, three years for burglary, and five years for armed robbery. He never "ratted out" anyone else and he earned a Caporegime's position after being released from prison the second time. At thirty-five, he commanded an organization of fifty soldiers, and earned $400,000 per year.

When the mob moved into Las Vegas, Benito was placed in charge of casino operations for the Luciano organization. And finally, as his own wealth allowed him to buy the necessary shares, he took over the Parthenon Hotel/Casino. In recent years, he had not needed to rely on the violence that made his earlier career. But Carter knew that if anyone crossed him, Benito could be a deadly adversary.

Benito looked up at Carter, and squinted through his cigar smoke. "Come in, Johnny. Sit. Tell me about the 'whiz kids'. You got an angle? What?"

Carter strode to one of the chairs in front of the desk, sat down and began the concise briefing he knew his boss liked. "Sollie, both women gave bogus birth records on their marriage licenses. That's very unusual. A marriage license is — sacred to a woman. It's the last document in the world she would want to be found invalid. It would be justification for an annulment."

"So? They're 'wet-backs'?"

"I doubt it, Sollie." He turned the news photo of Stephanie and Maria toward him. "They both look pretty Anglo."

"So they're illegals from — what? — Sweden?"

"Sollie, did you see in the news that one of them, the Hanley woman, helped save some kids in the ocean?"

"Yeah, I saw that. She swam faster than the lifeguard."

"That's right, Sollie. And he was a distance swim champ. That's also unheard of, for a woman to beat a man in competition swimming."

"You got more? What else?"

"The Hanley woman also lied about going to the University of Hawaii and lifeguarding in Honolulu. Also, the other one's husband, Washburn, is a computer scientist. He's got a Ph.D. in Artificial Intelligence and he's into robots."

"*Robots?*"

"Yes. I called one of his prof's at M.I.T. He said that Washburn had been interested in humanoid robots for years. And," Carter paused for affect, "the maiden names of both of the 'roulette whiz kids' are the same as the prof: Winthrop. And he says they're not related." Sollie squinted hard at Carter through his smoke.

"Here's the kicker. Cappie's been studying the videotape of the Hanley woman. He says she stops breathing for as long as two minutes at a time."

Benito focused on his cigar for a moment, and then asked quietly, "So if they're robots, what's the opportunity for us, Johnny?"

Carter turned the Sports Page with the picture of the boxer toward Benito. "If Washburn can make a robot that can beat a champion swimmer . . . "

"Can he make a robot that can beat a champion *boxer*?" Benito finished the sentence, grinning.

"We're talking big bucks, Sollie," Carter pointed to the page where he had high-lighted the estimated television and video revenue at $100-million. "If you had, say six boxing champions. I mean, you *owned* 'em, and each one defended his title twice a year, here, at the Parthenon, the revenue could be over one-billion-dollars."

"A *billion* dollars? Jesus Christ!" Benito tapped his cigar ash into the gold ashtray on his desk, and studied his cigar for a moment. Then returning his gaze to Carter, he asked, "What makes you think Washburn'll go for it?"

"Let me go talk to him. I'll take Cappie with me. They know him, and I think — trust him. Cappie said the Hanley woman kissed him good-bye."

"She kissed him?" Benito picked up the news-photo and stared hard at Stephanie's image. "She can kiss me, anytime," he leered. "Anywhere." Then his expression became serious again. "OK, Johnny. This sounds interesting. Owning a fighter. A champion. Maybe a bunch of 'em. I like it. Let's go for it. See what you can do. Take the Lear."

"OK, Sollie. I'll keep you informed." Carter got up, and headed toward the door.

As his hand reached the knob, Sollie yelled after him, "Hey, Johnny!"

"Yes, Sollie?"

"If you're right. If these are robots", he held up the newspaper with Stephanie's picture, "bring me one that looks like this." They both laughed.

\* \* \* \* \* \*

As Carter walked past Gwen's desk, he said, "Get Capodilupo on the phone for me."

Within thirty seconds, Gwen buzzed him, "Mr. Capodilupo, on Line One."

Carter grabbed the phone, "Cappie, I talked to Mr. Benito about your investigation of the Hanley and Washburn women. We agreed that it is possible that they are robots. And if that is true, then we see a possible opportunity for our organization."

"No foolin', John? What opportunity?"

"If Dr. Washburn has built a female robot that out-swims a male champion, we're wondering if he can be induced to build a male robot for us — that could out-box a champion."

"Jesus! Are you serious? You mean like some kind of man-fights-kangaroo exhibition matches?"

"No. I think not. I think it would be better to keep the nature of the fighter confidential."

"I don't know what to say, John . . ."

"Cappie, this could mean a great deal of money to this organization. With live, closed-circuit-television broadcasts, videotape sales and rentals, this could be very big. I'd like very much for you to work with me on this project, Cappie. I think it could be an exciting opportunity for both of us."

"Well, sure, John. It sounds good. What would you want me to do?"

"For starters, we've got to talk to Washburn. The first order of business is to confirm that the women are, in fact, robots. If we can establish that, then the next item is to ascertain if he can make a male robot that could be a champion boxer. And if so, would he be willing to do that — for us — at some agreeable compensation?"

"So, you want me to try to set up a meeting?"

"Exactly, Cappie. He knows you, and you've already established a certain degree of rapport with him."

"Yeah, that's true. OK, John, I'll call him. How soon do you want to do this?"

"The sooner the better. Mr. Benito's given us the use of the Lear jet. We could fly out this afternoon, and meet with him this evening."

"OK, John, I'll get right on it."

"And Cappie, don't tell him the details. Just let him know that we want to talk to him, and that we *may* have a business proposition for him. If he's concerned that we want our money back, you can set his mind at ease. Tell him that as far as we're concerned, that matter is closed. The money is theirs. But I would rather not have him fore-warned regarding the nature of our possible offer."

"I understand, John. I'll get back to you as soon as I talk to him."

After they hung up, Cappie pulled the Hanley-Washburn file out of his drawer. He turned to the TRW report on Washburn, scanned the page for Harry's telephone number, and dialed his home.

Maria answered.

"Mrs. Washburn. This is Anthony Capodilupo at the Parthenon Hotel in Las Vegas. How are you and Dr. Washburn?"

"We're fine," Maria said. She hesitated. "Is there some problem?"

"Oh, no. There's no problem whatsoever, Mrs. Washburn. I hope you're all enjoying your winnings. Is your husband available?"

"Yes. He's right here."

Harry took the phone, "Mr. Capodilupo," he laughed nervously. "I hope you don't want your money back . . ."

"Hello, Dr. Washburn. Not at all. As I told your wife, your winnings are a closed matter. The reason I'm calling, Sir, is that I'd like to meet with you to discuss a possible business proposition."

"What kind of business proposition," Harry asked in a guarded voice.

"I can't discuss any details on the phone. But I'd like to come to your home — tonight, if possible — say 8:00PM? We can discuss it then."

"Well — I guess that would be OK . . ."

"Good. Thank you very much, Dr. Washburn. Oh, and Mr. Carter, the Parthenon's lawyer will be with me. He'll just be there to sign for the hotel, in case we do enter into a business agreement."

"OK — but I'd like to have Mr. Hanley present also. I'd value his advice on any kind of a business contract."

"Well, I think that would be OK . . . Yes. Fine. We'll see you then."

Cappie hung up, then immediately called Carter. "OK, John. Washburn will meet us at his home at eight tonight. He wants Hanley there too. They're close friends, and he wants his business advice, if we do make an offer."

"Excellent, Cappie. Meet me in the lobby at five."

Carter hung up and buzzed Gwen on the interphone. "Call the airport, and tell the pilot I want to leave for Orange County at 5:30PM. Have a limo meet me at the front door at 5:00."

Carter called his home, but Norma did not answer. At that moment, her tennis lesson over, she clung passionately to her lover. Carter left a terse message that he had been called out of town, and would not be back until very late.

At 4:55, Carter rode down in the elevator with his briefcase clutched tightly in his hand. When the door opened in the lobby, Cappie stood waiting for him. Carter nodded to him and they strode together toward the front door.

Twenty minutes later, they arrived at McCarran Airport. The limo drove onto the apron at the executive terminal, where the jet waited, its engines running. As the limo drove up, the airplane's ramp lowered, and a flight attendant hurried down the steps. "Good afternoon, Mr. Carter," she smiled. She wore a blue uniform, and she filled it well. Carter felt himself stir as he followed her up the ramp, but the weight of his briefcase reminded him of his purpose. As soon as she closed the door, the plane started rolling, and Carter's mind returned to business again.

\* \* \* \* \* \*

The plane touched down at John Wayne Airport in just under an hour. As they taxied to the terminal, the flight attendant said, "We'll be waiting here for you, Mr. Carter. Unless Mr. Benito needs us back in Vegas."

"OK." He hurried down the stairs to the waiting limo.

# CHAPTER 15

At exactly 8:00PM, the driver parked in front of Harry's house. Cappie pointed to the red sports car in the driveway. "That's Hanley's 'Z'."

Carter's brow furrowed. "How do you know that?"

"It was in the DMV report."

Carter nodded and added a half-smile of approval. "Excellent memory for detail, Cappie."

"Once a cop, always a cop," Cappie replied, shrugging.

As the driver opened the limo's door for him, Carter stepped out and strode toward the house. Reaching the door, Carter nervously adjusted his necktie and cleared his throat, while Cappie pressed the doorbell.

After a moment, Maria opened the door. "Hello, Cappie." She took his hand warmly.

Carter could not help but respond to Maria's beauty. He immediately saw the resemblance to Denise Moran. As Cappie introduced them, he took her hand. "Mrs. Washburn, you are even more lovely than your pictures."

Maria smiled graciously. "Why thank you, Mr. Carter. Please come in, gentlemen." She ushered them into the living room where Harry sat in a large arm chair. Stephanie and Jack sat together on a couch. Cappie shook hands with Harry and Jack.

Stephanie walked directly to him, kissed him on the cheek, and grinned, "Wanna play some cards, Cappie?"

During the laughter that followed, Carter took his first good look at Stephanie, then turned to Jack. "Mr. Hanley, I must tell you and Dr. Washburn that your wives are two of the most stunning women I have ever seen."

"Why, thank you, Mr. Carter," Stephanie remarked, turning her radiant smile on him. "If we do play cards, you can be my partner." They all laughed again, sat and made themselves comfortable.

"Now, Cappie," Harry asked, coming directly to the point, "just exactly what kind of business proposition did you have in mind?"

Carter quickly said, "Before we discuss any specific proposal, Dr. Washburn, we need to verify some preliminary points."

Harry turned to Carter. "And what points are those?"

"Well, Dr. Washburn, if I may say so, it is obvious to us, and to anyone who has read a newspaper or watched the television news in the past week, that your wife and Mrs. Hanley are extraordinary women."

"Thank you," Harry replied evenly.

"I mean to say, we are aware that in addition to their phenomenal ability in roulette, Mrs. Hanley also out-swam a State champion — a male swimmer no less."

"Yes," said Harry, again without expression.

"Now," said Carter, choosing his words carefully, "I sincerely hope that none of you will be offended if I tell you that we have done a certain amount of research into your backgrounds." He added quickly, "Again, this was done while we were still concerned that you might have been using computers while playing roulette."

"I see," said Harry, his eyes narrowing. "And what did you find?"

"Well, sir," said Carter, "we know that both ladies did not give accurate birth data on your marriage licenses." Maria pulled her legs closer to her chair. Stephanie's hand seemed to fly almost involuntarily to her neck. Because of Jack's experience in sales negotiations, he recognized these as body-language signals of increased tension. He assumed that Carter, being a lawyer, would note them, also.

Carter pressed on, "And we know that Mrs. Hanley did not attend the University of Hawaii, and was not employed as a lifeguard in Honolulu."

Jack jumped in, feigning irritation, "And of what possible interest is all of this to you?"

Carter glanced at Jack, but said nothing. He turned back to Harry and said quietly, "And we know, sir, that you are a highly-regarded computer scientist, specializing in Artificial Intelligence, particularly robotics." The room fell silent. Carter went on, "Finally, in studying the videotape of Mrs. Hanley's roulette demonstration, we found several instances where she does not appear to breathe for periods of time exceeding two full minutes."

"So you think I'm a *robot*?!" exclaimed Stephanie.

"Mrs. Hanley, as I mentioned earlier, I certainly do not wish to say anything that would be offensive — to any of you. But, the facts are — that you and Mrs. Washburn are clearly extraordinary . . . "

Jack interrupted him, "Are you saying that because my wife and Mrs. Washburn are so extraordinary — not normal human beings — that we should return our winnings?"

"Not at all, sir," said Carter smoothly. "The matter of your winnings is completely closed. Please do not be concerned about that." He turned to Harry and continued, "If I may be so bold, Doctor, since Mrs. Hanley is so extraordinary that she can out-swim a champion . . ." He paused. No one moved. "Is it possible, that a male, a male so extraordinary . . . " He hesitated, then his words came in a rush, "Could a male capable of out-boxing a champion exist?"

Jack jumped in again, "He wants to know if you can build him a robot boxing champion!"

Harry and Jack stared at each other. Jack raised his eyebrows slightly, and his friend responded with a slight nod. Jack turned to the attorney, "My wife and Mrs. Washburn are not robots. They are human beings, who have some extraordinary capabilities. Their vision, hearing and math skills, as you've seen, enabled them to win at roulette. My wife is an Olympic-class swimmer. She can also out-run me, and I was a running-back in college. Mrs. Washburn has the equivalent of a Ph.D. in Biology, and she acquired that knowledge in a few months of self study.

"But — they were not 'born'. They are, as far as we know, the first genetically-engineered human beings." Jack paused to let his words sink in.

After several seconds, Carter turned to Harry, "But your field is Artificial Intelligence — robots. How did you get from that to genetically-engineered people?"

"I was approached," Harry replied, "by a molecular biologist. He was working on the Human Genome Project, a massive effort to construct a complete genetic map of a human being. He realized the enormous complexity of the problem meant that even the most powerful computers would require some fifty years to perform the necessary processing."

"And he thought that you, as an artificial intelligence scientist, could help him solve it sooner?" asked Carter.

"Yes." Harry nodded. "We got it done in two years."

"And then you used that information to create these — incredible women?"

"Yes. Actually, the biologist and I created my wife. Unfortunately, he died soon after. But after studying in the field extensively, my wife was able to use his notes, and we then created Mrs. Hanley."

"Remarkable," said Carter as he stared first at Maria, then Stephanie, with obvious admiration. Then his expression clouded, and he slumped back in his chair. "I suppose these extraordinary ladies required the usual time to reach maturity — I mean," he continued carefully, "they appear to be in their mid-twenties . . ."

"Nope," Stephanie interjected exuberantly. "it only takes six months."

"Six months!" the attorney sat up straight. "How can that possibly be?"

Maria answered, "Gene splicing. Our maturation was accelerated by inserting genes from another lifeform."

Carter turned back to Harry, "Well then, Dr. Washburn, shall we get to the heart of the matter? It appears that you could create more genetically-engineered people who would possess exceptional capabilities. Am I correct?"

"Yes," said Harry carefully, "I suppose that we could."

"Excellent," breathed Carter. "Now, our proposition. Would you be willing to make a genetically-engineered male, capable of becoming a boxing champion, for appropriate compensation?"

Maria interjected, "Mr. Carter, is it your intention that this boxer would be your company's property?"

"Well," said Carter, "we would not, of course, *own* him. He wouldn't be a slave. However, we would certainly want to have him under exclusive contract for his boxing services. I expect we would have a significant investment here. We would wish to protect our investment."

"And what kind of 'investment' might we be talking about?" Jack asked.

"I believe my company would be prepared to offer one-million-dollars," said Carter carefully.

"Mr. Carter," Jack said, off-handedly, "I think it's fair to say that championship fights generate as much as 100 million dollars in revenue. I would suggest that a more realistic offer would be an initial fee of one million dollars to cover development costs, plus ten percent of revenues generated by event attendance and television rights."

Carter turned to Harry, "Doctor Washburn, is Mr. Hanley acting in an agency capacity for you?"

"Yes, he is," Harry nodded. "Because of his experience in business negotiations, I have asked him to assist me."

"Very well." Carter turned to Jack, "The expenses involved in staging a professional boxing match are enormous. Salaries alone, for a manager, trainers, and sparring partners are considerable. The facilities and equipment costs are also very high. And to make the event profitable, there must be an enormous investment in promotion. Advertising would be in the millions of dollars. No," he shook his head. "We could not entertain a counter-offer of a percentage of revenue. There is too much risk. However, a percentage of the profits — say two percent — is a possibility."

"Well, then, I'm sorry," Jack said, gravely, "but I do not feel I could recommend to Dr. Washburn that he accept your offer. The potential for excessive costs, chauffeured limousines, private jet aircraft, and many other things is very great. They could all be charged off as fight expenses. Dr. Washburn would have no control over them and he would receive no tangible benefits from them. They could reduce the 'profits' to zero."

Carter studied Jack for several moments. Hanley knew how to keep his face a mask. He had been through this kind of negotiation often enough to be relaxed and confident. But he also recognized Carter's skill.

The "game" lasted five hours. By 1:00AM, they had reached agreement. The fighter would be completed within six months. Harry would receive a one-million-dollar cash advance immediately, and a second million when the boxer signed a contract with the Parthenon Corporation. Prior to being offered a contract, the fighter would have to pass a qualification test, consisting of a five-round bout with an opponent provided by Parthenon.

Beyond that, Harry would receive seven-and-one-half-percent of the revenues from ticket sales, and television royalties, from all bouts performed while the fighter remained under contract to Parthenon, against a ten-million-dollar annual guarantee.

Maria typed up the contract on a word processor, then printed copies. Harry and Carter both signed, and Cappie and Stephanie signed as witnesses. Putting down the pen, Stephanie said, "Well, we didn't get to play cards, Cappie. Wanna bet on our boy's first fight?"

"Not against him, and not against you, Mrs. Hanley," Cappie laughed.

# A.N.G.E.L.S., Inc. 163

"Think it's time you started callin' me Stephanie." She kissed his cheek. "See you at the fights, Cappie."

As soon as the limo pulled away, Maria yelled, "Yes! Stud Muffins, we're gonna be rich!"

"We all are," Harry beamed.

Maria got a bottle of champagne. As Harry popped it open and filled their glasses, he said, "We need a name for our new enterprise."

They all paused for a moment. From where Jack stood, a light behind Stephanie made a radiant glow through her fine blonde hair. "How about Angels?" he asked.

"The California Angels? No, it's been done," laughed Maria.

"How about Angels, Inc.?" suggested Stephanie.

"Hey," Jack exclaimed, "put periods after each letter. Then it's an acronym."

"What's it stand for?" asked Harry.

"Well, the 'A' could stand for American." Jack thought for a moment. "And the 'G.E.L.S' can stand for Genetically Engineered Life-forms."

"Wow! I love it," Harry pounded Jack on the back.

"What about the 'N' honey?" asked Stephanie.

"I don't know," Jack said. "Can't be National, since we already got American in the name. How about you guys? Think of anything that would fit? Maybe neuro-something?"

"Neural networks?" asked Harry. "That's the branch of Artificial Intelligence dealing with computers that learn."

"Hmm — no," Jack said slowly. "That smacks too much of robots."

"Neuroscience?" suggested Maria. "That's the branch of life science that deals with the anatomy, physiology, biochemistry, and molecular biology of nervous tissues — especially their relation to behavior and learning."

"Yeah, Sis!" exclaimed Stephanie. "That's perfect."

"OK," Jack said. "American Neuroscientific Genetically Engineered Life-forms."

"To A.N.G.E.L.S., Inc.," said Harry solemnly. The four of them raised their glasses, clinked them, and held them together for a long moment.

The classic scene from "The Three Musketeers" flashed into Jack's mind and, trying to keep a straight face, he said, "All for one . . . "

"And one for all!" they all yelled together. Laughter again filled the room.

"Well said, D'Artagnan," Harry grinned.

"Nah, he's 'Lover Buns'," said Stephanie, and she drained her glass.

# CHAPTER 16

The next day, Harry, Maria, and Stephanie started work on the fighter. Jack decided to keep his job at Global Nutrition, until the "big bucks" started rolling in, or until the new enterprise required his full-time effort.

The first day, they re-activated Harry's clean room, which had been idle since he and Maria made Stephanie. A tightly-sealed, plywood chamber, sixteen feet long, eight feet wide, and eight feet high, it filled half of Harry's garage. Large fans with air filters, built into each of the two end-walls, provided a constant flow of filtered air. Harry called it a laminar-flow clean room. He and Maria talked about air-flow in cubic-feet-per-minute, and particulate impurities in microns-per-square-millimeter.

After they assembled the clean room, they filled the rest of the garage with special equipment: an electron microscope, optical microscopes, an x-ray machine, refrigerators, heaters, and computers. When Jack arrived after work, the place looked to him like something out of a science-fiction movie.

Stephanie studied everything she could get her hands on, beginning with James D. Watson's "Molecular Biology of the Gene", and Maria tutored her intensively.

At dinner one evening, Maria quizzed Stephanie, "What are the four nucleotides that comprise DNA?"

"Adenine, cytosine, guanine, and thymine," Stephanie recited.

"Good. Now, what's the difference between mitochondrial and nuclear DNA?"

"Mitochondrial DNA is inherited unchanged down the maternal line. Nuclear DNA carries genes from both parents."

"Right. Give me a definition of cloning."

Stephanie recited confidently, "Cloning: Manipulating a cell from an animal so that it grows into an exact duplicate of that animal."

"OK, but, be more specific."

"Nuclear transfer," Stephanie replied without hesitating. "First, the nucleus is removed from an unfertilized egg while leaving the surrounding cytoplasm intact. Then the egg is placed next to the nucleus of a quiescent donor cell . . . "

"Why quiescent?" Maria interrupted.

"Embryonic cells are undifferentiated. They are capable of growing a complete organism. Adult cells, on the other hand, have become differentiated. They're liver cells, or brain cells, or finger-nail cells. They've suppressed the ability to express themselves as the other cells in the organism. By making them quiescent, they regain the ability to grow into a complete organism."

"OK. Go on," Maria nodded.

"Finally, the donor DNA is fused into the egg with an electric current, and implanted into the uterus of the surrogate mother — or incubator," Stephanie added, smiling at Harry.

"Good." Maria also smiled, obviously pleased with her student. "Now, define the human genome."

"The human genome: A complete genetic map of a human being, identifying and sequencing the three-billion nucleotides."

"What do you mean by sequencing?"

Specifying the location of each nucleotide, along the 23 pairs of chromosomes in each cell."

"OK, Sis." Maria raised her eyebrows. "Final question for tonight. It's a tough one . . . "

"Go, Teach," Stephanie bubbled with her usual enthusiasm.

"Describe the structure of a DNA molecule."

Jack stared at Stephanie, as his wife launched into a detailed description of how the component nucleotides joined to form the ladder-like, double helixes of DNA. It took several minutes, and she drew sketches on her napkin as she talked.

When Stephanie finished, Maria hugged her. "All right, Sis. You earned your dinner tonight!"

"Amen!" Harry agreed emphatically.

In just a few days, Stephanie absorbed enough knowledge about genetic engineering to become a useful member of their team. They talked about chromosomes and genes by identification codes: complex series of numeric and alphabetic characters. It meant absolutely nothing to Jack, but the three of them understood each other very well.

A cashier's check for $1,000,000 arrived three days after Harry signed the contract with Carter. Jack took a day off from work to visit an attorney who specialized in setting up new corporations, and got him started on the Articles of Incorporation for their new company. Jack called Harry from the attorney's office, and they decided that Harry, Jack, Maria, and Stephanie would each hold twenty-five-percent of the stock.

Harry also insisted that Jack accept the title of President of the company because of his business experience. Jack reluctantly agreed. He still felt that the whole basis of the company was Harry's work, but Harry wanted to immerse himself in the technical detail, and needed Jack to run the business.

Later that night, as Jack and Stephanie got into bed, she snuggled against him. "And now, Mr. President, I've always wondered just what might be the duties of a First Lady . . ."

\* \* \* \* \* \*

For the next few weeks, the three of them worked increasingly longer hours. Jack never went into the clean room. He wouldn't have been useful, and every time someone went in, they took contaminants in with them. Harry, Maria, and Stephanie wore surgery garb: gowns and boots over their clothing, caps and masks, and surgeon's gloves, whenever they entered the sanitized environment.

# A.N.G.E.L.S., Inc.

There were no windows in the clean room, so Jack had not seen the fighter. But he knew that he would be a heavyweight, six feet, four inches tall, and would weigh 240 pounds.

Six months after Harry signed the contract with Carter, as Jack returned to his office after a meeting, his intercom buzzed.

Picking up the phone, he heard his secretary say, "Jack, your wife called. No emergency, but she wants you to come to Dr. Washburn's house after work."

Jack glanced at his watch. 4:00PM. "Any major crises, Liz?"

"No, Jack. Nothing that can't wait 'til tomorrow."

"Well, I think I'll call it a day."

"OK, boss, it's a day."

Forty-five minutes later, he pulled into Harry's driveway. He went in the front door and through the connecting door to the garage. Stephanie, sitting at a computer, jumped up and ran to him, brimming with excitement. She kissed him quickly, then pressed an interphone switch. "Jack's here."

Maria's voice came through the speaker, "OK, we'll be right out." A moment later, the door to the clean room opened and Maria stepped out. "Hi, Jack." As casually as she could, she pulled her surgical mask down. He could see the excitement in her face.

Harry came out. He already had his mask off, and he beamed. He looked at his friend and said dramatically, "Jack, say 'Hello' to the next Heavyweight Champion of the World . . ."

A figure filled the doorway. He had to duck his head as he stepped through. He wore only a bathing suit and sneakers. Superbly muscled, he looked like a fighter in top condition.

As he cleared the doorway, he looked up. Jack's jaw dropped. He was looking at himself. Or more accurately, what he might have looked like at twenty-five, if he had spent many years training as a fighter.

# CHAPTER 17

Harry said, "Jack, this is Joey Hanley. He's your new kid brother." Dazed by the fighter's resemblance to himself, Jack barely heard the words.

The young man walked toward him, his relaxed manner masking the awesome power of his physique. He grinned, stuck out his hand, and said "Hi, Jack. I'm really glad to meet you."

As they shook hands, Jack stared into Joey's eyes. Joey returned the stare. Jack felt suddenly overwhelmed with emotion. He had never had a brother, and he felt as though he were looking in a mirror, or a time machine, taking him back to his mid-twenties. Jack's eyes stung as he fought tears. Joey saw Jack's emotion and his grin softened. He reached out and gripped Jack's shoulders.

Jack, too moved to speak, grasped Joey's arms. As Jack studied his face, he saw Joey also felt the intense emotion of the moment. Finally, Jack broke the tension. "Aw, hell, kid," he grinned.

Joey laughed, then spontaneously reached out and hugged his older brother. Stephanie and Maria both had tears in their eyes. Harry beamed like a proud father, which in a way he was, to all three of them. Jack returned the hug, a little awkwardly at first, then with the intensity of a man who has suddenly found a long-lost brother.

Finally, Jack stepped back, cleared his throat and asked, "How did you do it? I mean he looks so much like me . . ."

Harry proudly said, "Jack, Joey is a clone of you, with a few minor genetic improvements, which make him potentially the strongest, and fastest fighter that ever lived."

"But how did you . . . ?"

"Oh, that was easy," Harry laughed. "Stephanie brought us facial tissue scrapings from your electric razor, fingernails, hair, and — another source of your genes — I won't mention."

Stephanie blushed and stammered, "I hope you don't mind, Sweetheart . . ."

Jack grinned. "I'm flattered."

"Good," Joey said. "Now can we eat? I'm starved."

Harry barbecued steaks. Jack's eyes bugged out when Maria served two of the huge slices of meat to Joey. During dinner, the conversation revolved around boxing.

"During Joey's incubation," Harry explained, "our computers read to him."

"Just as they did to our *Angels*," Jack said, smiling at his wife.

"Yes," Harry continued, "but Joey's reading list included every available book, magazine, and newspaper article on boxing." Turning proudly to the fighter, Harry expounded. "In addition, every film or videotape on boxing that I could find was shown to him."

"Films? Tapes?" Jack asked.

"Oh, yes." Harry said emphatically. "The nature of his special skill is kinetic."

"Kinetic?"

"Pertaining to, or caused by, motion," Maria interjected.

Jack considered that for a moment. "OK," he nodded. "I sure watched my share of game-films when I played football. I can see why it was important for him to watch other fighters in action."

Joey added, "I've memorized detailed scripts of hundreds of boxing matches, especially heavy-weight championship fights." He speared a piece of steak with his fork, and stuck it hungrily into his mouth.

Patting his protégé on the shoulder, Harry beamed, "It's all available for instant, nearly-perfect, recall."

"My grandfather . . . " Jack turned to Joey. "*Our* grandfather saw Gene Tunney take the Heavyweight title from Jack Dempsey in 1926. He also watched Joe Louis destroy Max Schmeling in 1938."

"Yeah, I know," Joey's expression turned serious. "He was avenging racist slurs the Nazi had made about blacks." Joey went on to relate, blow-by-blow, the terrible beating Louis had given Schmeling. Then he described several of Louis' other fights. "I believe that Louis, who held the title from 1937 to 1949, was the greatest fighter in history." He concluded solemnly, "I chose the name 'Joe' in honor of this great champion."

Jack stared at his new "brother" in open admiration.

The room was silent for a moment, then Harry said smartly, "Ten o'clock, Joey. Time to hit the sack. You got road-work at 6:00AM."

"OK, Boss." Joey rose. As he shook Jack's hand, he asked, "How 'bout doin' some road-work with me?"

"I'd be glad to, Joey. But, if you can run as fast as your sister, we wouldn't be in the same county after ten minutes."

"No sweat, Brother," he grinned. "You get to ride the bike."

\* \* \* \* \* \*

The following morning, Jack arrived promptly at 6:00AM. Joey stood in the driveway holding a ten-speed bike with a small computer mounted on the handle-bars. He showed Jack how to use the computer to keep track of elapsed time, distance covered, and average speed.

"OK, let's do it." Joey started jogging. About one-half-mile from Harry's house, a Santa Fe Railroad track ran from Los Angeles to San Diego. Dirt roads on both sides of the track provided miles of excellent running trails. When they arrived at the dirt road, Joey stopped. "OK, I need to run for three minutes, then rest for one, fifteen times."

Jack started the computer and said, "Go!"

Joey took off, practically sprinting. Jack could not believe how fast he ran. When he caught up to Joey and matched speeds with him, he hit the "Compute Speed" key. The display showed twelve-miles-per-hour. At three minutes, Jack yelled "Time," and stopped.

The computer showed that Joey had run 0.55-mile. After a one-minute rest, Jack yelled "Go!" Again, the fighter ran for three minutes and rested one minute. They repeated the cycle for the required fifteen rounds, then Joey jogged home and went directly to the shower.

Harry asked, "How'd he do?"

"I can't believe it. He ran so fast he almost *sprinted!* He covered nine miles, in forty-five minutes. That's five minutes-per-mile!"

"Perfect," Harry nodded. "That's right on the profile."

"What do you mean?"

"Well, I doubt if anyone will ever go fifteen rounds with him, but I want his reserves to be able to handle it. And running five-minute miles is just about the same speed as a world-class marathoner covering twenty-six miles in two hours, ten minutes."

"My God!" Jack exclaimed. "Marathon runners look like they're made out of pipe cleaners. Joey weighs 240. Nobody will ever go fifteen rounds with him!"

"And you haven't seen him punch yet."

Jack quickly said, "I hope you don't think I'm going to spar with him."

"No. No," Harry laughed. "We need your brains unscrambled for future negotiations. We'll let Carter provide the sparring partners. But he'll work out with a heavy bag this afternoon, and you won't believe how hard he can hit."

After lunch, and another hour to rest and digest his food, Joey got into his trunks and boxing shoes. Harry taped his hands, then helped him slip on the bag gloves. They all went out to the garage, where a 120-pound bag hung from the rafters.

Harry started his stop watch, and said, "Go." Joey started throwing punches. He moved with the fluid smoothness of a dancer, but the blows landed with incredible impacts. He threw punches continually until Harry yelled, "Time!"

Harry let him rest for one minute, then said, "Go." As in the morning workout, he trained for fifteen rounds of three minutes each, with one minute of rest in between. As Jack watched him carefully the second round, he noticed a definite pattern to the fighter's moves.

During the next rest period, he went over and asked Joey, "You're not just throwing punches at random, are you?"

"Very good, Brother," he grinned. "That was Rocky Marciano and Joe Walcott, September 23, 1952, Round Ten."

"And you, of course, were Marciano," Jack grinned back.

"You got it. Marciano KO'd him in thirteen . . ."

"Go," yelled Harry.

Joey's workout fascinated Jack. After each round the fighter would tell him which script he had used: "Joe Frazier and Jimmy Ellis, February 16, 1970, Round

Three. George Foreman and Joe Frazier, January 22, 1973, Round One. Muhammed Ali and George Foreman, October 30, 1974, Round Six."

Harry said to Jack, "He's going through a series of fights where the championship changed hands."

Finally, on the fifteenth round of his workout, Joey pulled out all the stops. He threw punches with a terrible, relentless, determination. Jack, Harry, and their wives stared at the awesome power of his attack. When Harry yelled, "Time!" Jack went over to Joey.

"That was Louis and Schmeling, wasn't it?"

"Yes," said Joey, and he didn't smile.

"Which round?" Jack asked, as he helped him take off his gloves.

"There was only one," Joey said coldly.

Jack looked carefully at him and saw the anger in his eyes. Like a method actor who immerses himself into the character he is portraying, Joey had stepped into the role of the aggrieved black man who had just devastated the hated Nazi.

After he got his gloves off, Joey walked into the house to have his shower, and they all gave him plenty of space until his emotions had a chance to cool down.

Jack, still stunned by the awesome display of the fighter's devastating power, exchanged glances with his wife and Maria. No one spoke. Harry busied himself by hanging up Joey's gloves, and securing the heavy bag against a wall.

Stephanie, sensing her husband's mood, touched Maria lightly on the shoulder. "C'mon, Sis. I'll help you fix dinner."

When they were alone, Jack turned to his friend. "My *God*, Harry!"

"What?" Harry looked up with a half-smile that told Jack his friend anticipated his next remark.

"I hope he doesn't *kill* someone. I mean, for Crisssakes, Harry, he attacked that bag like . . . "

"Jack."

"Yes?"

"You played football for what — ten years?"

"That's right. So?"

"You used to say lots of guys that tackled you tried to hurt you. I even remember you saying line-backers considered it their job to *punish* you for trying to carry the ball through their territory. So you'd be thinking about that the next time."

"Yeah, that's right." Jack nodded. "So?"

"So, lot's of sports are tough. Football, hockey, and certainly boxing. I mean, the whole *purpose* is to knock the other guy *unconscious*, for Christ's sake."

"I know, but . . . "

"But, bull crap! If we didn't want to build a fighter, we should have told Carter 'No' six months ago."

"Harry, let me get a word in edge-wise, will ya?" Jack gathered his thoughts for a moment, then went on. "What I'm tryin' to say, Pal, is just — I don't know — it almost doesn't seem *fair*, somehow. You know what I mean? This guy's like a new kind of being. How the hell can any normal man stand a chance against him?"

"Jack, every sport is constantly improving performance. Records are being broken all the time. Technological improvements of all kinds. Training methods, equipment, vitamins. Look at Steroids for Chrissakes . . . "

"Yeah, and they're *illegal*."

"Nevertheless, guys who want to play pro ball bad enough use that crap."

"That doesn't make it right."

"OK," Harry said, holding up his hands. "How about Mark Spitz. First man in Olympic history to win seven gold medals."

"So?"

"I saw him on a talk-show once. He worked out twice a day, from the time he was a little kid to get ready for that."

"What's your point?"

"Johnny Weissmuller didn't train that way. Kids didn't swim competitively in his day. Was that fair to him? That his records were broken by someone who had the benefit of better training knowledge?"

"That's still not the same, Harry. Joey is a superior being."

"Jack." Harry held his friend's eyes for a moment. "Joey is *you*. Younger, faster, stronger, and with the knowledge of hundreds of professional fights in his head. But, he's basically you."

"I could never fight the way he can . . ."

"You sure as hell could."

"What do you mean?"

"Ask the guy that mugged me, and the two guys that tried to rape that gal. You put them all in the hospital."

"I'm not in the same league with professional boxers."

"You were an All-state running back, in the biggest state in the country, my friend. And if you had chosen to go into boxing instead of football, you could have been a nationally-ranked fighter."

"You really think so?"

"I *know* it. And that's why we picked you for Joey's gene-source." Throwing his arm around his friend's shoulders, Harry said, "C'mon, let's go eat. And if you're still worried about Joey doing someone serious injury, we can tell him to take it easy."

Jack allowed Harry to guide him into the house, closing their discussion, but he still felt uneasy.

As they all sat down to dinner, Jack asked, "Joey, do you realize just how strong you are? I mean, you're not gonna kill someone, are ya?"

Joey glanced up from his steak and raised his eyebrows. "Ask yourself, Brother."

"What do you mean?"

"Jack, don't you know that personality is governed far more by combinations of behavioral genes than by environment?"

"Well, yes. I know that's supposed to be the latest theory."

"Nope. Not just theory anymore. The Behavioral Genetics people and the Environmental Psychologists have thrashed that one out."

"And the Behavioral Genetics guys won?" Jack asked.

Maria interjected, "Few psychiatrists today embrace the neo-Freudian view that the child's family environment is paramount in determining adult behavior."

"Alas, poor Freud," Harry said. "I'll miss the guy. He saw sex in everything."

Ignoring her husband, Maria pressed on with sincerity, "Jack, psychiatrists today are far more likely to assume that a father and son exhibit, for example, the same antisocial behavior because they share the same behavioral genes."

Joining the serious side of the conversation, Harry added, "Genes have been found that dictate alcoholism and other addictive personality disorders, depression, aggressiveness, even schizophrenia."

Jack nodded. "Yeah. I remember the big brouhaha about the 'Gay' gene."

Joey rejoined the discussion, "Tons of studies have been done on identical twins raised apart. They often drive the same car. Model *and* color. Usually wear similar clothes, and even marry people who resemble each other and have the same first name. There's no doubt about it, Jack. My personality is just about a mirror-image of yours." Joey put down his fork and stared straight into Jack's eyes. "So, ask yourself, Jack: Would you deliberately kill another human being, just to win a championship?"

"No."

"Of course you wouldn't." Joey picked up his fork. "And neither would I."

Jack called Carter the next day. They set up Joey's demonstration fight for the following Saturday.

# CHAPTER 18

They had exactly one week to finish Joey's training. Jack took some vacation time from Global Nutrition and became totally involved in the project.

The next few days, Joey had two work-outs each day. As they reached the end of the week, they reduced the length of his workouts from fifteen rounds to ten, then five. The day before his demo he rested completely.

They flew to Las Vegas on a Saturday morning. Carter and Cappie met their plane. Stunned by the resemblance between Jack and the fighter, the attorney exclaimed, "My God! You're identical twins."

But the former cop's practiced eye caught the differences. "Not quite," Cappie spoke slowly, his gaze darting back and forth between Jack and the fighter. "This guy is taller, about two inches. He's a little heavier too. I'd guess around 20 pounds. And he looks younger — maybe ten years or so."

"Very observant, Cappie." Harry smiled. "Jack is the principal source of Joey's DNA, but our young heavyweight here," he gestured toward Joey with obvious pride, "has a few improvements spliced into his genetic structure which make him potentially the fastest, strongest fighter who ever lived."

"Excellent. Excellent." Carter took a final appraising look at the fighter, then quickly led them to the waiting limo. When they arrived at the Parthenon, the attorney led them into the main showroom. A boxing ring had been set up, and bright overhead-lights glared on the canvas floor. Jack began to feel the pre-game jitters that had hit him before every game in his football career. Harry also seemed tense and nervous, but Joey walked coolly around the ring, inspecting it. He radiated confidence.

Cappie showed them to a dressing room backstage, where Joey pulled on his gear. Joey sat on a training table and they talked quietly while Harry and Jack taped his hands. As they helped him slide his hands into his gloves, Joey said, "These aren't training gloves."

"Damn it. Youy're right, Joey." Jack tapped one of the light-weight gloves. "I guess they want to make it more of a fight, and less of a sparring exercise. You OK with that?"

"Sure, Brother," he grinned. "That's what I'm gonna get paid for. Right?"

"OK," Jack said. "Just watch yourself — all the time."

Someone knocked on the door and announced, "We're ready, Mr. Hanley."

Joey slid off the table and said, "OK. Let's do it." The three of them walked out to the ring. Jack was surprised to see about 50 people seated in groups throughout the showroom. Cappie and Carter sat at ringside with a fat, mean-looking man who smoked a cigar. A number of off-duty casino dealers sat together. Some uniformed security guards made up another group. Several young women dressed casually in slacks and sweaters engaged in animated conversation. When they caught sight of Joey, they stopped talking and stared at him. Their extravagant hair-styles, heavy make-up and voluptuous figures caught Joey's eye.

"Wow," he grinned, "they've gotta be show-girls."

"Keep your mind on the fight, Joey," Jack cautioned him.

"Work now, play later," added Harry.

"Yes, Daddy," Joey said, winking at Harry. He turned his attention to his opponent, a very tough-looking character. Joey guessed his weight at 260, and his age in the mid-to-late-twenties. He was Caucasian, possibly Italian, with black hair and dark eyes. Joey noted the man's broken nose, cauliflower ears, and the scar tissue around his eyes. The eyes had a cold, deadly look, but Joey remained relaxed and confident.

The bell rang several times, and a man in a striped shirt motioned them to the center of the ring. The referee introduced Joey to his first opponent, Tony Pascucci. The referee explained that the bout would consist of five three-minute rounds. He wanted a clean fight, and they better break clean when he yelled "break". They touched gloves, and returned to their corners.

As Harry took his robe, Joey asked, "How long do you want this to go?"

"You feel *that* confident?" Jack asked.

"This is gonna be a piece of cake, Brother."

Jack glanced down at Stephanie and Maria, who sat at ringside near Joey's corner. They both looked worried. "Joey," he said, "I want you to be cautious. Very cautious. We have no idea who this guy is, and what his history is. Don't let him hit you with anything. Use your speed. Jab him silly. Get him pissed. Let him throw hay-makers. But stay out of the way. Don't try to put him away this round."

Joey glanced at Jack, then looked at Harry questioningly.

"Jack knows a lot more about this than me. Do what he says."

Joey grinned at Jack, "OK, boss."

The bell sounded, and he moved out to meet his opponent. Pascucci came out swinging hard, but he fanned a lot of air. He was a slugger, not a boxer, and Joey made him look stupid. Joey moved around him with such speed and style it was a pleasure to watch.

For the first 30 seconds, Pascucci swung, and hit nothing. Then Joey started throwing jabs. Pascucci did not appear to care if he got hit with such light punches. He made little effort to parry the jabs, or even try to bob his head out of the way. He seemed to accept the jabs, and tried to counter-punch with heavier blows, which all missed.

The bell rang. Joey came back to the corner, sat on his stool, and let Jack take his mouthpiece. "Jack, I don't think he can stop me from hitting him."

"Are you *sure*, Joey? He doesn't *seem* to give a damn if you jab him."

"Yeah. I'm pretty sure he *can't* react in time."

"OK," Jack said carefully, "throw some heavier blows this round. Use some combinations. Maybe a series of jabs, then a quick cross."

"OK, boss." The horn blew, and Jack put Joey's mouthpiece in.

Joey jumped up. The bell rang, and he was waiting for Pascucci in the center of the ring. Pascucci's corner-men had apparently coached him to stop wasting his energy on air-punches. More cautious now, he seemed to wait for Joey to make a mistake.

Joey threw more jabs, and put more sting into them. Jack noticed the louder slap of Joey's left glove on Pascucci's face, and he could see Pascucci's head jerk backward with the impacts. Pascucci led with a right cross. Joey easily blocked it. Then Joey threw a series of three quick jabs, and a right cross that landed solidly in Pascucci's midsection. He staggered, then grabbed Joey in a clinch.

The referee tapped them both on the shoulders and yelled, "Break!" Pascucci released Joey, but as they moved apart, he dragged the laces of his left glove across Joey's cheek.

"You laced me, you bastard!" yelled Joey.

Pascucci grinned nastily. "Fuckin' A, Pretty-boy. Welcome to the fight-game."

Joey moved in. Pascucci let one of his hay-makers go, a left hook. Joey bobbed his head under it. Pascucci fired another hard punch, an overhand right. Joey weaved to his right and dodged that punch as well.

Joey came out of his weave with a right cross that slammed into the center of Pascucci's chest. The fighter froze, helpless, and his legs crumbled. Joey threw a left hook that smashed into the side of Pascucci's head with an impact so loud everyone in the audience reacted with a chorus of "Oh's!" The punch lifted Pascucci sideways, completely off his feet. He crashed to the canvas and lay motionless.

Joey immediately went over and looked hard at the other fighter. Then he spat out his mouthpiece and yelled, "Maria, give me a hand! Jack, help me get out of these!"

Jack jumped into the ring, but Maria dodged past him and knelt beside the fallen fighter. Jack cut the laces off Joey's gloves. Joey threw them down and raced over to help Maria. The referee grabbed Joey's gloves and felt carefully inside each one. Jack ran over to Pascucci. Maria breathed air into his lungs, and Joey pumped his chest.

"Jesus Christ! That bad?" Jack asked hoarsely.

"No respiration, no carotid pulse," Joey said as he grimly pumped Pascucci's heart.

Capidolupo arrived in the ring, holding a cellular phone to his ear. He watched Maria and Joey giving Pascucci CPR, and he spoke loudly into his phone, "Well, *page* him! I need him *here*! *Now*!"

Beads of sweat dripped from Joey's face as he worked on the stricken man. "Don't die," he begged. "Come on, man. Please don't die."

Stephanie joined Jack and said quietly, "Paramedics are on the way, Honey."

A few moments later, the hotel doctor arrived.

"Where did he get hit?" he asked as he pulled out his stethoscope.

Joey stopped pumping Pascucci's chest so the doctor could check his heart. "Solar plexus," said Joey, looking down. "And the head."

After a moment, the doctor said, "He's in fibrillation. Keep going." Joey immediately resumed the rhythm.

Five minutes later, the paramedics arrived. One of them slipped an oxygen mask over Pascucci's face, and another took over from Joey. After a few moments, the doctor said, "OK let me check his heart." The paramedic stopped pumping Pascucci's chest. The doctor listened for a moment. "OK, we got a good heart-beat. Take him in."

Jack and Joey helped the paramedics lift the unconscious fighter onto the stretcher. Parthenon security guards held the ring ropes apart, while the paramedics carried the stretcher down the steps. The doctor went with them, and they moved quickly through the crowd that had gathered at the showroom door.

Joey, Jack and Harry walked up the aisle and headed toward the dressing room. Jack noticed the contingent of showgirls stared at Joey with excitement written all over their faces. He briefly thought of Sherry Tyler's reaction when he had scored his first touchdown. Jack also noticed that Joey stared back in their direction. One of the women left the group and walked directly to them. At close range, the men could see she had long blonde hair, beautiful green eyes, and a gorgeous figure.

She handed Joey a slip of paper, and said, "I'd like to take you to dinner. Please call me."

Joey smiled at her, and looked at the paper she had handed him. Then he looked back at her and said, "I'd like that, Sheila. Thank you."

She gave him a smile that Jack thought could melt rocks. Then she turned and walked slowly back to her friends. The three men stood for a moment and watched her go. Then they heard Stephanie's voice behind them, "OK, Hanley, keep it in your pants."

Joey turned with a laugh and said, "What, Sis? I'm single."

"Not you," she said whacking Jack on the butt. "Lover Buns."

They all laughed and walked together to Joey's dressing room. Harry and Jack cut the tape off Joey's hands, and he went into the shower room.

The door opened, and Cappie, Carter, and the man with the cigar came in. Carter introduced them, "This is Mr. Benito, Chairman and CEO of the Parthenon." As he said their names in turn, Benito shook hands. Surprised by the strength of his grip, Jack thought, underneath all that fat, this is one tough character. When Jack looked into Benito's eyes, he saw a hardness that made Pascucci look like Mother Theresa.

"Your brother has one hell of a left hook, Mr. Hanley."

"Pascucci's in X-ray," Cappie said. "They think he might have a fractured skull."

"Jesus Christ!" Harry exclaimed.

Joey came out of the shower room, with a towel wrapped around his waist. "Did you say he's got a fractured skull?"

"Don't worry," said Benito, waving his cigar in dismissal. "He had it comin'. The bastard laced ya." Then extending his hand, he said, "I'm Salvatore Benito. I own the hotel. I'd like to have you fight for us. I hope we can come to an agreement — tonight."

"That's up to Jack," said Joey, turning toward him. "He's my brother — and my manager."

Everybody looked at Jack. Looking Benito straight in the eyes, he said, "We came here so you could see Joey fight, Mr. Benito. And to sign a contract. Let's do it."

Benito grinned, and said, "I like you guys! You don't play no games. OK. You guys go with Carter and work out the details. Then I want you all to join me for dinner tonight."

Joey said quickly, "I'm sorry, Mr. Benito, but I already have other plans for dinner."

Benito grinned at him, "I know, Joey. Bring Sheila. Please. I want my new fighter, and his friends, to enjoy my hospitality." Before Joey could answer, Benito swept out the door, saying to Cappie as he went, "Be sure they all get the best rooms."

"OK, ladies," Joey announced. "I need some privacy."

"Jeez, brother," grinned Stephanie, "we were changing your diapers just a few weeks ago. . . "

"That's right," said Maria. "And since he's a clone of you, Jack," she breathed her sexy impression of

Denise Moran, "I feel I know you — *oh* — so much better."

They all laughed as the women went out. Joey threw on his clothes. Harry swabbed the scrape on his cheek with hydrogen peroxide, and taped a square of gauze over it.

They all trooped up to the fifteenth-floor executive suite, where Carter led them into a mahogany-paneled conference room. Jack found the attorney did not press as hard in this negotiation, as he had six months before. He assumed that Carter had been instructed by Benito to get Joey under contract, quickly.

Three hours later, they had signed the contract. Joey got $100,000 as a signing bonus. Beyond that, he got a percentage of the revenue from his fights. Although nominal at first, the percentage would increase if he became a contender. As a challenger for the title, and for any defense of the title, if he did become the champion, he would receive seven-and-one-half-percent of the revenue from both ticket sales and television rights.

After they signed the contract, Cappie showed them to their suite, which had three luxurious bedrooms and a spacious sitting room.

Later, they met their host at the main showroom for dinner. Benito and Carter were accompanied by their secretaries. Both were voluptuous blondes, and Jack guessed correctly that they were former show-girls. Sheila joined them and sat beside Joey. They talked quietly, and were soon engrossed in each other. A very interesting table, Jack thought, five beautiful women: three showgirls and two *Angels*.

Benito was a gracious host. They ate lobster and filet mignon. Excellent wines accompanied each course, and the service was impeccable. During the show, Harry remarked that he thought the lead dancer was particularly talented.

"Don't say that too loud," Sheila laughed. "She's my understudy. Mr. Benito arranged for me to be excused from tonight's shows." Then, again giving Joey the smile that could melt rocks, she said, "So I could help his new fighter feel welcome."

After dinner and the show, Jack, Stephanie, Harry, and Maria thanked their host and headed for their rooms. Joey and Sheila left to "see another show".

"Starring Sheila, I'll bet," Stephanie whispered to Jack as they left arm-in-arm.

\* \* \* \* \* \*

And the following morning, when they met for breakfast in the sitting room of their suite, there were six of them.

# CHAPTER 19

Both Joey and Sheila wore Parthenon robes. They did not try to hide the fact that she had spent the night with him. Jack worried about Joey. Although his head contained the knowledge of thousands of books, his emotions were very young. The previous night had been the first time he had slept with a woman. Jack feared he could not know the difference between infatuation and love.

After breakfast, they had a second meeting scheduled with Carter to work out the arrangements for Joey's training. Stephanie and Maria asked Sheila to go shopping with them, while the "boys" were at the meeting.

As the three men walked toward the elevator, Jack said, "Joey, it sure looks like you and Sheila are moving pretty fast."

He grinned and said, "You got that right, Brother."

Speaking as gently as he could, Jack cautioned, "I hope you don't get hurt, Pal."

"Jack, do you mind if I ask, how well did you know Steph, before you . . . "

"We made love the third time we were together. But I'd been having sex for nearly twenty years. And I'd even been married once before. So I knew the difference . . ."

"Jack," Joey interrupted him, "I know you're only trying to look out for me, and I appreciate it, but Sheila isn't a 'bimbo'. She has her degree, in English, and she's just working as a dancer to save for Grad school. She wants to teach, disabled kids.

"You're right about one thing, though. I don't know the difference between 'true love' and sexual gratification. I told her I loved her after the first time, last night. She laughed and said 'You tell me that again, after we've known each other for a few months, and then we'll talk'."

Jack breathed a sigh of relief. "OK, Brother, I'm impressed. She sounds like a smart lady."

They arrived at Carter's office, and his secretary ushered them into the conference room where Carter and Cappie waited. They sat down, and Gwen brought coffee. This meeting was not a negotiation. They just needed to agree on the logistics of Joey's training.

Carter cleared his throat, picked up some papers, and whacked the bottom edge on the conference table. "Gentlemen," he began, "we would like to have Joey train here." Turning to Joey, he continued, "The Parthenon Corporation owns several condominium complexes in Las Vegas. We would be pleased to either sell, or lease a condo to you, well below the market rate. Many of our employees take advantage of this." He smiled condescendingly at the younger man. Before anyone could reply, the attorney hurried on, "We will hire a team of fight professionals to work with you: a manager, a trainer, a 'cut-man', and sparring partners."

Jack and Harry looked at Joey. The fighter turned to Carter, and replied, "Sir, I prefer to live in California, near my brother, my — creator," he grinned at Harry, "and their wives — who are like sisters to me." Glancing at Jack and Harry again, he continued, "They can handle my training. They've done a great job so far. And Jack *is* my manager," he said emphatically.

The attorney started to protest, but Joey raised his hand, cutting him off. "I don't need a 'cut-man'. I'm not planning on getting cut. And I don't want sparring partners. I don't want to hurt anybody else, just for practice."

After several minutes of discussion, they agreed on a compromise. They'd try it Joey's way, as long as he won. But if he lost a fight, then they'd do it Carter's way. Joey would move to Las Vegas, and let them run him.

Later that day, after Cappie drove them to McCarran Airport, Jack, Harry, and their wives sat inside the Parthenon's Lear jet. Joey and Sheila said their good-byes at the foot of the plane's stairs. They clinched a long time. When Joey came into the cabin, his eyes were damp, and nobody kidded him about it.

That night, Stephanie told Jack that she and Maria had been very impressed with Sheila. Definitely no bimbo, they agreed. Sheila said she had been attracted to Joey because he had moved so quickly to help the injured fighter. And listening to the other girls in her group, she knew that Joey would have more than one room key dropped in his lap that night. She had decided to move quickly and directly.

"Ah, yes," Jack said, doing a fair impression of W. C. Fields. "The direct approach. I seem to remember my little chickadee taking me by the hand, and leading me into our love nest."

"Oh, really?" she said, giggling. "And then what, Mr. Fields?"

"Ah, let me see, my dear," he said, as he took her in his arms. "I think it was this way . . ."

\* \* \* \* \* \*

In the next few weeks, they made some changes. Jack and Stephanie used their roulette winnings to buy a four-bedroom house, just a few blocks from Harry and Maria. They converted the garage to a gym, installing weight-lifting equipment, a heavy-bag, and a speed-bag. Joey moved into their guest room.

Jack had a long talk with Mike Barclay, his boss at Global Nutrition. He explained that he wanted to work full-time with Joey. Mike was so good about it, Jack felt guilty. They agreed that Jack would take a leave of absence for a few months. Then, if things didn't work out with Joey's career, Jack could come back.

A month after Joey's demo, Carter lined up his first fight for money. His opponent, Vincent Lemay, a former contender, was forty years old and way out of condition. Joey sparred with him the first round, landing sharp jabs at will. The ex-contender lumbered around the ring, unable to connect on a single punch. When the bell rang to end the round, Joey sat on his stool with a disgusted look on his face. As Jack took his mouthpiece, he said angrily, "Jesus Christ, where did Carter find this guy? In a friggin' bar?"

"Keep cool, Brother," Jack said calmly. "This is only your first pro fight. You can't expect Carter to get guys with a decent record to fight you. Not yet."

"I know, Jack. But — God dammit! I feel sorry for him!"

"Joey, listen. Do you want to be a fighter?"

"Yeah. Sure. That's why we're . . ."

"You want to be a contender? The Champion?"

"Yes, I do, Jack." He looked his brother squarely in the eyes.

"Then do your job." The horn blew, and Jack put his mouthpiece in. Joey nodded and jumped up. "Put him away, Joey. Quick." Jack ducked between the ropes.

Joey waited for his opponent at the center of the ring. As the 275-pound man moved slowly toward him, Joey stepped forward quickly and fired a series of three stinging jabs, then a right cross to Lemay's head that knocked him down. Lemay climbed to his feet before the mandatory eight-count. When the referee released him, he lunged at Joey and threw a roundhouse right. Joey parried the blow, almost casually, with his left arm, and countered with another right cross that smashed into Lemay's head. Lemay crashed to the canvas and did not get up for a full minute.

As before, they were given a first-class suite at the Parthenon. Benito insisted they be his guests at a large dinner-party at his home. He wanted to show off his fighter to some of his friends: local politicians, businessmen, and newsmen.

Joey and Sheila had not seen each other for a month and they were eager to be alone. They gamely did their duty until 11:00PM, before they fled to her apartment.

The next day, Cappie drove them all to McCarran Airport. Jack, Harry, and their wives climbed the steps into the plane and waited for Joey and Sheila to say good-bye. After a few moments, Joey followed, plopped onto his seat, and said irritably, "This is gettin' kind of old."

Jack asked, "Well, Brother, what's next?"

"Nothin'," he said, still annoyed. "At least for now. She won't discuss livin' together, either in Vegas or Irvine. And she doesn't even want to hear me tell her I love her, until — I don't know — another few months, I guess."

"Well, she sounds like a smart lady," said Stephanie, gently. "Try to be patient Joey. If it's right for you to be together, it'll happen."

Sheila came to see Joey two weeks later, and stayed for three days.

Two weeks after that, Carter lined up Joey's next fight, and they all returned to Las Vegas. Carter had found a 24-year-old, in good condition. Unlike Joey's first two opponents, Stanley Washington, a black fighter, could box. His record stood at five wins, five losses, and he had won his last three fights.

# A.N.G.E.L.S., Inc.

In the first round, Washington stayed out of Joey's reach, most of the time. They jabbed at each other for three minutes, but neither fighter took a serious hit. They parried each other's blows well, and they both bobbed and weaved, constantly.

After the first round, Jack asked Joey, "Well, is this guy a real boxer?"

"Yup. But I'm gonna kick his ass!"

"You got him figured out, already?"

"I'm gonna suck him in, and close the trap."

In the second round Joey slowed his pace a half-step. He let Washington land a series of jabs. Joey looked surprised. Washington pounced, and threw a right cross at Joey's head. Joey bobbed under it, and came up with a crushing left to Washington's ribcage. Stunned, and flatfooted, Washington could not avoid the right cross that smashed into his head. He had to be helped to his dressing room, and Joey went in to see if he would be OK.

Later that night, after the obligatory dinner party, Joey and Sheila stole away. And the next morning, as before, the six of them had breakfast together at the hotel. After he finished his usual steak-and-eggs, Joey sipped his coffee, deep in thought. Then he turned to Jack, "Last night's fight taught me somethin'."

"What's that, Joey?"

"All the fight knowledge I've got is great, but I've got to do more boxing in my training. It's a skill that will only improve with practice. I need to develop more *muscle memory*."

"That makes sense, Joey. There's a gym in Westminster where boxers train. That's about thirty minutes from Irvine. Or we could go to plan 'B', and let Carter set you up with sparring partners here."

Joey looked at Sheila. She returned his look and said, "Why don't you try Westminster, Honey? I'll take a week's vacation and come to California, if you like?"

Later that day, when Cappie took them to the airport, Sheila brought a suitcase. Joey grinned the whole flight, when he wasn't kissing her.

For the next month, Jack and Joey drove to the Westminster Boxing Club three days each week. The Club manager gave Jack the names of several heavyweights who sought sparring partners. Joey's boxing skills improved dramatically. In just two weeks, they found that only professional sparring partners could give him a challenging workout.

Carter had arranged Joey's next bout with another young boxer, Andy Hamada. Undefeated in his previous five fights, Hamada's overall record stood at eight wins against five losses. He was the fastest fighter Joey had faced. Although Hamada was not known as a slugger, Jack cautioned Joey that he must respect the potential punch of any fighter over 200 pounds.

In the first round, Hamada's speed surprised Joey. The Asian landed sharp jabs that stung Joey's face. When Joey tried to counter-punch, Hamada slipped away.

When Joey sat on his stool, he said, "Shit! This son-of-a-bitch is fast!"

"He is, Brother. But stay with him, and you'll nail him."

Round Two was a repeat of Round One. Jack knew that Hamada had gone ahead on points. "Take the fight to him, Joey. Bore into him. Back him into a corner if you can. Use your strength. He's no match for your power."

At the bell to start Round Three, Joey met Hamada at the center of the ring and lunged into him. Joey threw a series of three jabs, and a right cross. Hamada avoided all of Joey's punches, but had to back-pedal. Joey stayed with him and forced him into the ropes. Off balance, Hamada threw a desperation cross that grazed Joey's cheek. Joey countered with a heavy body-blow that lifted Hamada off the canvas and left him stunned. Joey attacked like a panther. He pounded Hamada's ribcage with four more body-blows, alternating right, left, right, left. They all landed. Hamada lowered his arms to protect his mid-section. Joey threw a right cross that smashed into Hamada's head. He was helpless. Joey threw his left hook. Everybody in the place yelled "Oh!" when it connected, and Hamada hit the canvas like he'd been shot.

When the fighter opened his eyes, five minutes later, the first thing he saw was the concerned look on Joey's face. Assured that Hamada would be OK, Joey left his opponent's dressing room. Sheila waited for him. She walked straight up to him and wrapped her arms around his neck. "Joey Hanley, you are the most caring man I've ever known."

"And . . ?" Joey asked, hopefully.

"And", she turned on her devastating smile, "I love you."

Joey gathered her up with his still-bandaged hands, and kissed her. Flashbulbs started going off, and Jack knew the Las Vegas papers were going to have a great picture of their new heavyweight for the following day's sports page. He also knew that even though Joey had fought only four times, no one had lasted more than three rounds with him, and his awesome left hook would garner some serious coverage.

# CHAPTER 20

At breakfast the next morning, they pored over the Las Vegas newspaper. Joey dominated the front page of the sports section with two pictures: the left hook smashing into Hamada, and, as Maria called it, the "Joey-Sheila" clinch.

One of the writers had done some digging. He revealed the fact that Joey's left hook had put Pascucci in the hospital. Although X-rays had shown his skull wasn't fractured, he had a concussion that kept him under observation for three days. That, coupled with Hamada's trip to "La-la land", caused the writer to compare Joey's hook to Jack Dempsey's and Joe Louis'.

Later that day, they met with Carter. He wanted to know if Joey could fight more than once each month. They realized he would not be considered a serious contender until he had accumulated at least 20 victories.

And at the present rate, that would take about two years.

Joey shrugged, "I feel like I could fight every day. I mean, I've only boxed a total of nine rounds in four fights. Let's go for it. Schedule me as often as you want. I'll let you know if I need a break."

Carter looked at Jack, and he nodded.

"OK," Carter said, "I'll get working on it. I'll see if I can line one up every two weeks."

"You can line 'em up every week, if you want to," Joey said.

A smile broke across Carter's face, "The Parthenon Fight-of-the-Week! *Excellent!*"

They settled down to a weekly schedule of flying to Las Vegas every Saturday morning. Joey would fight that night, and they flew home on Sunday. Joey faced progressively better fighters, but he also improved with every fight. In the following seven weeks, he had seven fights. He won them all, by knockouts, usually with his awesome left hook. The Parthenon "Fight-of-the-Week", featuring their undefeated heavyweight, began to draw good-sized crowds. A group of serious fans began to yell "Bam!" whenever Joey threw the left hook. A local sportswriter nicknamed him "Bam-Bam" Hanley.

In the following ten weeks, he won ten more fights, all by knockouts. Joey discovered that his fans would be disappointed if they did not get to see the left hook, and get to yell: "Bam!" He had 20 wins, all by knockouts, against no losses. He started to receive serious national press coverage. Every one of his fights sold out, and the last ten were televised on cable TV in

# A.N.G.E.L.S., Inc.

Las Vegas. Carter negotiated a major network deal for a package of Joey's next ten fights. He even made the cover of <u>Sports Illustrated</u>.

The press wanted to know about Joey's earlier life. Carter hit on the idea of saying that he went to school in Europe, starting at an early age. He somehow had documentation set up, regarding Joey's educational career in a small town near Palermo, Sicily. And he even got some retired school teachers who would say what a bright, but tough, kid he had been. Jack didn't ask Carter how he had arranged all that.

Sheila quit her job and moved in with Joey. They bought a house in "The Ranch", just two blocks from Jack and Stephanie. Sheila enrolled at U.C.I. Since Harry was still on the faculty, he helped her get in. "Not much of a problem," he said. "Her grade point average is 3.87."

Joey's next opponent, Mickey Robinson, was a very serious contender. The sixth-ranked heavyweight in the world, he had a record of 26 wins, against eight losses. A powerful slugger, Robinson had 19 knock-outs, and a streak of 12 consecutive wins, all by KO's, when Joey faced him.

Robinson accomplished something that night that had never been done before: he knocked Joey down. He caught him with a hook, late in the third round. But Joey bounced up immediately, and the referee had to force him to accept the mandatory eight-count. As soon as the referee released him, Joey attacked Robinson with a fury that none of them had ever seen. He blasted his opponent with a series of punishing body-blows, and then decked him with a right cross, just two seconds before the bell. Robinson had to be helped to his corner.

During the break, Joey's fans started a chorus: "Bam!, Bam! Bam!" The arena became a madhouse. When the bell rang to start the fourth round, Jack could hardly hear it. Joey charged into Robinson like a tiger. He threw another series of devastating body-blows, and then he threw the left hook. Joey's fans screamed: "Bam!" as Robinson crashed to the floor.

When the referee shouted, "Ten!", Joey became the sixth-ranked heavy-weight. As usual, he tried to visit his fallen opponent, but Robinson had been taken to the hospital. Like Pascucci, he had a concussion, and they kept him overnight for observation.

Joey continued to fight every week. In nine more weeks, his record stood at 30 wins, all by KO's, and he was still undefeated. The only argument among fight fans centered on whether his left hook equaled or surpassed Joe Louis'. The fans and the press demanded a title fight.

The Champ, a powerful black named Willy Kramer, had 44 wins, 35 by KO's, and no losses. But he was not anxious to fight Joey. A sports columnist in Las Vegas wrote a strong article suggesting that the WBA threaten to strip Kramer of the title if he failed to defend it against the popular challenger. The call was repeated in L.A., Chicago, and New York. The television networks picked up the issue, and Kramer finally agreed to fight Joey. The contract required that they fight at Caesar's Palace. Further, if Joey won, he would be bound to give Kramer a re-match within six months, also at Caesar's.

They all helped Joey train hard for his title shot. With Carter and Cappie's help, they got videotapes of Kramer's important fights. Jack and Joey studied them, looking for any weakness. They hired several top-notch fight managers as consultants to study the tapes. The experts agreed. Kramer did not have a weakness. The Champion stood in a class by himself: a superb boxer, with a deadly punch.

Joey trained so hard Jack could not believe it. In roadwork, he increased his speed to a phenomenal 15 miles-per-hour, the equivalent of a four-minute miler. In his sparring, he used three partners for five rounds each. He yelled at them to throw everything they had at him, but he did not throw heavy punches at them. He wanted to practice slipping punches, bobbing and weaving, and always moving so fast that none of his partners could last more than five rounds. His dedication was phenomenal, and his endurance increased to the point that he seemed tireless.

As the date of the fight approached, the national news media descended on Joey's training facilities. He could no longer do roadwork beside the railroad tracks near his home. They had to rent the entire gym in Westminster for his sparring workouts, and hire security guards to keep the press out.

A month before the fight, they moved their operations to Las Vegas. Carter rented a sports complex with a fully-equipped gym. There was also a running track surrounded by high, cyclone fencing. They had canvas hung on the fence for greater privacy. Cappie stationed a crew of armed security men around the complex whenever Joey worked out.

Joey's motivation reached incredible heights. He drove himself to run faster and punch harder than ever. He focused on the fight exclusively, as he and Sheila reluctantly put their love-life "on hold". Joey bore down with an awesome intensity. Mealtimes became serious affairs. The usual kidding evaporated, and they confined their conversation to a single topic: The Fight. Joey's manner became deadly serious, and as Jack told an interviewer, "We're all anxious for this one to be over."

# CHAPTER 21

Now the big fight was over. His brother had won the Heavyweight Championship of the World, and during the victory celebration, Joey and Sheila had announced their plan to marry. Jack finally drifted off to sleep, as the morning's first light woke the birds in the nearby eucalyptus trees.

\* \* \* \* \* \*

Sollie gave them a magnificent wedding. Jack served as Joey's best man, Stephanie and Maria as Sheila's bridesmaids. In exchange for a generous donation, a well-known television preacher agreed to perform the ceremony. Eight hundred guests filled the Parthenon's main showroom, which had been completely renovated and configured as a church sanctuary. A major television network paid one million dollars to cover the ceremony. The new champion's wedding to the stunning former showgirl was a national event.

Jack stood beside his brother at the front of the "church", facing the doors at the back of the huge hall where the procession would soon begin. The TV minister stood on his mark, his hair perfectly coifed. His white teeth gleamed as he smiled magnanimously at the audience. A television camera dollied across the front of the set, stopped, and swung toward the minister. The red light on the front of the camera flashed, and the minister beamed into the lens.

Joey spoke quietly to Jack out of the corner of his mouth. "Jesus, you'd think it was a freakin' coronation or somethin'!"

"Well, Brother, in a way it is. They often refer to boxing championships as 'crowns', and that means you're like a king to your fans."

The processional music began, a lilting romantic melody. Maria started down the aisle, slowly and with great dignity. She wore a pastel green dress, and Jack thought she looked as lovely as he had ever seen her. Stephanie followed Maria, wearing an identical dress. As Jack looked at his wife, he thought again how much he loved her, and how lucky he was to have her. He recalled his early misgivings about her, and wondered why he had questioned the nature of her existence. As the two bridesmaids walked down the aisle, all heads turned toward them, and excited whispers rustled throughout the room. Jack supposed the TV anchorman reporting the scene, probably recounted the story of the roulette whiz kids, as they moved gracefully to the front of the hall, and took their places.

The traditional wedding march began with a flourish. The audience rose and turned to face the rear of the hall. Sheila stepped through the doorway on Sollie's arm. She wore a white satin dress, with a veil so long two little girls had to carry the ends. She was even more stunning than ever. Jack glanced at his brother. Joey's eyes eagerly followed his lovely bride as she slowly approached. His face glowed in adoration.

The ceremony lasted forty-five minutes. Joey and Sheila had written their own vows, but had not recited them during the rehearsal the previous evening. They wanted to savor the spontaneity of that moment during the actual ceremony. Joey had written a moving testimony of his love for Sheila. He had memorized it, and spoke his words with great feeling as he held Sheila's hands and gazed into her eyes.

The minister held the microphone in front of Sheila and nodded to her. She took the microphone from him, and on cue, music began to play. To the audience's surprise, Sheila sang her vows to her groom, in the form of a love song: "The Power of Love." She had a beautiful voice. Jack knew she had been a dancer, but he had never heard her sing. Her lovely song moved Jack deeply. He looked at Stephanie and Maria and saw tears rolling down their cheeks. He glanced at Joey and saw tears forming in his brother's eyes as well.

The network just got their million bucks worth, thought Jack. After the ceremony, they moved to a second showroom for the reception. Sollie provided an extravagant celebration for the champion and his bride. They ate lobster and filet mignon and drank champagne.

Joey and Sheila had their first dance. They moved with such grace it almost seemed like they were skating. When Jack got his turn to dance with the bride, he found she anticipated his moves better than any woman he had ever danced with before.

"Sheila, you are an extraordinary dancer." Then with a laugh, he said, "You could even make a rhinoceros look good."

"Oh, you're just sayin' that cuz I'm your sister now."

"Speakin' of your talents, Sister, where did you learn to sing like that?"

"Oh, it's no big deal, really. Anybody who wants to be serious about show business has to do it all. Act, sing, dance, comedy, drama, you name it. You can't make a living in the business until you've accumulated a string of credits. And to get the roles, you have to audition for everything that comes along."

"Are you thinking about getting back into show business?"

"Nope. Been there. Done that." She laughed. "Dancing for two years at the Parthenon was enough. Now I'm retired. I'm just gonna stay home and raise kids with your brother."

Jack knew that all of the angels were infertile and he assumed that Joey must have discussed that with Sheila. He didn't want to mention it then, so he said nothing. But Sheila had noticed the troubled expression that flashed across his face.

"Jack, I know about the genetic defect that's prevented Stephanie and Maria from having children. And I also know that Joey will have — a similar situation. But we could adopt, or there's artificial insemination. One way or another, we're gonna have a bunch of rug rats."

Joey swung by with Stephanie. "Hey Brother. Don't get my bride all tired out. I got big plans for her later." They laughed and changed partners. Jack took his angel in his arms as Joey and Sheila spun away.

After two more hours of dancing, Sheila tossed her bouquet. Several showgirls, friends of Sheila's, laughed as they struggled to catch the prize. A young Hispanic woman won the contest, and held her trophy high. Jack recognized her as the flight attendant from the Parthenon's Lear jet. She was immediately approached by Carter. After a moment's conversation, she nodded, then they began to dance together.

A few minutes later, Joey delighted the crowd by removing his bride's garter from her shapely leg, with his teeth. He then shot it over his shoulder. A boisterous group of young bachelors scrambled for the prize. The winner was a handsome, blonde, athletic-looking, young man. He searched the crowd for the attractive woman who had caught the bouquet. Spotting her dancing with someone else, he stood awkwardly for a moment.

Norma Carter approached him. "You're supposed to win a prize with that garter, Brett."

"I know," he said sheepishly. "But the girl who caught the bouquet is otherwise occupied."

"Yes," Norma said coldly. "I know."

Noting her expression, he asked, "Is that your husband she's dancing with?"

"Not for much longer. I filed for divorce last week."

"What? I had no idea you were leaving him." Then looking at her closely, he said, "I've never seen you look so beautiful."

"That's because you've never seen me in anything but my tennis togs." Looking down, she laughed, "Or out of them."

While Carter continued to dance with the flight attendant, Brett led Norma to his car.

Joey and Sheila were oblivious to the romantic intrigues developing at their reception. They sat in the Parthenon's Lear Jet, and stared deeply into each other's eyes, as the sleek jet headed for the South Pacific.

# CHAPTER 22

Joey and Sheila honeymooned for a full month in the Polynesian Islands. In Papeete, Sheila quickly learned the Tahitian hula, a more suggestive dance than its Hawaiian counterpart. One night at a luau, the master of ceremonies asked for volunteers from the audience to join the performers on stage. With a laugh, Sheila skipped up the steps to the raised platform. One of the male dancers swayed in front of her, urging her to roll her hips as he demonstrated. She immediately went into a vigorous wiggle. The band leader signaled the drummers to increase their tempo. The beautiful former showgirl glided across the stage, dancing an alluring hula, to the delight of the other tourists, and even the natives.

After her dance and the enthusiastic applause, the MC leered at Sheila, then turned to the audience and wisecracked, "How'd ya like to wind that up and set it to go off at midnight?"

Sheila leaned toward the microphone and said innocently, "I guess you'll have to ask my husband — Joey. He's right over there." She pointed toward the table where her husband sat, stonefaced.

Following the direction of her forefinger, the man suddenly recognized the champion. The color drained from his face. After a moment, he recovered and said quickly, "Well, thank you very much for joining our dancers, Mrs. Hanley. I hope you and your husband enjoy the rest of your stay."

Joey's favorite island was Bora-Bora. Less populated than Tahiti, fewer people recognized him and asked for autographs. "I just want some privacy, to enjoy being with you, Sweetheart," he told his wife, as they lay together on the warm sandy beach.

"I know, Darlin'. Sheila caressed his cheek with her fingertips. "But this is the price of fame, and we're going to have to get used to it." Then with an impish look, she whispered, "But there's *one* place where people can't bother us . . ."

"Yeah!" Joey jumped to his feet, and they raced, laughing, toward their bungalow.

\* \* \* \* \* \*

When they returned from their honeymoon, the well-rested champion eagerly resumed training. Kramer had spent three days in the hospital after losing his title to Joey, and did not care for a re-match. The new champion, anxious to emulate his namesake, wanted to fight often. He urged Carter to line up his first title defense as soon as possible.

Joey's title fights would all be held at the Parthenon. Carter, representing the champion, negotiated from a position of strength. He arranged Joey's first title defense with a top-ranked contender, a young Swede, Thor Garborg. At twenty-six years of age, Garborg stood six-foot, three, and weighed 230 pounds. With a record of thirty-five wins, twenty-three by knockouts, against eight losses, the challenger had captured a gold medal in the Olympics two years before, and won all of his last ten fights by knockouts. Sports writers predicted that Joey might need five rounds to defeat Garborg. The Las Vegas odds-makers picked Joey, eight-to-one.

Joey prepared well for the fight, but he seemed more relaxed than he had been during his intense training for the championship fight. Jack felt that everyone seemed to be having fun again. Good-natured kidding flew around the table at mealtimes, and Joey refused to abstain from making love to his new bride.

On the night of the fight, Cappie knocked on the door of their penthouse suite. One group of guards escorted Stephanie, Maria, and Sheila to Sollie's private box at ringside. Cappie and another group of guards walked Jack, Harry, and Joey to the elevator. Cappie inserted his security key, locking out any unwanted stops. The express elevator took them to the sub-basement where more Parthenon guards patrolled the corridor to Joey's large dressing room.

"How do you feel, Brother?" Jack asked, as he taped Joey's right hand.

"Relaxed. Confident. This Swede is no Willy Kramer."

Harry, taping Joey's left hand, looked up. "You'll make schmorgasbord outa him!"

"Listen," Jack said firmly, "Garborg's put his share of guys on the mat. Don't be too damn cocky."

"OK, Boss," Joey smiled at his brother.

At the start of Round One, Joey hit Garborg with a series of lightning-like jabs. The Swede's head bobbed backward like a basketball being dribbled. The last of Joey's jabs was so hard, it knocked Garborg down. Joe Louis had been famous for being able to knock a man out with a six-inch jab. Joey had nearly done it himself. The champion's fans were delighted with his new feat, but they still wanted to see the left hook. As Garborg pulled himself to his feet, the fans started yelling "Bam! Bam! Bam!"

Joey moved in and threw another series of quick jabs. Garborg seemed defenseless. He had not landed a punch. The crowd continued to chant, "Bam! Bam! Bam!" Joey threw another series of jabs and then a solid right cross to the head that knocked the challenger down again. He did not get up.

Joey's first title defense had lasted only forty seconds. Disappointed that they did not get to see the left hook, Joey's fans nevertheless continued to praise their champion as the greatest fighter in modern history.

\* \* \* \* \* \*

Two months later, Carter signed a black fighter, Lucas Calvin, to challenge Joey. Light for a heavyweight at 210, Calvin had a reputation for quickness and polished boxing skill, but he did not have a heavy punch. His record stood at a respectable 30 wins versus six losses, but he had only eight knockouts.

Calvin tried the same strategy that Joey had used when he took the title from Kramer. He used his speed to stay away from Joey's heavy punches. Both fighters boxed well in the first round, but no serious punches landed. In Round Two, Calvin appeared more confident. He threw a series of three jabs, and then a right cross that missed. Before Calvin could recover, Joey countered with a right cross of his own, that staggered the challenger. Joey stepped into him and threw the left hook. Calvin dropped as though he had been shot with a bullet, and did not move for two minutes.

\* \* \* \* \* \*

The third contender to face Joey, Leo Fantone, made a bad mistake. Fantone, a 240-pound slugger, came out swinging in the first round. He threw a flurry of hard punches that all missed, except the last one. It landed below the belt. As the referee stepped between the fighters to warn Fantone, Jack caught the look on Joey's face. So did everyone else in the audience.

Thousands of words had been written about Joey's reaction to being hit with a low blow when he took the title from Kramer. Thousands more had been written about the punch to Pasucci's solar plexus that almost killed him after he deliberately laced Joey. "You're dead meat, Fantone!" yelled Benito.

"Bam! Bam! Bam!" Joey's fans demanded retaliation. The champion caught his breath, nodded to the referee that he felt OK, then lunged at his prey. Joey's first punch, a smashing left to the body, cracked two of the challenger's ribs. Joey fired a right cross to the head that knocked Fantone out, but before he could fall, Joey followed it up with the left hook. Fantone spent six days in the hospital.

A popular late-show comedian joked, "My second most un-favorite thing would be to stick my hand, bleeding profusely, into the shark tank at Sea World. My *first* most un-favorite thing would be to hit Joey Hanley below the belt!"

\* \* \* \* \* \*

Two months later, Joey defended his title again. Andy Hamada, whom Joey had knocked out early in his career, had fought well in the intervening two years and earned a title shot. Still one of the fastest heavyweights in the game, Hamada stayed out of harm's way until the third round. As in their first match, Joey backed him into the ropes. Trapped in a corner, Hamada fought back desperately and threw everything he had, but he was no match for Joey's great strength. He succumbed to the awesome left hook for the second time in his career.

As before, the first thing Hamada saw when he opened his eyes in his dressing room was the concerned face of Joey Hanley, who quipped, "We gotta stop meetin' like this, Andy. People are gonna talk." In spite of the ache in his head, Andy laughed.

By the end of his first year as champion, Joey had fought four times and he won them all by knockouts.

His second year was more of the same. He fought six times and KO'd all of his opponents. In defending his title ten times, no one had lasted more than three rounds with him. Joey, Jack, and Harry all became multi-millionaires. The three men and their wives enjoyed the good life. Stephanie, Maria, and Sheila decided only one thing was missing: children.

# CHAPTER 23

They discussed the issue of children for a long time. Harry again explained the genetic failure that prevented Stephanie, Maria and Joey from being fertile. Jack could not follow Harry's explanation, but Maria and Stephanie understood it very well. Joey, absorbed in his career, just accepted it. But the women grew more restless with their maternal instincts unsatisfied.

One night, after they had gone to bed, Stephanie turned to Jack. He saw tears in her eyes. Before he could speak, she put her fingers on his lips and said, "Sweetheart, I have to ask you something. Would you be willing to father a child, by artificial insemination, that we could raise as our own?"

He didn't have to think about it long. "My darling Angel, you'll be the best mother any child could have. I'd love to have a child that we could raise together." The floodgates opened. He took her in his arms and kissed away her tears. After a moment, he asked,

"Have you thought about who the surrogate mother would be?"

"You've already got that figured out, haven't you, Honey?"

"Sheila?"

"Yes, Sweetheart. In fact, we've talked about her carrying two children. You and I would raise one. She and Joey would raise the other."

"Sounds like you girls have it all worked out. But — does it have to be *artificial* insemin . . . "

"Watch it, Lover Buns," she dug him in the ribs with her knuckle, "or I'll tell your kid brother, and you'll become the forty-second notch on his gun."

"OK, OK. Nobody gets any more notches on their guns."

"Good." She dropped her voice to a sexy purr, "Now, wanna practice, Daddy?"

\* \* \* \* \* \*

A few days later, Stephanie, Sheila, Jack and Joey visited a fertility clinic in Century City. Harry and Maria decided to wait. Harry worried about the responsibility of parenthood. Maria hoped that if he did agree to father a child, they could find a brunette who resembled her to be the surrogate mother.

At the clinic, the four of them signed legal forms, by the dozens it seemed. Jack left a sample for testing, and Sheila got an instruction sheet. She had to take her temperature daily to determine her most fertile time. The next day, they received word from the clinic regarding Jack's sample: "Fertile as a turtle."

Two weeks later, Sheila called Stephanie, "I'm ready to make a baby!"

They all trooped back to Century City. Jack made a fresh "donation". Sheila asked Stephanie to come into the examination room with her while the doctor performed the procedure. When they came out, Sheila was glowing. "It took! I know it did!"

The doctor smiled at her enthusiasm and explained it would be highly unusual for a woman to conceive a child by artificial insemination on the first try. He cautioned Sheila to be prepared for numerous attempts.

One week later, a disappointed Sheila called Stephanie and Maria to report that she had started her period.

It took six attempts before they received the news that Sheila was pregnant. The women had a wonderful time buying a nursery full of furniture, baby clothes, toys, bottles, and everything else they could think of. One thing became immediately clear. Even though Joey and Sheila would officially raise this first baby, there would be two other "Moms" living close by.

In the meantime, it was business as usual for Joey, Jack and Harry. During Sheila's pregnancy, Joey successfully defended his title five more times. His record stood at 46 wins, all by knockouts, and no losses. He had defended the title a total of 15 times. No one appeared on the horizon who could be considered a serious threat, but that did not stop the contenders from trying. Joey gave them all a shot. Sports writers began to ask: "How soon could he break Louis' record of 25 title defenses?"

Joey told Carter not to schedule a fight within two months of Sheila's due date. He devoted all of his time to helping his wife prepare for their baby.

One night, eight months into Sheila's pregnancy, Stephanie cooked pasta for the six of them. Jack, Joey, and Harry sat in the family room watching a football game on TV and drinking beer. The women chatted in the kitchen. Suddenly, Sheila squealed and grabbed her swollen abdomen. Before Jack or Harry could blink, Joey launched himself off the couch and sprinted to his wife's side.

"What is it, Honey? Are you OK?" He held her arms and looked into her face with concern.

"Oh, I'm just being silly," she said with an embarrassed laugh. "That little tiger in there just gave me a kick strong enough to get a tryout with the Rockettes!"

Stephanie and Maria rushed over and put their hands on Sheila's stomach to feel the infant's movements. Sheila's face glowed with warmth and excitement. A strange series of emotions washed over Jack, as he thought about the fact that he had fathered the baby that grew in the body of his brother's wife.

Four weeks later, the phone rang beside Jack and Stephanie's bed. Instantly awake, Stephanie reached across Jack and grabbed the phone. Glancing at the clock, Jack noticed it was 2:30AM. Stephanie yelled "OK, Joey, we're on our way!" Then, hanging up the phone, she said to her husband, breathlessly, "Sheila's started labor, Honey."

Jack rolled out of bed, and threw on his clothes. Stephanie had already dressed and raced down the stairs into the garage. They drove the two short blocks to Joey and Sheila's house and met them at the door. Joey and Jack eased Sheila into the car. Stephanie drove them carefully to the hospital.

In the labor room, Joey held Sheila's hands, kept track of her pains, wiped her forehead, and spoke tender words of encouragement, his face close to hers. He stood by her side for four hours and never took a break.

A no-nonsense OB nurse examined Sheila and announced, "OK, folks, she's dilated ten centimeters. We're transferring this party to the delivery room. Only the husband is invited."

Joey followed his wife as two nurses wheeled her out of the labor room. Jack, Stephanie, Harry, and Maria went to the waiting room. One hour and forty-five minutes later, Joey burst into the room, wearing surgical greens soaked in sweat and a huge grin on his face.

"We got an eight-pound boy! He's perfect! Sheila's doin' great. Everything's great."

Jack leaped up and hugged his brother. Stephanie rushed over and threw her arms around both men. "I'm so happy for you, Joey." Tears ran down her cheeks. Maria and Harry joined them, and Jack felt they were all bound even more tightly as a family, since a child had been born.

# CHAPTER 24

Sheila and Joey named their son Joseph Hanley, Junior. He should have been terribly spoiled, with three doting "Mothers"; but, surrounded by love, he responded in kind, a happy and lovable baby. Stephanie and Maria spent hours at Sheila and Joey's house every day. Sheila smiled with patience and love as she shared her son with them. They all took turns feeding, changing, bathing, and dressing Joe, Junior.

Six months later, Jack and Harry watched Joey knock out his 49th opponent in Las Vegas. Stephanie and Maria followed the fight on television at Sheila's house. After the bout, Sheila turned to Stephanie and smiled. "How about driving me up to Century City tomorrow?"

"Oh, Sheila!" Stephanie cried. "Already? Are you sure?"

"Yes," she nodded. "I feel great, thanks to you two 'God-Mothers'. And the time is right. So let's go to the baby store again!"

The following day, when the women met their plane, Stephanie ran to Jack and threw her arms around his neck. He felt the tears on her cheek as she clung to him.

"What is it, Honey?"

"Oh, Jack. Sheila wants us to take her to the clinic today. She's ready to try for our baby!"

Again, it took several tries before Sheila conceived. When they finally got the report that she was pregnant, Stephanie, Sheila, and Maria went on another shopping spree. The bedroom in Jack and Stephanie's house, which had once been used by Joey, became a lovely nursery.

Stephanie attended classes with Sheila and prepared to be her coach during childbirth. Jack watched the special bond grow between the two women, as Sheila nurtured the baby in her body, which would soon become a precious gift to Stephanie. When the baby moved, Sheila and Stephanie held Jack's hand on Sheila's swollen abdomen to feel the life growing there. Strong emotions again swept over Jack as he felt the baby kick. He knew that for the second time, a child had been conceived from his seed, but grew in the womb of a woman who was not his wife. The fact that the mother was his brother's wife made the intimacy of the moment even more awkward for Jack. But Stephanie and Sheila both seemed to accept the situation happily and without question.

Maria became more quiet. Jack sensed she feared missing out on this wonderful part of life if Harry did not change his mind about being a parent. It saddened Jack to see Maria's delightful sense of humor slip away.

Harry continued to work with Jack as a corner man for Joey's fights, but he also turned back to his original love for computers. He wrote programs which he used for making investments. Expert Financial Decision Systems, he called them. In a few months, he increased the value of his portfolio by twenty percent. Jack and Joey asked him to handle their investments, and Harry did so well for them that Carter, Benito, and Capodilupo asked him to manage their portfolios, also.

Harry soon gained a reputation as a financial guru among Benito's friends in Las Vegas, and people approached him with offers to manage their investments for a fee. Harry opened an office in the Newport Financial Center and hired a small staff of licensed stock brokers, financial planners, and CPA's. Everyone knew that Harry, and his ingenious computer programs, were the real "brains" behind the operation.

But as Harry's financial success reached greater heights, Jack saw that his friend seemed further away from any desire to have children. Sensing the depth of Maria's unhappiness, Jack became concerned. One Saturday night, as the six of them had gathered at Harry and Maria's house for their usual weekend dinner of steaks and Cabernet, Jack joined Harry at the barbecue, out of earshot of the others. "Harry, I'm worried about you and Maria."

"What do you mean?" Harry asked, not looking up from the grill.

"I mean, Maria's unhappy. She wants what Sheila's got, and what Stephanie's about to have."

"You mean a baby." Harry finally glanced up at his friend.

Jack noted the stubborn set of his jaw. "Yes, Harry. Maria wants a baby. Christ! What's wrong with that? Most women do. It's in their genes . . ."

"What the hell do you know about genes?"

Hearing the sudden irritation in Harry's voice, Jack realized how much of a sore subject this must have become for his friends. "Harry, if I didn't love you guys so much, I'd back off from this. But I can't. You know, Pal, you've got everything going for you. We all do. Christ, you must be worth — what? — twenty million by now? So you don't want to baby-sit a kid? OK, hire a Nanny. Hire ten of 'em."

"It's not that simple, Jack."

"OK. Explain it to me."

"Maria and I have been seeing a counselor."

"Jesus! I didn't know you had *that* kind of trouble."

"We don't. I mean, it's *me*. I'm having trouble — with the whole idea of sharing Maria with someone else. You know? If we had a child, that would become terribly important to her, probably the main focus of her life. I need to be Number One with her. I know it's selfish, but with my background — I mean all the years of loneliness — and then with Francine's infidelity . . ."

Jack softened his tone. "OK, Pal," he put his arm around his friend. "I'm glad you're workin' on it. I know you'll come up with the right answer." Harry nodded and again looked down at the grill.

\* \* \* \* \* \*

During Sheila's second pregnancy, Joey fought three more times. His record stood at 52 wins, all by knockouts, and no losses. He had defended his title 21 times.

When Sheila went to the hospital to have the baby, Stephanie stayed with her every step of the way. They were a terrific team, and Jack felt great pride as he watched his wife helping the mother of their child as she labored. The doctor arranged for both Jack and Stephanie to be present in the delivery room. Jack could feel the tension in the room increase as the doctor announced, "OK, it's on the way. Push for me, Sheila. Atta' girl. Push again."

Suddenly the doctor said, "I can see the head! Push, Sheila. Push hard!" She bore down, and Stephanie strained with her. Jack's eyes stung with tears. In a matter of minutes, the doctor held the child in his hands. "It's a girl!"

Stephanie hugged Sheila, both in tears. Jack moved to them, wrapped his arms around the two women and lay his face next to his wife's. Tears ran down his cheeks and mingled with theirs.

"Boy. Ain't we all a bunch of bawl-babies," laughed Sheila through her tears.

One of the nurses cleaned the baby and gently placed her on Sheila's chest. She held the infant for a moment and kissed her tenderly. With a smile, she said,

"OK, Darlin', now meet your Mommy." She handed the baby to Stephanie.

As Stephanie took her daughter in her arms for the first time, tears streamed down her cheeks. She could not speak. But she looked at Sheila, and her expression spoke volumes.

# CHAPTER 25

During the next six months, Joey defended his title three more times. He needed only one more fight to tie Louis' record of 25 title defenses. No one could be considered a serious threat to his crown. Very few fighters had even gone more than five rounds with him.

Jack negotiated product endorsements for his brother, and Joey's name appeared on athletic equipment, vitamin supplements, breakfast cereal, orange juice, and milk. He donated his image and his efforts to various charities and other social causes he believed worthwhile. He encouraged kids to stay off drugs, liquor, and tobacco. He told them to stay in school and out of gangs. The President of the United States asked Joey to chair the Citizens Council on Health and Fitness. He appeared frequently on television and became a popular guest on talk shows.

On the home front, Stephanie glowed with the joy of mothering her daughter, whom she and Jack had named Michele.

Sheila, completely wrapped-up in Joe, Junior, turned down repeated offers to re-enter show business. A record producer had called her regularly since hearing her sing at her wedding, and she had been offered an important role in a Broadway musical, but Sheila could not be coaxed out of retirement. Her world revolved around her son and her husband.

Maria made the rounds between Sheila's and Stephanie's homes every day. She loved both children, and Stephanie and Sheila lovingly shared Michele and Joe, Jr. with her, but they all sensed her lack of contentment.

For Joey's attempt to tie Louis' record, Carter found a giant of a man named Bronco Kowalski. He stood six-feet, ten inches tall, and weighed nearly three hundred pounds. He had been an All American football player in college, a linebacker with a reputation for hurting people. As a professional fighter, he had 30 wins, 25 by knockouts, and five losses. He had knocked out his last ten opponents. Kowalski had a quick temper and a nasty mouth. He got plenty of press coverage, but he made a very bad mistake six weeks before the fight. In response to a reporter's probing questions, he lost his temper and yelled, "I'll hurt Hanley so bad his old lady's gonna have to go back to showin' off her boobs in Vegas!"

Kowalski's comment made the front page of newspaper sports sections nationwide. When Joey read it, he tore his paper to shreds and stormed into his gym.

He pounded the heavy bag for an hour. Sheila finally went into the gym and touched her husband's shoulder. His clothes drenched in sweat, the exhausted fighter looked at his wife. The pained look on his face brought tears to her eyes. She threw her arms around his soaked body. He held her tightly for a long moment. "I gonna kill him, Honey."

She nodded, then wiped her face and said brightly, "OK, Sugar. Into the shower with you." She took his hand and led him into the house. "I'll fix you a nice breakfast."

For the next few days, whenever a reporter asked him about his reaction to Kowalski's remarks, Joey eyes would turn to ice, and he would quietly say, "I'll do my talkin' in the ring."

As the day of the fight approached, scalpers sold seats for $1,000. The excitement built as reporters covering Kowalski's training camp wrote about the intensity of his preparation. He made more headlines by hospitalizing one of his sparring partners.

Joey trained with a grim determination that Jack had not seen since his brother's preparation to capture the title. Again, the laughter and good-natured kidding evaporated, and all conversation focused on the fight. Cappie obtained videotapes of Kowalski's previous 15 fights. Joey studied them tirelessly, stopping the tape, backing it up, and re-playing sequences over and over.

Late one night, shortly before the fight, Jack found Joey sitting in the living room viewing a tape. As Jack sat beside his brother, he noticed Joey using the VCR's jog-shuttle feature to replay a sequence, frame by frame. "Find something, Joey?"

"I sure as hell *did*!" The measured intensity of Joey's reply made Jack look at him. He saw excitement in the fighter's eyes.

"What is it, Pal?"

"Watch Kowalski's recovery, after he misses a right cross."

Jack studied the screen. Kowalski jabbed twice, then threw a right cross which did not connect. Kowalski appeared awkwardly off balance for six frames. "Jesus! How long was that in real time?"

"About three-tenths of a second," said Joey, with a grim smile.

"He's a sittin' duck for your left hook." Jack returned his brother's grin.

"Yeah, he sure is. But I'm not gonna give it to him 'til late in the fight."

"What do you mean?"

"Jack, I've got mad at a couple of guys, hittin' me with a low one or somethin', but I've never felt like this before. I really hate this son-of-a-bitch."

"And . . ?" Jack asked, knowing the answer.

"I'm going to really hurt him, Jack."

\* \* \* \* \* \*

On the night of the fight, Jack and Harry taped Joey's hands in the dressing room. There was little conversation, and Jack could feel Joey's tension, like a bomb ready to explode. When they got into the ring, Kowalski waited impatiently. As they stood before the referee getting their instructions, the challenger stared at Joey with an ugly leer. Jack, standing beside Joey, felt the full impact of Kowalski's impressive size. He towered a full six inches over Joey, and outweighed him by sixty pounds.

At the opening bell, Joey met the giant in the center of the ring and threw a series of six sharp jabs at the challenger's face. Jack could see Joey snap his wrist downward as each jab connected. After a few seconds, the challenger started to blink, and the first traces of blood appeared. Joey continued to work on Kowalski's face. He threw another series of jabs, snapping his wrist down with each impact, tearing the man's skin.

Although bleeding, Kowalski did not seem badly hurt, and he counter-attacked with a hard jab. Joey brushed it aside. Kowalski threw a right cross. Joey stepped back, easily dodging the blow, then moved in quickly and fired another series of cutting jabs. By the end of the round, Kowalski bled from cuts above and below both eyes.

Between rounds, his corner men worked on the cuts. The referee checked the challenger's corner. "Jesus! I hope he doesn't stop the fight," Joey said, frowning.

"If you don't want it to be over too quick, Brother," Jack cautioned, "you better lay off his eyes for awhile."

Joey nodded grimly and jumped up at the horn. In the second round, Joey pounded Kowalski's rib cage. He hammered away with punishing intensity, alternating lefts and rights. The challenger absorbed the beating, and threw everything he had. He tagged Joey solidly twice, a left hook to the head, and a right uppercut to the chin. Joey, uninjured, continued to punish Kowalski with the unrelenting attack on his body. By the end of the round, Kowalski's pained grimace bore mute testimony to the pounding his rib cage had taken.

Between rounds, Joey said, "OK. I'm gonna put the bastard away this round."

At the start of Round Three, Joey went back to work on Kowalski's face. The challenger's energy had obviously been drained by the punishing body blows in the previous round. Joey repeatedly snapped jabs at the defenseless Kowalski's eyes, quickly re-opening the cuts. Sensing that the referee might stop the fight, Joey threw the punch he had used only once before, a tremendous right cross to the center of Kowalski's chest. As the punch smashed into his solar plexus, the giant froze, paralyzed. Joey launched the left hook. Kowalski fell sideways into the ropes, and hung helplessly across the top strand. The referee grabbed Joey. Kowalski slid off the ropes and lay face down, motionless.

Joey strode to a neutral corner, and glared at Kowalski's fallen body, as the referee counted him out. Kowalski's corner men dashed into the ring. His manager peered at the fallen fighter's face for a moment, and yelled above the crowd's roar, "Doctor! We need the Doctor!"

The ringside physician had already run up the steps. He ducked between the ropes and fell to his knees beside the motionless man. He listened through his stethoscope for a moment, then said something to Kowalski's men. One of them started pumping Kowalski's chest, another breathed air into his lungs. The crowd noise suddenly hushed. Jack noticed the expression on his brother's face. Never before, in any of his fights, had Joey failed to show concern for an injured opponent, but he watched the scene before him without remorse.

Jack and Harry walked carefully over to Joey, and slipped his robe over his shoulders. Capidolupo's men quickly surrounded them, and they moved toward the dressing room.

Later, in the post-fight interview, reporters fired questions at Joey. One asked, "Hey Champ, the paramedics had to defibrillate his heart. What did you hit him with?"

"Right cross. To the solar plexus. Must have shocked his heart."

The room was still for a moment. Then one of the reporters asked, "Jesus, Champ! Did you know that — at the time? *Before* you hit him with the left hook?"

Everyone in the room looked at the champion. The coldness in his eyes startled them. Even the most-seasoned fight reporters stopped writing and stared.

Joey's reply was deliberate. "Maybe in the future — he'll keep his filthy mouth shut about my wife."

# CHAPTER 26

Fight fans nationwide anticipated Joey's next fight, the historic attempt to break Joe Louis' record of 25 title defenses. Sportswriters devoted columns to the fact that Louis' career had been interrupted by four years of military service during the Second World War. Other writers countered that Joey defended his title so often he could challenge any record set by Louis, even if the "Brown Bomber" had been able to fight four more years.

For Joey's attempt on Louis' record, Willy Kramer decided to come out of retirement. Kramer had not fought since Joey had taken the title from him four years before. Many writers claimed that Kramer could not possibly make a decent showing against Joey, without "tuning up" with at least two or three fights. Rumors circulated that Kramer had been training hard for more than a year, and that he was leaner and meaner than he had ever been.

Jack cautioned Joey to be ready for the "new" Kramer. "You have to assume he's studied the tapes of every one of your fights. Whether he's leaner and meaner remains to be seen, but it's a sure bet that he'll know your style better this time."

"You're right, Jack," Joey nodded in agreement. "What kind of strategy do you think he might try?"

"Well, you beat him last time by stayin' away from his heavy stuff until you wore him down. He'll probably try to get you to mix it up early. Maybe he'll come at you from the opening bell. He might try to suck you in, by makin' you think you've tagged him harder than you really have." Jack thought a long moment, then said, "Joey, remember how he finally got his toe-to-toe with you last time?"

"Sure. He hit me with a low one. Got me mad."

"Right. And that was Round Ten, and he was tired. If he had done that earlier, while he still had some gas . . ."

"Jesus, Jack! Are you sayin' you think Kramer might hit me with a low one, on purpose? To get me pissed?"

"I think it's a possibility. And if he did it early in the fight, while he's still fresh . . ."

"C'mon, Jack. Kramer's got more class than that. He was a great champion."

"Think about it. The whole world saw what you did to Fantone when he hit you with a low one. And they know the only two guys you've ever hit in the solar plexus were Pascucci and Kowalski. And Pascucci laced you, and Kowalski shot off his dirty mouth."

Joey thought for a moment, then said decisively, "Nope. I can't believe that about Kramer."

"OK, Brother. Maybe you're right, but just keep it in the back of your mind. He might try somethin' to get you mad, early. And if that does happen, try to hold your temper in check. You're still younger than him, and there's no way he can go fifteen rounds with you."

"OK, Jack. I'll keep it in mind."

"Good. Now, here's another thing I've been thinking about. What's the one punch he's gonna be lookin' for most?"

"The left hook."

"Correct. And what's your second most deadly weapon?

"Right cross."

"Correct again. Now, what punch don't you use a lot?"

"Uppercut?"

"No good. You gotta be in too tight. That's where Kramer's most dangerous."

"What then?"

"Overhand right."

"Overhand right? I *never* use that!"

"Exactly, my boy." Jack smiled with satisfaction. "He's never seen it. It's not on the tapes he's watchin' right now."

"I don't know, Jack," Joey said thoughtfully. "It's a risky punch. If you miss, it's hard to recover fast, and you're wide open for a hook."

"For most guys, yes. But not for you."

"What do you mean?"

"I want you to spend the next three weeks workin' on it. Every day. I want you to work with the fastest sparring partners we can get our hands on. I want you to get your recovery time down so fast that they can't counter-punch you, even when they know what you're doin'."

"Hmm," Joey murmured. "Might work. OK, Jack. Let's go for it."

\* \* \* \* \* \*

The next day, Joey worked on the overhand right. He used three sparring partners, for five rounds each. They knew he was going to throw a lot of overhand rights, and their job was to counter-punch when he missed. Joey got hit plenty the first day.

At dinner that night, Sheila looked at Joey's red face. "Honey! What happened to you today?"

"Oh, I'm tryin' to learn a new secret weapon." He smiled. "My sparring partners are havin' some fun until I get it down pat. That's all."

"Aren't you wearing a helmet?" she demanded.

"Sure."

She looked closely at her husband's face again, then turned to Jack. "Well, take it easy on my man, will you, Jack?" Then quickly changing her mood, she said, "I think you better let me kiss that to make it better." She walked behind her husband's chair and caressed the back of his neck. Joey winked at Jack, and followed his wife upstairs.

\* \* \* \* \* \* \*

The next day, Joey got hit less often when he missed with the new punch. The third day, only one of his sparring partners could catch him with a counterpunch. After the third day, no one could. In the second week, he used five partners every day, for three rounds each. No one could catch him.

Jack also had him pound the heavy bag incessantly with the new punch. Joey's power increased daily, and Jack thought his new weapon had become nearly as lethal as his famous left hook.

During the third week, Jack reduced the number of rounds Joey trained every day. On the day before the fight, Joey rested completely.

At the weigh-in, they got their first good look at Kramer. The rumors were true. He had lost weight, and he not only looked leaner, he even looked younger than he had when Joey had taken the title from him.

"Jesus," Joey whispered in Jack's ear, "I wonder if this is a *clone* of Kramer?"

Jack chuckled and whispered back, "Well if it is, you'll kick his ass too."

When Kramer stepped on the scale, the official read his weight and announced, "Two-twenty."

Kramer had lost fifteen pounds. He hopped off the scale like a teenager and smiled at Joey. "See you tomorrow night, Champ."

"Yeah, tomorrow night," Joey returned his smile. "Seems like old times, Willy."

"Not *just* like old times, I hope, Champ."

That brought a laugh from everyone present, and the sports-reporters dutifully recorded the gentlemanly exchange.

\* \* \* \* \* \*

The next morning, Jack looked at his brother across the breakfast table. "You look like a coiled spring, Joey."

"Yup." Joey did not smile. "Feel like one, too." Jack knew he probably was going through one of his scripts, so he left him alone.

That night, when Cappie arrived with his crew to escort the champion to his dressing room, the former LAPD cop departed from his usual vigilance for a brief moment. "Well, this is a big night, Champ. Good luck." Then he quickly became all business again, as he opened the door and led them down the hall.

After Jack and Harry had laced Joey's gloves, they made their way into the arena. As Joey stepped through the doorway, his fans erupted. They began chanting "Bam! Bam! Bam!" as Joey walked down the aisle to the ring. It seemed the entire crowd joined in, cheering their popular champion. "Bam! Bam! Bam!" The arena rang with their chant.

As they climbed the stairs into the ring, Jack glanced at the challenger, who had arrived first and awaited the champion. Unlike their first bout, Kramer did not seem amused by the fans chanting for "Bam-Bam" Hanley. Kramer was all business, his face tense, as he paced nervously near his corner. Jack could feel his tension across the ring.

"Joey, I think he's gonna come at you like gang-busters, right from the start."

"I think you're right, Brother. But I'm gonna have a little surprise of my own, waitin' for him."

The horn blew. Jack stuck Joey's mouthpiece in, and Joey stood up, calmly. The bell rang. Joey moved toward the challenger. As Jack and Joey had anticipated, Kramer lunged into Joey with a flurry of hard punches: three jabs, and a right cross. Joey parried them all, and launched the overhand right. It caught Kramer completely by surprise, landed squarely on his forehead and knocked him down. The crowd roared their approval. Joey quickly retreated to a neutral corner, and the referee began counting. Kramer got to his feet by the count of four, and shook his head to clear it. The referee released him after the mandatory eight-count.

Kramer lunged at Joey again, landing a lab, then missing a follow-up right cross. Joey countered with a left to the ribcage, which landed solidly. Kramer grabbed Joey in a clinch. Joey, now twenty pounds heavier than Kramer, easily pushed him away. Joey jabbed twice. Kramer parried the first, slipped the second, and then fired a quick series of four jabs of his own. Joey parried the first three, but the last one caught him squarely, and popped his head back. Kramer fired a right cross. Joey bobbed under it, and wove to the left, to avoid a left hook. Joey came out of his weave with a left hook of his own. Kramer was ready for it, and stepped back. Kramer countered with a right to Joey's rib-cage that connected solidly.

Joey back-pedaled a few steps, and the challenger moved in. Joey threw another overhand right. Again, Kramer did not see it coming, and it smashed solidly into his nose. He fell backward onto the seat of his pants. He scrambled up quickly, but the referee held him for the eight-count. Kramer started to bleed from his nose, but he moved gamely back into the fight as soon as the referee released him.

Joey threw a series of three sharp jabs. Kramer parried the first two and slipped the third. Kramer fired a flurry of six hard body blows, alternating lefts and rights. Joey blocked the first four, but the last two landed solidly. Kramer charged in, directly into another overhand right, which knocked him down again. The fans screamed so loudly Jack could hardly hear the bell.

When Joey sat on his stool, Jack said, "You're three-for-three on the new punch, but sooner or later he'll figure it out."

"They're workin' on it right now," Harry warned.

Jack glanced at Kramer's cornermen as they talked to the challenger, gesturing with overhand rights.

"OK," said Jack, turning back to Joey. "As soon as he starts slipping the overhand right, feint with it, then hammer him with a left hook."

"Gotcha," Joey acknowledged, taking his mouthpiece at the horn. The bell rang, and Kramer again lunged aggressively toward Joey. Kramer jabbed twice. Joey parried the first, slipped the second, and countered with a right cross to the head. Kramer bobbed under it, and came up with an uppercut, which caught Joey squarely. Kramer charged in. Joey threw an overhand right. Kramer saw it coming in time to slip it, then countered with a left hook. Joey, after three weeks of drills, easily ducked under the punch. Kramer moved in and fired three sharp jabs, and a right cross. Joey backed away from the punches. Kramer chased him. Joey feinted with the overhand right, and fired a left hook. It connected solidly enough to knock Kramer down. Although Joey's fans screamed "Bam!", Jack knew the punch would not end the fight.

Kramer scrambled up quickly. When the referee released him at the count of eight, Kramer moved back into the fight. He came at Joey with a flurry of hard body blows. Most of them landed. Jack could see that Joey felt them. He circled away from the challenger. Kramer chased him and fired a right cross that landed solidly on Joey's head. Joey clinched. The referee separated them, and Joey got on his bicycle. Kramer, trying desperately to catch Joey before he could recover, lunged again. He missed with a left hook, and another right cross. Joey moved smoothly around the challenger and fired off three jabs. Kramer parried them all and countered with another right cross, which missed.

The bell rang, and the crowd cheered lustily. Jack knew that although Joey had won the round because of the knock-down, Kramer had made a better showing than he had in Round One. The surprise of the new punch was gone. Kramer had that wired. Joey sat down on his stool, hard.

"OK." Jack frowned. "Back to Plan A."

"Stay on the bicycle, right?"

"Yep. Just like before. Tire him out."

"OK." Joey took a mouthful of water and spat it out.

In Round Three, Joey stayed out of Kramer's reach. The fans wanted more of the slug-fest and voiced their disapproval, but Joey stayed with his strategy and avoided Kramer's heavy punches. Joey fired three sharp jabs, and blood spurted from Kramer's nose. At the bell, Jack felt the round was even. Kramer had been the aggressor, taking the fight to Joey, but Joey had landed more punches, even though they were just jabs.

Between rounds, Jack cautioned Joey, "Watch out for the low one."

"I still don't think he'd stoop to that."

"Just be ready to protect your jewels." The horn blew. Jack stuck Joey's mouth-piece in and finished his warning, "And don't let him piss you off."

Joey grunted and stood up. The bell sounded and he moved toward Kramer. The challenger threw a series of six punches, alternating rights and lefts. Joey circled to his left, and the first five punches missed. The sixth punch landed, in his crotch. Joey saw it coming in time to catch most of the impact with his arm, but he fell to the canvas and writhed as if in pain. The crowd erupted in outrage. Benito screamed "You're a dead man, Kramer!"

The referee gave Kramer a stern warning, then checked on Joey. The champion pulled himself to his feet with apparent difficulty and walked slowly to his corner.

"You hurt, Brother? Jack asked.

Looking over his shoulder and spotting the referee talking to the challenger again, Joey replied, "I'm OK.

I blocked most of it. Just goin' for a delay to keep my cool."

"Good job, Joey. If you can keep your temper reined in, there's no way he can beat you."

"I still can't believe he'd stoop to this."

The referee came over. "Are you able to continue, Champ?"

Joey nodded, and the fans roared as he moved toward Kramer. A fan with a foghorn voice yelled, "Somebody call 9-1-1! Kramer's gonna need it!"

As the fighters came together in the center of the ring, Kramer fired a series of three jabs. Joey parried the first, slipped the second, and was tagged by the third. Kramer followed with a right cross that connected solidly in Joey's mid-section. Joey grabbed him in a clinch.

"You hit me low on purpose, Kramer. That was beneath you."

"I want my title back."

Joey pushed Kramer away so hard he slipped and almost fell. Catching himself, Kramer bored back into Joey, throwing hard punches at his body. Joey expertly parried, twisted, and slipped them all. Then he circled around Kramer's attack, firing sporadic jabs. Kramer kept up his attack, but could not connect with a solid punch.

When the bell rang to end the round, Jack said, "I think he's a half-step slower."

"Yup," Joey agreed. His face was tense with anger.

Jack looked closely at Joey's eyes. "You still got your temper under control, Brother? I think you should stay away from him for a few more rounds."

"I'm OK. He admitted he did it on purpose."

"Well, make him pay, but wait a few more. OK?"

"OK."

The next four rounds, Joey circled Kramer, firing jabs. Kramer parried some, and slipped others, but whenever Joey connected, he snapped his wrist downward. By the end of Round Eight, Kramer was bleeding from a series of cuts around his eyes. His cornermen worked on the cuts between rounds, and the referee peered over their shoulders. Jack could see Kramer tiring. He carried his arms low, and made no unnecessary moves.

Just before the bell rang to start Round Nine, Jack said, "Put him away this round, Joey."

Joey replied by springing off his stool. At the bell, he charged into Kramer and fired three sharp jabs, and a right cross to Kramer's head, which all landed. Joey threw a series of hard body blows, lefts and rights. Kramer staggered. An over-hand right knocked him into the ropes. Joey bored into him with another devastating series of body blows. Kramer tried to clinch. Joey pushed him away. Sensing the end was at hand, Joey's fans chanted "Bam! Bam! Bam!"

Joey threw a right cross to the head. Kramer staggered. Joey fired the left hook. "Bam!" screamed Joey's fans. Kramer dropped like he'd been shot, and lay motionless. Joey turned his back on him, and strode to a neutral corner.

In the post-fight interview, a reporter asked, "What about the low blow in Round Four?"

Joey replied simply, "I think it was deliberate, and I'm disappointed. Kramer was a great champion and that was beneath him."

"How about a re-match?"

"If he wants one. I've never turned anyone down."

Andy Hamada, working as a color commentator, drew a round of laughter from the other sports-casters by interjecting, "But nobody's stupid enough to want to collect three of your left hooks, Champ."

# CHAPTER 27

Joey, Jack, and Harry lived on the road a lot, not only when Joey fought, but when he made personal appearances. The demands on his time were endless, and they had to select carefully the events he could reasonably handle.

In Houston, for a Cystic Fibrosis fund-raiser, Jack got a call in his hotel room. As he picked up the phone, he heard his wife crying. "Jack! Maria collapsed. She's in the hospital . . ."

"My God, Honey! What is it?"

"It's her heart, Jack. They're doing tests . . ."

"Oh, no! How can that be? She's only — what? I mean, it's like — she's only thirty-two or thirty-three!"

"That's right, Jack. Her equivalent age is only thirty-three, but her EKG shows she's definitely had a coronary."

"Oh, God! Is she conscious?"

"She comes in and out. They've got her medicated."

"OK, Sweetheart. I'll get us on a plane. I'll call you back as soon as I get a flight number."

Jack went into Harry's room and gave him the news. Harry, beside himself with worry, immediately called Stephanie at the hospital. She could not tell him any more than she had told Jack.

Jack woke Joey up, and they caught the next flight back to LA.

On the plane, Joey fell asleep almost immediately, but Harry stared out the window and could not stop fidgeting. Jack felt his friend's worry and tried to bolster his spirits.

"Don't worry, Harry. She's gonna make it. She's in a good hospital with great doctors. Steph and Sheila are with her, and we'll be there in a couple more hours. It's going to be . . . "

"I know all that," Harry blurted as he turned away from the window and stared at Jack. "It's just . . . " His voice trailed off and he abruptly turned back to the window.

Jack looked at the back of Harry's head. "What? What is it, Harry?"

Harry just shook his head, still facing the window.

Jack tried to figure out his friend's unstated concern, but could not identify it. Obviously, Harry was frightened about his wife's condition; but they had been close friends for so many years, Jack could not understand Harry's unwillingness to talk with him. He decided to give Harry some space, but began to feel vaguely uneasy.

Stephanie met their flight, her face taut and tearstained. At the hospital, the doctor let Harry see Maria right away. Jack, Stephanie, Joey, and Sheila waited outside.

A half-hour later, Harry came out, his face ashen. "How is she, Harry?" Jack asked.

Harry could not meet his friend's eyes, but stared at the floor for several seconds. When he looked up, his eyes brimmed with tears and his lips quivered. "They won't know for sure, until they get all the test results, but the cardiologist says . . ."

Jack stepped forward quickly and put an arm around Harry's shoulders. "It's OK, Pal. We're all here together, and she's going to be . . ."

"Jack!" Harry's face twisted in his agony, "the cardiologist says her EKG . . ."

Something about Harry's manner suddenly gave Jack a premonition. He felt his stomach tighten. "What? Harry! What the hell . . . ?" Jack felt like a huge vice squeezed his gut.

Harry blurted, "Her EKG is so weak — it looks like — it looks like the heart of an *elderly woman*!"

Jack felt Stephanie stiffen beside him. "Harry," her voice quivered. "What are you saying?"

Harry looked at her, and the tears spilled down his cheeks. "I'll need to look at a tissue sample — under the electron microscope . . ." He struggled to finish. "I'm afraid this might be related — to the accelerated-growth gene . . ."

"God damnit!" Jack exploded. "I thought you said you turned that thing off somehow."

Harry turned a miserable face toward his friend. "I thought we did, Jack. That's what Feingold said — when we made Maria — and I used the same procedure for . . . " He turned toward Stephanie, but could not finish.

Stephanie's hands flew to her mouth. Her eyes opened wide with fear. Jack reached for her and held her tight, trying to protect her from something he could not understand. With a cry, Sheila rushed to Joey and clung to him. Her face contorted as she began to sob.

The five of them stayed at the hospital. About midnight the doctor returned. "She seems to have turned the corner, and is out of any immediate danger."

"Thank God!" Harry breathed. "Any idea how long she'll have to stay here?"

"That's difficult to predict at this point, Dr. Washburn. If she continues to improve, perhaps a week or ten days."

"How about her long-range prognosis?" Harry asked tentatively.

"Well, that's also very hard to say just yet. As I mentioned to you earlier, this is a very unusual case. Your wife seems to be in very good health, with the exception of her heart. Unfortunately, there appears to have been considerable damage to the heart muscle by the coronary. At this point, we must hope for the best — but be prepared for the worst."

"And what would be — the worst case?" Harry asked, his voice faltering.

The doctor said quietly, "Perhaps a year. Perhaps two."

Stephanie's knees buckled. Jack, still holding her, helped her to a couch, and sat beside her. Sheila clutched Joey, sobbing uncontrollably.

The doctor went on, "I recommend that you all go home and get some sleep. Dr. Washburn, you will be notified if there is any change in your wife's condition."

Harry continued the conversation with the doctor for a few moments. Then, the five of them went home.

* * * * * *

Maria continued to improve, and the doctor released her from the hospital six days later. As soon as Harry got her home, he, Maria, and Stephanie went immediately into the garage, and set up the electron microscope. Using tissue samples from Maria, they worked for hours.

Jack, Joey, and Sheila waited nervously in Harry's living room with the two children. Finally, Harry, Maria and Stephanie came out of the garage and joined the others. The grim expressions on their faces told the story. Stephanie went immediately to her husband, and shuddered as he took her in his arms. Harry and Maria sat on the couch and held each other's hands, tightly. Sheila and Joey also clung to each other.

Harry started to speak, his voice hollow. "The telomeres in Maria's heart tissue are very short . . . "

Jack interrupted, "What's a telomere?"

"It's the tip of the chromosome. It regulates the number of times a cell can replicate itself. Each time a cell divides, its daughter cells have shorter telomeres.

After about 100 replications, the cell reaches its Hayflick limit . . . "

"What that?" Jack demanded, not trying to conceal his concern.

Maria said, "Leonard Hayflick discovered that after 100 replications . . . " She blinked as tears formed in her eyes, then continued bravely, "the cell dies."

Jack met her gaze for a moment, then looked down and asked softly "So what's the bottom line?"

Harry responded, "Jack, the bottom line is — the accelerated-growth gene . . ." His voice faltered. He took a breath and steeled himself. "The accelerated growth gene did not get turned off in Maria's heart. I have no idea why — except that heart tissue is quite different than any other muscle in the body."

"Well, can't you fix it? Can't you splice in the correct gene now?" Jack demanded.

Harry slowly shook his head, and looked at the floor. "I can't, Jack. It's too late. You can't manipulate the genetic code in a mature being. That's something that has to be done at the beginning."

"Well, what about a heart transplant? Surely Maria, at thirty-three, would be a prime candidate. Wouldn't she?"

Harry shook his head again, still looking at the floor, and tears formed in his eyes. "I've taken tissue samples from different parts of Maria's body. Many of her organs are the same way — kidneys, liver . . ." His voice trailed off again.

"I thought you said the heart was the different kind of tissue. Why are those other organs affected?"

Exasperated, Harry retorted, "Jesus! I just don't know, Jack. All I know is that, for some reason, her skin, and the muscles of her arms and legs are very youthful — while many of her internal organs are aging at the accelerated rate."

Jack remained silent for a long moment. Then he looked up and searched Harry's face. "So what's the — you know, what's the prognosis?"

Tears rolled down Harry's cheeks. When he spoke, his voice broke into a sob, "I'm going to lose her. Oh Jesus! I'm going to lose her." He collapsed into Maria's arms. Although she was the one who was dying, and she knew it, she comforted her husband. She led him out of the room and toward the stairs.

After they had left, Stephanie said quietly, "Guys, Maria will probably be gone within six months."

She gave Jack, Joey, and Sheila a few moments to absorb that. Then she continued, "We also looked at some tissue samples — taken from — me." She squeezed her husband's hands, and looked bravely into his eyes. "I have the same problem. It's not as advanced. I might have a year."

Jack had been praying silently for the past several minutes. When Stephanie confirmed his worst fears, he burst into tears, and reached for his wife. As Stephanie comforted her husband, she looked over his shoulder and met Sheila's and Joey's eyes.

Sheila, searching Stephanie's face, asked, "And Joey?"

Maria walked into the room. "I gave Harry something to make him sleep." Then turning to Joey and Sheila, she said quietly, "We think, Brother, that you're probably affected too. I'd like to do a test to confirm it."

Joey stood up quickly. "Let's do it, Sis."

Sheila took his hand and they followed Maria through the door into the garage. An hour later, Joey and Sheila walked slowly back into the living room, both in tears. Nobody had to say anything. They sat like statues, lost in their thoughts.

Until a few days ago, they had been three happy couples, very much in love and financially secure beyond their wildest dreams; but now their wonderful, perfect worlds crumbled around them. Jack looked at Michele, as she slept in her Porta-crib. Joe, Junior, slept on the floor, his favorite truck in his grasp. Nobody wanted to talk. Jack needed to be alone with Stephanie. Maria smiled bravely as she kissed them goodnight at the door.

# CHAPTER 28

In bed that night, Jack held Stephanie, and they both cried for hours. Jack had never felt such grief. He could not accept the fact that he was going to lose her. His emotions swung from unspeakable sadness and guilt, to anger and helplessness, and then back to grief. He did not know how or when he finally fell asleep.

When he awoke the next morning, he lay in bed for a few seconds before he remembered what had happened. His grief again flooded back, and tears stung his eyes. He reached out to touch his wife, but her side of the bed was empty. He jumped out of bed, threw on a robe, and hurried down the stairs.

He found her in the kitchen, dressed in a bright yellow sundress, fixing breakfast. Michele sat in her highchair, happily patting her applesauce with a spoon.

"Honey," he said, surprised, "you're up awfully early."

She answered brightly, "I decided that we've got a year, and starting today it's going to be the best year anyone could want. No more tears. OK, Honey?" She came to him, with a brave smile.

As he took her in his arms, he had never felt greater love for her.

Later that day, Stephanie called Maria and Sheila and asked them to bring their husbands over. The six of them sat outside, by the pool. Stephanie, in her matter-of-fact way, quickly presented the idea that they needed to spend their remaining time together with as much happiness as they could. The others all eagerly agreed and took "The pledge," as Stephanie called it. "No more tears." Then Stephanie suggested that they go to Hawaii and live on the beach. Her enthusiasm helped them all to agree.

It only took a week to pack the things they wanted to take and arrange for a realtor to handle their homes. They decided to lease them for a year, furnished. The realtor glowed while she imagined what she could get for the Heavyweight Champion's house.

They realized that Joey would have to resign his title. Joey felt he owed it to Sollie to tell him personally, before they announced it to the press. Jack and Harry flew to Las Vegas with Joey. Sollie surprised them by his reaction. Jack had thought he would be furious, and even expected that the former Mafioso might demand that Harry create a new champion for him.

Sollie looked like he'd been kicked in the stomach, then he said quietly, "You been almost like a son to me,

Joey. I am sorry for your trouble. I thank you for the honor you have given me — to be your sponsor. You are a great champion. No one may ever break your record. I wish you, and Sheila — all of you — all the happiness you can have," and he kissed Joey's cheeks.

Carter did not make an appearance. Jack assumed the lawyer had no further interest in them, since Joey would not be bringing any more millions into the Parthenon's coffers.

Cappie drove them to the airport. As Jack shook the ex-cop's hand, he saw the craggy face grimace to ward off tears.

"Tell that little lady of yours that . . . " His voice broke and he clenched his jaw.

Jack clutched the brawny shoulder. "I know, Cappie. I know."

Cappie nodded to them, and not trusting himself to speak again, turned and walked quickly away.

\* \* \* \* \* \*

They left for Maui the next day. As their plane glided down into the lush, tropical forests surrounding Kahului Airport, Jack glanced down at his wife's face. Stephanie dozed with her head snuggled against his chest. The plane touched down with a gentle bump. Stephanie's eyes flickered, then opened. She saw her husband gazing at her, and she smiled up at him. Jack continued to gaze at his wife. "Your eyes are still the most incredible shade of blue I've ever seen, Angel."

Before Stephanie could reply, the flight attendant announced, "Aloha, ladies and gentlemen. Welcome to the island of Maui."

*Maui*. Jack remembered the beach bag Stephanie had used when he first met her. The whimsical lettering on the bag came into his mind, "Here today, gone to Maui . . ." He felt his eyes begin to smart, and he quickly turned away and looked out the window on the far side of the plane, trying to divert his thoughts. He struggled to keep his "No more tears," pledge.

* * * * * *

They found a four bedroom house, on a secluded cove a few miles from Lahaina. The three couples became even more like one family, eating all their meals together. The women shared the child-rearing and housekeeping duties. The men barbecued almost every night, alternating between steaks and the fresh fish they speared while snorkeling before dinner.

In many ways, it seemed like a wonderful, extended vacation as they lay in the warm sun and swam in the clear Pacific. But the nagging reminder that these would be their last happy times together, forced its way into each of their thoughts, many times every day. Jack had promised to make it the best year he could for Stephanie, and he worked especially hard to keep his promise, for both of them.

On Joe, Junior's second birthday, he sat on his Daddy's lap and blew out the two little candles on his cake. Michele also had a small cake, even though she would not have her first birthday for a few more months. They gave presents to both children.

Joe, Junior had mastered dog-paddling in shallow water, and Joey had bought his son a little skin-diving set: fins, mask, and snorkel. Stephanie helped Michele unwrap a present, a doll, of a blonde angel. Jack looked at his wife, and her unspoken smile said, "Just so she'll always remember me." Jack had to fight to keep his promise not to cry.

\* \* \* \* \* \*

Maria died a few months later, in her sleep. They were all grateful that she did not suffer a painful death, and that she could be with her husband and all her "family" during her last few months. They had a quiet service in a local chapel and buried her in a small cemetery in Lahaina. Harry asked Jack to help him select the casket and the gravestone. Harry noticed a stone with the carved image of Mary, the Mother of Jesus. "What do you think, Jack?"

"I don't know, Pal. She wasn't a Catholic, was she?"

"No, but she believed in God. And her name is — was — Maria . . ." His voice cracked.

"Well," Jack said quietly, wrapping an arm around his friend's shoulders, "then I think we should get this one."

Harry had the stone engraved, "Maria Washburn, 1978-2011." Maria, of course, had not actually lived 33 years, but he decided against using the actual date of her "birth". He did not want to raise any eyebrows with the last line, "Beloved wife of Harry."

Harry tried very hard, but it soon became obvious that he could not cope with the loss of his wife. He was desperately unhappy. For the last several years, she had been the light of his life, and he missed her beyond belief.

Jack realized the depth of Harry's grief, and the terrible guilt he carried, as they walked together on the beach a few days after Maria's death. "I can't help wondering if I'm being punished because I tried to play God. Maybe it would have been better if I had never met Jim Feingold, and never . . ."

"Harry, I'm no scientist, and I'm no philosopher. I'm just a guy who loves his wife, very much. And if she'd been conceived in the usual way, or by artificial insemination, instead of by cloning, I couldn't love her any more than I do this minute. Stephanie is the most wonderful, most loving person I've ever known. She's a wife and mother with unbounding love. I'll miss her, terribly, when she's gone, but I'm thankful for the six wonderful years we've had together."

"I know what you're sayin', Jack. I feel the same way about . . ." His voice broke as he said his wife's name, "Maria. But I still can't stop feeling that I let my loneliness get in the way of my scientific judgment. We didn't know enough about the process. Maybe we never will . . ."

"Damn it, Harry. Don't punish yourself for the failure of the gene-splicing technique. The history of medicine, in fact all of science, has had its share of honest mistakes. Look at the Thalidomide babies. That was the result of a sincere effort to help pregnant women with morning sickness."

Harry turned slowly to Jack. His eyes darted back and forth across his friend's face. "I don't know, Jack. I hope . . . " Harry's voice trailed off for a moment, then he said, "I *pray* that — that my motives were — right."

"I guess we've all been doing a lot of praying lately."

"Do *you* think He's listening to us?" Harry searched his friend's face for an answer. "Do you think He's — *punishing* us?"

"You mean because our wives weren't born the usual way?" Jack considered that for a moment. Then shook his head emphatically. "Nope. I don't buy that. I've never been a bible-thumper, but I certainly believe in God . . . "

"So do I," Harry interjected.

"And I *don't* believe," Jack continued, "in a fire-and brimstone God."

"What kind of God do you believe in, Jack?" Harry asked earnestly.

Jack responded at once, "I believe in a God of love, not hate. A just God." Touching his friend's shoulder, Jack went on, "And I believe your heart was right when you made Maria and Stephanie. Your motive was love. Nothing to be ashamed of. You were a good husband to Maria."

"And you to Stephanie," Harry smiled weakly.

\* \* \* \* \* \*

A week later, Harry had his will changed. He left everything equally to Jack, Stephanie, Joey, and Sheila. His net worth totaled just over $200 million. That night, after dinner, he said he was going out for a walk. He kissed the kids "goodnight", and as he walked by Jack's chair, he brushed his hand across his friend's shoulders.

The next morning, when he didn't come down for breakfast, Jack checked his room. His bed had not been slept in, and an envelope lay on the bedside table. Jack saw his own name, printed neatly on it, the way an engineer would do it. Jack opened it. The letter was also neatly printed:

> Jack,
> I'm sorry, but I can't go on without her.
> She was my whole life for eight years.
> I've gone to be with her.
> Please try to make Stephanie, Joey, and
> Sheila understand.
> Thank you for your friendship.
> I'll see you later.
>   Harry

Jack found Harry in the cemetery, an empty bottle of sleeping pills on the ground nearby. Harry lay beside Maria's grave, with his arm draped protectively over the newly sprouting grass. Jack supposed they had slept together in the same way. He had died with a gentle smile on his lips. Jack hoped it meant Maria had come to take him home.

They buried him beside Maria, and had his stone inscribed, "Harry Washburn, 1969-2011, beloved husband of Maria."

The night after Harry's funeral, Stephanie slid into bed and turned to her husband with a serious expression. "Jack, I want you to promise me three things. Remember that after I'm gone, you'll still have a daughter who'll need you . . ."

"Oh, Honey! I'd never . . ."

She put her hand over his lips. "Second, you are a wonderful father, but girls need a mother, too. A role model. Someone to tell them how to deal with the little boys in their lives . . ."

"I couldn't even begin to think of another . . ."

Her fingers gently squeezed his lips. "And you are still a young man. In your early forties. Full of life, and love." She continued to hold his lips, gently, but firmly. "When the time comes, you and Sheila are Joe, Junior's and Michele's natural parents. She's a good woman, a loving wife, and a wonderful mother. Joey and I have discussed it, and we both feel the same. When the time comes. End of conversation. No response is needed."

She quickly replaced her fingers with her lips on his mouth. She kissed him tenderly, and he felt her tears as they fell gently from her cheeks onto his.

# CHAPTER 29

After the deaths of Maria and Harry, Jack, Joey, and their wives clung even more tightly to each other and the children. The women had formed an extraordinary bond, when Sheila carried Stephanie's daughter in her womb, and the men had always considered themselves brothers, as close as any pair of twins. After the deaths of two of their "family", the cold reality of what lay ahead drew them ever closer as they sought comfort from each other.

Jack and Joey took long walks together on the beach and spent hours talking. They reminisced over Joey's extraordinary career, the excitement of his climb to the title, and breaking the "Brown Bomber's" record. With his near-perfect memory, Joey could recount, blow by blow, every fight in his career.

Joey never tired of hearing the story of how Stephanie and Maria had beaten the roulette wheels. He considered them both his sisters, and he loved them dearly. He laughed as Jack recounted the child-like delight of the women as they became the "Roulette Whiz Kids".

Their talks turned serious more than once. One day, Jack carefully broached a sensitive subject. "Joey, I know Harry felt terrible guilt over the genetic failure." He paused for a moment, choosing his words with care. "I hope you can find it in your heart to forgive him — all of us . . ." His voice trailed off.

Joey put his arm around his brother's shoulders and slowed his pace as he thought deeply for a moment. Then he said quietly, "Jack, when I knew I was going to die, probably within a year or so . . . I won't lie to you, Jack. I was devastated. Chewed up with anger. I think I even felt — hatred for awhile. It was so damned unfair! I wouldn't see my son, probably after he's three. And Jesus, I can't tell you how it tore me up to see Sheila cry, knowing we were going to lose each other. But, you know what pulled me out of it?"

Jack shook his head.

"Your sweet wife, my sister. Her attitude, remember? 'OK, we can't change the end, so let's take what we've got and live it together with all the love and kindness we can have for each other.' I mean, I realized the same thing's happening to all of us, and if she's got the guts to live it as best she can, by God I oughta do the same — for Sheila — and all of us."

Jack, too moved to speak, reached up and patted his brother on the shoulder. After a few moments, Joey broke the silence. "Although my life will be short, I've done more already than most guys will do in 80 years. I've climbed to the pinnacle of success in my career, and it's been a fantastic adventure. Out of the millions of men to walk this Earth in the past century, only a few of us have achieved the Heavyweight Championship of the World. I've been treated like a king. I've had all the best that life can offer. I've got the most wonderful wife any man could want. She's gorgeous, talented — and she's given me all the love — my heart can hold." His voice broke.

Jack squeezed his brother's shoulder. "I know, Joey. She's an incredible woman. Stephanie and I both love her for what she did to help us have a child."

Looking out to sea, Joey cleared his throat. "And speaking of that, Brother, Stephanie and I both hope — that you and Sheila will — you know, raise the children together — after we're gone."

Jack searched for the right words for a moment. Following Joey's gaze out to sea, he said quietly, "I know, Joey. Steph mentioned that." After a pause, he continued, "I can't think of another woman in my life just now, but I *promise* you this: I'll always be there to protect Sheila and Joe, Junior — all my life."

Joey, still looking away, nodded and said, "Thanks, Brother. I know you'll look out for 'em. That's all I ask." They turned and walked back to the house, and never spoke of the subject again.

* * * * * *

Because he had disciplined himself to endure the intense physical conditioning of his boxing career, Joey hid any outward signs of the aging and weakening of his internal organs. One evening, he and Jack skin-dove in twenty feet of clear water, as they searched for dinner. Joey jackknifed his body, and his powerful legs quickly propelled him to the bottom. He finned lazily above the sand, scanning from side to side.

Floating on the surface, Jack breathed deeply, recovering from his last dive. As he watched his brother, he saw Joey drop his Hawaiian sling, and grab his chest. Jack dove to help his brother, driving himself downward with his fins. He grabbed Joey under the armpits and swam for the surface as hard as he could. Towing his brother's limp body slowed him down, but he kicked with all his strength. As they burst through the surface, Jack spit out his snorkel and yelled, "Joey! What's the matter?"

Joey's face twisted in agony. He gasped, "Heart! Jack . . .!" He lost consciousness.

Treading water and supporting his brother in his arms, Jack turned toward the house and yelled, "Steph! Sheila! Help!"

The screen door banged as Stephanie ran out onto the porch. "What is it?"

"It's Joey! His heart! Call 911!"

Stephanie yelled over her shoulder to Sheila, who had just appeared in the doorway. Then Stephanie ran down the steps. As she raced across the sand, she kicked off her shoes, and ripped off her skirt. She plunged into the water and swam to her husband and his brother with the same lightning strokes Jack had seen years ago when she helped rescue six children caught in a rip tide.

As she reached them, she felt for a carotid pulse on Joey's neck. "Damnit!" she cried out in despair. Then she gathered her wits, and said grimly, "This isn't going to be easy, Jack. You tow us toward the beach, fast as you can. I'll do the best I can with CPR." She immediately clamped her mouth over Joey's and forced air into his lungs. After three breaths, she tried to squeeze his chest. She swam beside Joey's body, held one hand under his back, and pushed with the other on his chest.

After a moment, she said, "This isn't working, Jack. I can't get enough compression on his chest out here. I'm not strong enough. Change with me, Honey."

Stephanie swam to Joey's head and started towing him toward shore. Jack swam beside them. With his greater strength he squeezed Joey's chest and prayed that he circulated some blood to his brain. He squeezed five times, then blew a breath of air into his brother's lungs. Then he repeated the cycle. They swam that way for several minutes.

As they neared the shore, paramedics waded out to meet them in waist-deep water. They quickly got Joey onto the beach. Using a resuscitator, they worked to restore his breathing and heart beat. Listening through a stethoscope, one of the paramedics said tensely, "Hospital. Now!"

Jack helped the paramedics lift Joey's 240 pounds onto a stretcher. They loaded him into the ambulance as quickly as they could. Sheila rode with her husband to the hospital.

A crowd of neighbors had gathered. Jack asked one of them, a middle-aged woman they knew, to baby-sit the children. He and Stephanie ran into the house, pulled on dry clothes and rushed to the hospital.

They found Sheila in the ER waiting room. She ran to them and cried, "Oh my God! They've been working on him since we got here. I'm so scared, Steph! I'm afraid I'm going to lose him!"

Stephanie reached out to Sheila and held her, caressing her forehead and speaking quietly in her ear. Jack wrapped his arms around them both. They stood for several moments, comforting Sheila as best they could.

A doctor walked slowly out of the ER, his surgical greens soaked in sweat. Jack searched the man's face as he approached them. He had a grim expression. He met Jack's eyes and shook his head slightly. Then he touched Sheila's shoulder. "I'm sorry, Mrs. Hanley. We did everything we could . . . "

Sheila's knees buckled. Jack caught her, and carried her to a couch. Later, Jack and Stephanie took her home.

\* \* \* \* \* \*

They buried Joey beside Harry and Maria. Sheila decided against a gravestone. She thought souvenir hunters might carry it away, one piece at a time.

# CHAPTER 30

For the first few days after Joey's death, Sheila cried almost continually. Stephanie comforted her, almost like a mother. "It's good to let your grief out, Sheila. Don't be concerned about anything else. I'll do it." Stephanie took over all the responsibilities for both children, while Sheila dealt with her loss.

A month later, Jack awakened suddenly, thinking he had heard a noise downstairs. He slipped out of bed and padded quietly down the stairs. He found Sheila sitting in the living room, with an unopened book in her lap. She looked up as he came into the room. "Jack, I hope I didn't wake you."

"It's OK, Kiddo. You all right?" Suddenly aware that he had only his underwear on, Jack grabbed a pillow from the couch and held it awkwardly in front of himself.

"Oh, I'm having trouble sleeping," she smiled weakly.

"You take any of those pills the Doc' gave you?"

"Oh, I hate to take sleeping bills. Scares me, you know? I knew so many girls in Vegas that got their heads screwed up, taking one kind of crap or another."

Jack smiled. "You're beginning to sound more like the ol' Sheila."

"Yeah." She stood up quickly and started to walk past him toward the stairs. Glancing pointedly at his underwear, she said coyly, "I see you're a 'briefs-man', Jack."

"Sorry. I was expecting a burglar."

As she hurried up the stairs, she murmured something quietly. He realized she probably did not think he would hear it, but he thought she said "Lucky burglar."

\* \* \* \* \* \*

Jack tried spearfishing by himself. Stephanie had wanted to go with him, but he feared it would put too much strain on her heart. In the water by himself, Jack was overcome with loneliness. He kept seeing the image of his brother, as he had practically died in Jack's arms. He swam back to the beach, fighting tears. He hung his fins and mask on a peg in the garage, and did not try spearfishing again.

Jack observed Sheila's grief, and dreaded the time when he would lose his wife. Stephanie did not tell Jack that she felt herself growing weaker, but Sheila seemed to sense that her sister-in-law could no longer handle both children alone. Realizing that she was needed more, Sheila seemed to grow stronger, and assumed more of the load every day. Every night, Stephanie slept cuddled in Jack's arms. She seemed to need his closeness all night. Jack noticed that his wife began to sleep more, as the days passed.

One day Stephanie said earnestly to Jack, "I miss the ocean, Honey. Please take me for a dip. I promise I'll take it easy. I just want to get wet. OK, Honey?"

Jack could not refuse her. He knew how much she loved the ocean. They walked into the blue-green water, hand-in-hand. "Oh, this is wonderful," Stephanie breathed, as the small waves washed over her body. Jack held her in his arms, in chest-deep water. She wiped her hands over the top of her head, and her face glowed. "This reminds me of our first date, Sweetheart."

"Yes," he smiled into her eyes, as he cradled her tenderly in his arms. "I remember thinking how much you seemed to be in your natural element, that first time I saw you swim in the ocean. Even that lifeguard said you were a 'fish'."

She laughed. Then jerking her head from side to side she haltingly said, "Well — he — never — saw — me — breathe."

Jack laughed, "Golly, it's a robot-lady."

She reached both arms around his neck, and kissed him tenderly at first, then her kiss grew passionate. "Make love to me, Darling," she breathed.

"Right here? Now?"

"Yes. The water's deep enough. Nobody can see. C'mon, Honey," she said urgently, caressing him through his bathing suit.

He slid his suit off his hips, and she came into his arms. They made love with great tenderness. Afterwards, she sighed, "That was sweet, Jack." Then abruptly changing her mood, she giggled. "Thanks for the swim, Lover Buns."

"Any — time — Ro — bot — la — dy," he laughed haltingly.

As they walked hand in hand up to the house, Sheila sat on the porch with the children. "How's the water?"

"Wonderful," said Stephanie. She and Sheila exchanged a look that spoke volumes. Few men, including Jack, would have recognized it. But in that unspoken exchange, Sheila's expression said "I can see that you've just been loved. I'm happy for you, but I miss my man."

And Stephanie's sad smile said in reply, "Yes, but I have so little time left with him."

\* \* \* \* \* \*

Three weeks later, Stephanie woke her husband in the middle of the night. "Jack. Honey," she said urgently. As he took her quickly in his arms, her breath slipped away. He kissed his sweet *Angel* for the last time, and the tears he tasted on her lips were his own.

# CHAPTER 31

They buried Stephanie next to Maria. Jack selected a stone with a delicately carved angel and had it inscribed: "Stephanie Hanley, 1980-2012, beloved wife of Jack, and mother of Michele."

Sheila and Jack continued to live in the house on Maui. The children handled the transition more easily than Jack had expected. Joe, Junior was almost three years old. He understood that "his Daddy had gone to be with the angels", and he would not see him again. He continued to call Jack "Uncle Jack" for awhile. But he had been raised in a loving environment, surrounded by six adults who cared deeply for him, and he soon accepted Jack in his new role.

Michele, just 18-months old, missed Stephanie, but seemed to sense the special bond between Sheila and herself. She started calling Sheila "Mommy" almost immediately.

Jack and Sheila continued to work through their grief. Having the children was a Godsend. They could not just sit in a dark room and feel sorry for themselves. They had two small children who depended on them for everything. Because of that, they had purpose. They were needed, and they went on.

Sheila slept in her room, and Jack slept in his. It was the first time in many years that he had been celibate for such a long time, but he didn't think about it much.

\* \* \* \* \* \*

Three months after Stephanie's death, as their "family" finished breakfast, Jack grinned at the children and asked, "OK! Whose ready for the beach?"

"Me! Me!" Michele squealed with delight.

Looking at Joe, Junior, Jack asked, "How 'bout it, Pal? You up for it?"

Continuing to stare at his empty cereal bowl, the little boy replied tentatively, "Can we go skin-diving?"

Jack felt a sudden stab of grief, as the image of his stricken brother again rushed into his mind. He thought of making some excuse, but he knew how much Joe, Junior loved to snorkel in shallow water. Jack took a breath, then sat up. "OK, but I'll have to teach you some stuff — if you're going to be my dive-buddy."

His interest piqued, the boy looked up. "What kind of stuff?"

"Oh, all about rip-tides, and sting-rays, and — sharks, so you can help me if I need it."

The boy's eyes widened. "Really?!"

"Sure, Joey. That's what dive-buddies are for."

"Oh, boy!" The lad jumped off his chair and ran to get his fins, mask, and snorkel.

Jack glanced up at Sheila and was surprised to see her watching him intently. He met her gaze for a moment, and then raised his eyebrows. "We'll stay in close . . . "

Her soft green eyes smiled back at him, "You're a good daddy, Hanley."

"Oh, thanks," he said, relieved.

Sheila continued to gaze at him. Jack thought he had seen her look at her husband that way before, and he felt a strange series of emotions sweep over him.

Sheila suddenly stood and turned away. "You guys go ahead. I'll clean up these dishes first, then I'll come down."

Jack held each child's hand as they hurried down the wooden stairs and raced across the hot sand to the water's edge. Later, after Sheila joined them, Jack took Joey out for "deep-water training". While the water only reached Jack's chest, it was over the little boy's head, and he responded to the challenge eagerly. He floated face down on the surface and kicked his little flippers like a baby dolphin. He swam circles around Jack and pointed excitedly as small fish darted around them.

After thirty minutes, Jack thought the boy should rest. "Hey, Joey. Let's take a break."

"Naw. Not yet. Please?"

"Your Mom's probably brought some apple juice."

Appropriately bribed, the boy swam for shore. Jack waded out of the water, his pockets bulging with the shells and rocks Joey had collected.

"See you got some treasures," Sheila laughed.

"Yep. I'm just an ol' pack-mule. Right, Joey?"

"Between gulps of apple juice, the little boy gasped, "Right, Dad."

Jack glanced at Sheila. "I hope you don't . . . "

She cut him off quickly, "Jack. You *are* his father." The warmth of her smile made him think again of times he had seen her gaze lovingly at her husband.

Jack returned Sheila's gaze, suddenly aware of her stunning figure, barely covered by the green bikini. "Your bathing suit matches the color of your eyes," he said, his voice slightly hoarse.

"Thank you, Hanley." She smiled, then continued, "Sounds like you could use some apple juice yourself." She popped open the lid and handed the can toward him.

"And thank *you*, Hanley," he laughed as he reached for the drink. The can was so small he touched her fingers as they made the exchange. They both reacted, and the can fell to the sand. They both laughed nervously as they watched the golden apple juice pour out onto the sand.

Then Sheila stopped laughing and said, "This is silly, Hanley." She reached out and took Jack's wrist, held it firmly, and slapped another juice can into his palm. "There. That wasn't so bad, was it?"

"No it wasn't," Jack said sheepishly. "I don't know what's the matter with me."

# A.N.G.E.L.S., Inc.

"Yes you do," Sheila said evenly. "Same thing's the matter with me."

Jack looked into her eyes. "You're right, Sheila. I guess it's time to stop dancin' around it. We've both been recently widowed, and we're both hurting — something awful. But for all of that, I find you . . . "

"Attractive?" she tipped her head slightly.

"Of course. You're *gorgeous*, for God's sake."

"Good," she said. "I like you too."

He felt butterflies in his stomach. "So, what's next?"

"I think dinner would be nice — and dancing."

Jack's face fell, and his eyes filled with tears.

"Oh, God. What is it, Jack?"

He just shook his head, and could not speak.

"Oh, Jack. That was a special memory for you, wasn't it?"

He nodded as tears rolled down his cheeks.

"Jack, I'm so sorry." She reached for him and held him tight. She comforted him and wiped away his tears. She kissed his cheek. Then again. She drew back and looked at him for a long moment. He gazed forlornly back into her lovely green eyes. She smiled slightly, bent toward him tentatively, and kissed his lips, lightly at first. Then he pulled her to himself and kissed her. The weeks of grief poured out of his heart, and tears again rolled down his cheeks. She kissed him tenderly and lovingly, and he somehow felt her accepting his grief with understanding. Then, he felt the intense emotion begin to change, and the pent-up loneliness and longing of several weeks rushed into him.

She responded with her own longing. They kissed for a long time.

Finally, she leaned her head back to look at him again, as they still held each other. "Well," she sighed. "Glad to see we haven't forgotten how to do that."

"No," he laughed sheepishly. "What's that old line about riding a bicycle?"

She smiled back at him, and began to gather up the children and their toys. As they walked back to the house, he reached for her hand. She quickly took his and squeezed it.

\* \* \* \* \* \*

That night, after the children fell asleep, Sheila came to Jack's room and slid into bed beside him. As he turned to her, she came into his arms, and it seemed the most natural thing in the world, to love her.

Maybe it was easier for her, because he looked so much like Joey. Maybe it was more difficult for her, because he looked so much like Joey. They had been sleeping together for about a week, when one night, as she reached the peak of her passion, she called out Joey's name. They cried in each other's arms.

Without knowing exactly when it happened, Jack realized one day that he loved her. Maybe he always had, in a different way, of course, when she was his brother's wife. As his feelings grew for Sheila, he found that he could begin to remember the happy times he had with Stephanie, without feeling such crushing grief.

One night they toasted marshmallows over a fire on the beach. Michele had fallen asleep. Sheila cradled their daughter in her arms, and gazed lovingly at her face. "You do good work, Hanley," she said quietly.

"Thanks, Hanley. So do you."

"Think we should make another one?" she asked tentatively.

"Only if you'll make an honest man out of me first."

"Oh, you drive a hard bargain, Hanley," she said, with a gentle laugh.

"You wouldn't even have to change your name," he offered, raising his eyebrows and smiling hopefully.

"Yes, I would," she replied softly. "It'd me Mrs. *Jack* Hanley."

He suddenly was flooded with emotion. "You know, I love you, Sheila."

"I love you back," she laughed again,

"And . . . ?"

"I think I'll be free Sunday afternoon." Holding Michele with one arm, she reached out with her free hand and drew his face to hers. He kissed her with great tenderness.

# ABOUT THE AUTHOR

Dr. Robert W. Bliss is a Computer Systems professor at Saddleback College, California, where he has taught since 1977. Prior to that, he was a technical writer. His article "Hybrid Computers" made the cover of <u>Machine Design</u> magazine, in October 1967.

He has an AA degree in Physical Science from Cerritos College; BA and MBA degrees in Management from California State University, Fullerton; and a Doctorate in Education from NOVA Southeastern University.

He has made three television series. In one, viewers phoned in questions, which he answered, live. In a second, Saddleback videotaped 28 of his Computer Systems lectures and broadcast them as a telecourse. In 1990, he made the "Computer Literacy with Dr. Bliss" series at KOCE-TV, for John Wiley & Sons.

A futurist from an early age, he read his first Sci-Fi story at age seven. At his high school Science Fair, he lectured on space flight — four years before Sputnik. In 1968, he won an employee suggestion award for recommending a machine we now call the Fax. His current interests are artificial intelligence and genetic engineering. In a recent sabbatical, he visited AI Departments at Harvard, Dartmouth, and MIT.

Since 1994, he has created two science fiction novels: "A.N.G.E.L.S., Inc." and "Dream Machines" which deals with intelligent robots.